Death in Cyprus

By the same author
The Far Pavilions
Shadow of the Moon
Trade Wind
Death in Zanzibar
Death in Kenya

Death in Cyprus

M. M. Kaye

St. Martin's Press
New York

Library of Congress Cataloging in Publication Data

Kaye, M. M. (Mary Margaret), 1911-
    Death in Cyprus.

    I. Title.
PR6061.A945D34   1984   823'.914   83-24434
ISBN 0-312-18614-2

First Published in 1956 under the title *Death Walked in Cyprus* by
Staples Press

First U.S. Edition

10 9 8 7 6 5 4 3 2 1

To
MAXINE
and the Enchanted Island

Author's Note

Back in 1949, while my husband's regiment was stationed in Egypt, and we were living in an army quarter at Fayid in what was then known as the 'Suez Canal Zone', a friend and I decided to spend a painting holiday in Cyprus. We went there on a ship sailing from Port Said to Limassol, and once on the Island, hired a self-drive car for the duration. (Incidentally, cars in those days were still build with running-boards, and had a luggage-grid instead of a boot!) We stayed in the enchanting house in Kyrenia that I have described in this story, and the plot was practically handed to me on a plate by a curious series of incidents that occurred during our stay. But owing to the fact that I was too busy painting and, later, because of a multiplicity of army moves, I did not get around to writing it for almost five years. Reading it now, I am interested to see that even during that halcyon holiday I must have been aware that the Cyprus I was living in and painting was much too good to last, and that one day greedy quarrelling factions were bound to destroy it. That day came sooner than I thought; and nowadays the Island is divided into two hostile sections. Kyrenia and Hilarion, lovely Aiyos Epiktitos and beautiful Bellapais, and most of the places I knew best, are now held by the Turkish Cypriots, while the Greek Cypriots, who hold the remainder, have turned their sleepy little coastal towns into roaring tourist resorts, complete with vast holiday hotels and 'recreation complexes'. *'O world! O life! O time!'* ... Shelley said it all.

1

Amanda had not been really frightened until she found the bottle. Horrified certainly: shaken by incredulity and shock, but not with fear. Not with this cold, crawling apprehension of evil . . .

One minute Julia Blaine had been alive and talking in that high, hysterical, sobbing voice. And almost the next minute she was dead — sprawled on the floor of Amanda's cabin in an ungainly satin-clad heap.

It had all happened so suddenly, and without a word of warning. Or had there been a warning? Somewhere in the happenings of the past few days or weeks had there been nothing to suggest that such an ugly and fantastic thing might possibly occur . . .?

Amanda Derington had been staying with an aunt at Fayid in the Suez Canal Zone while her uncle and guardian, Oswin Derington of Derington and Company, looked into his business affairs in the simmering stock-pot of the Middle East.

A night raid on London during the autumn of 1940 had left Amanda an orphan, and she had been subsequently and arbitrarily annexed by her Uncle Oswin. This despite the fact that there had been several sympathetic aunts only too ready and willing to take charge of the child. But then Oswin Derington, a bachelor and a misogynist, had little or no opinion of any of them, and a great many opinions on everything else: including the upbringing of children.

The head of Deringtons — that ubiquitous firm whose name and multitudinous activities crop up like measles spots wherever

9

the shoe of the white man has managed to gain a foothold — was a stern moralist in whom the blood of Calvinistic ancestors ran strongly. He was, in addition, successful, egotistical, selfish and frequently inclined to pompousness, and it was his firm conviction that the majority of his fellow-men led sinfully immoral lives. Anyone hearing him holding forth on his favourite subject might well gain the impression that, in the mind of the speaker at least, the entire population of the world was given over to sinful and riotous living with the solitary exception of that pillar of uprightness, Oswin Greatorex Derington.

Uncle Oswin apparently included Amanda's aunts among the ranks of the ungodly, for his action in assuming sole charge of his brother Anthony's only child was prompted as much by a desire to save a tender brand from the burning, as to put into practice various long-held theories on the correct method of bringing up the young. And Anthony having left a will in which he had light-heartedly named his brother as trustee and sole guardian of his daughter, there was nothing that anyone else could do about it.

The outlook for Amanda might well have been bleak, had it not been for the fact that she had inherited her mother's physical beauty, together with much of her father's gaiety and courage. Three useful legacies that a series of strict boarding schools, constantly changed, and her Uncle Oswin's selfish and Victorian ideas on the correct behaviour of young ladies, had done nothing to diminish.

In the years that followed on the heels of Hiroshima, and saw a startling shrinkage of those pink-tinted portions of the map that depicted territories governed by or owing allegiance to the Crown of Great Britain, the trading empire of Derington and Company saw many changes. A number of branches, mainly in the Far East, had been compelled to close down with unexpected suddenness. But other and newer branches had sprung up to replace them, and there came a time when Oswin Derington (whose harassed but resourceful medical adviser had recommended him to take a long sea voyage) decided to combine business with the pursuit of health, and personally inspect a few selected Outposts of the Derington Empire.

He had taken Amanda, now aged twenty, with him; in pursuance of a favourite and often expressed theory that women have an instinct in the matter of irregularities, and that no Branch Manager however efficient occupied — at least in Mr Derington's opinion — the position of Caesar's wife.

He intended to visit Alexandria, Cairo, Aden, Mombasa and Nairobi, and to return via Tripoli. But finding that travel in or to various of these cities was likely to prove full of unpleasant surprises, he had, on reaching Cairo, ordered his niece to return to England forthwith, while he continued the journey alone. There being no return passage immediately available, and as he had a rooted objection to flying (except on those occasions when it happened to suit his convenience) he had packed her off to the temporary care of one of his sisters whose husband, a Brigadier, was stationed in Fayid.

Amanda enjoyed Fayid, and had ultimately administered an even more unwelcome surprise to her Uncle Oswin than his discovery of a strange tendency among certain coloured races to take an actively unappreciative view of Empire builders. She had announced her intention of remaining in Fayid for several months and, later, of visiting the Island of Cyprus.

Since she had in the meantime celebrated her twenty-first birthday and come into control of a small but adequate income, there was little that her Uncle Oswin could do about it beyond losing his temper, which he had done to exhaustion and no effect. His niece had remained sweetly adamant; aided and abetted by her aunt, who had waited a good many years for a chance to repay Oswin for a few forceful criticisms he had uttered on the subject of her choice of a husband, in the days when the Brigadier had been a high-spirited subaltern in the Horse Artillery.

Amanda had extended her stay in Fayid, and eventually carried out her intention of visiting Cyprus, where she had planned to put up in some hotel in Kyrenia. But here, after several weeks of sulky silence, Uncle Oswin had once more intervened:

Deringtons, it appeared, owned a wine business in Cyprus: a post-war venture that was not of sufficient importance to warrant a personal visit from Derington of Deringtons. The management of the business was in the hands of a Mr Glennister Barton, and — wrote Uncle Oswin — if Amanda insisted on gallivanting all over the Middle East in this unmaidenly and unladylike manner, it was only right that she should have some consideration for his good name, if not for her own, and, as an unmarried female, stay in some respectable private house rather than in a public hotel. He had therefore taken it upon himself to appraise the Bartons of his niece's arrival, and demand that they should put her up for the duration of her stay, offer her all facilities and see that she came to no harm. He had already received a favourable reply, and Mr and Mrs Barton would meet Amanda at Limassol ...

'You are on no account to fly. I hear that there was an accident only last week. I am further informed that anti-British feeling runs high among those Cypriots who support Enosis and wish the Island to be united to Greece. If you had the slightest considera-tion for the name of Derington you would abandon this rash and unwomanly project and return to Hampshire,' wrote Uncle Oswin — but without much hope.

Amanda read the letter and sighed. She would have much preferred a hotel and independence, but although she could not be fond of her Uncle Oswin, she felt a certain sense of duty towards him. Despite his selfishness and pomposity, and his conviction that he had been sent into the world to reprove Vice and restore Victorianism, he was — or had been — her legal guardian. And if he had arranged for her to see Cyprus under the auspices of these Bartons, 'she did not feel like pouring oil on the smouldering embers of his disapproval by refusing to be their guest. She there-

12

fore wrote dutifully to say that she would be delighted to accept their kind hospitality.

To the dismay of her aunt and uncle, who pointed out that it would entail travelling to Port Said with an armed convoy and going through the Egyptian Customs, Amanda booked a passage on the S.S. *Orantares* sailing from Port Said to Limassol. They were, however, relieved to discover that others from Fayid, also bound for a holiday in Cyprus, had decided to travel the same way, and that she would be accompanied by Captain Gates, Major and Mrs Blaine and Persis Halliday.

Captain the Hon. Tobias John Allerton Gates was a pleasant young man whose more engaging qualities were at present somewhat obscured by the state of his emotions. Toby was in love — not for the first time — and his failure to make the present object of his devotion, Miss Amanda Derington, take him seriously was casting a deep gloom over a hitherto volatile nature.

Toby had not intended to go to Cyprus for his leave. He had had other plans that included Roehampton and Cowdray Park. But on hearing that Miss Derington meant to visit Cyprus, he had hurriedly cancelled these arrangements and booked a room at the same hotel in Kyrenia that his divinity had intended to patronize. And now it seemed that she was not to stay there after all. She would not even be staying in Kyrenia. She was staying instead at Nicosia with the manager of the Cyprus branch of some Derington & Co. enterprise, and Captain Gates wondered gloomily if it would be possible for him to cancel his room at the Dome Hotel and obtain one in some hotel in Nicosia instead?

Major Alastair Blaine of the 6th Hussars and his wife, Julia, were to spend three weeks with cousins who had a house in Kyrenia. They had intended to go by air, but the only passages available had been on a plane leaving on the 13th of the month, and Julia, a superstitious woman, had refused to fly on such an inauspicious date and had insisted on going by sea. The fifth member of the party from Fayid was Persis Halliday.

13

Mrs Halliday, although perhaps not so well known outside her own country, would have needed no introduction to anyone living within the bounds of the United States. Persis was a writer of romances, and unlike most of that sisterhood managed to look it. Her books sold by the hundred thousand and her name on the cover of any woman's magazine could be guaranteed to boost its circulation into astronomical figures. She had been widowed by an air disaster three years previously, and her presence in Fayid was accounted for by the fact that she had been on a world tour collecting material for Love in an Eastern setting, and was a friend of Amanda's aunt.

Persis, having heard Amanda mention that Venus-Aphrodite was supposed to have arisen from the foam off the coast of Cyprus, had immediately decided to visit the Island.

'Why, honey — it's a natural for me,' declared Persis. 'The birthplace of the Goddess of Love! Say, that's wonderful. You can count me in on the tour. I just can't miss it!'

'When one thinks of the money you must have made out of the woman,' commented Julia Blaine acidly, 'I suppose the least you can do is to pay her birthplace a visit.'

That had been at a dance at the Fayid Officers' Club, and Persis had raised her brows in real or affected astonishment at the vehemence of Julia's tone, and then laughed and drifted away on a wave of expensive scent.

'Twaddle!' said Mrs Blaine angrily, watching her go.

'What is?' inquired Amanda, startled.

'Her books. Silly, sloppy, sentimental twaddle with a nasty, slimy streak of sex. I can't think why anyone ever reads the stuff.'

'Escape,' said Amanda promptly. 'Just think what life must be like for millions of girls? A deadly, boring grind. Then they read something by Persis and they think, "That might be me!" and feel a lot better.'

'Do you mean to say that *you* read them?' demanded Mrs Blaine incredulously.

'I used to. My last headmistress banned them on the strength of one about a poor but honest hat-check girl who got mixed up with racketeers, dope peddling and white slavery. She emerged spotless of course — all Halliday heroines do — but the ban was enough to make us smuggle them into the dormitories by the dozen.'

Julia Blaine produced a sound uncommonly like a snort and said sharply: 'That merely bears out what I have just been saying. Only giggling schoolgirls would read them!'

She rose abruptly and walked away, angrily jerking at a long chiffon scarf that she wore about her plump, bare shoulders, the end of which had caught on the back of her chair.

'Sour grapes, I'm afraid,' said Amanda's aunt regretfully. 'Poor Julia. She used to write herself — or at least she tried to write. She once had a short story accepted by a magazine and thought that she had really arrived. But nothing came of it and she gave it up. Nothing has ever gone quite right for Julia.'

'Whose fault is that?' grunted the Brigadier, mopping the sweat from his brow and trying to edge his chair round so as to get a more direct blast from the nearest electric fan. 'I know she's your cousin, but the woman's a fool.'

'I know,' sighed Amanda's aunt. 'She is difficult. Poor Julia! She's always angry about something — usually something that doesn't matter at all, like Persis Halliday's books. If she hadn't anything to be angry about I believe she'd invent it. It's a habit of mind. Such a pity that she's never had any children. Alastair's father was one of a family of eighteen I believe, but only two of them married. Alastair is the very last of the Blaines of Tetworth and I think Julia feels it rather. Perhaps that's why she's turned so sour. She shouldn't be sour. Stout people are usually rather placid and jolly.'

'Probably the result of all those pints of lemon juice and iced water that she drinks,' said the Brigadier. 'Enough to sour anyone. Can't think why she does it!'

'To make her thin,' said Amanda's aunt. 'Not that it seems to do much good. All the same it's really very stupid of her to be rude to Persis. Persis may seem gay and good-tempered, and her books may drip with sentiment. But underneath all that she has a good hard streak of vanity and cast iron. She wouldn't have got where she has without it. And because she makes fun of her own books, it doesn't necessarily mean that she takes kindly to other people doing so.'

'Julia,' said the Brigadier, 'is jealous.'

'I know, poor dear. But then she's always been like that ever since she was a child. She's pretty — or she was pretty — and she's got plenty of money. But she would so like to have been fascinating and famous and filthy-rich. And she's automatically jealous of anyone who has anything she hasn't got.'

'I didn't mean that,' remarked the Brigadier. 'I meant Alastair.'

'Oh *that!*' said Amanda's aunt, and sighed. 'That's just an occupational disease with her. She wouldn't speak to Amanda for days just because he started giving her those riding lessons, and she still sulks every time he asks Amanda for a dance.'

Amanda laughed. 'I can't think why,' she said. 'He's very nice and he has charming manners. But he's as dull as — well I don't believe that ditch water is dull. Isn't it supposed to be simply teeming with weird and peculiar and wriggly forms of life? I don't believe that you'd find anything weird or peculiar about Alastair Blaine if you pushed him under a microscope. He's just a nice reliable glass of water — slightly chlorinated. The sort of thing you drink at every meal without thinking about it, and pass up at once if anything better offers.'

'Such as what?' demanded the Brigadier. 'Champagne? Seen anything yet that looks like champagne to you, Mandy?'

'Yes,' said Amanda, her dimples suddenly in evidence.

They had been sitting, all three of them, in a corner of the ballroom, and Amanda's aunt had turned in her chair to watch Persis Halliday and Major Blaine, who were dancing together.

16

Alastair Blaine was not a particularly good-looking man, but he possessed a pleasant tanned face, the lean lines of a cavalryman, thick blond hair and a pair of frosty blue eyes. He was forty, but did not look it, and was frequently taken to be at least five years younger than his wife's stout and embittered thirty-eight. He was popular, especially with men, and his manner towards his nagging, discontented wife was generally admitted to be beyond reproach, for Julia Blaine cannot have been an easy woman to live with. She had been the spoilt only child of rich and elderly parents, and as a plumply pretty debutante with a more than adequate income she had fallen in love with young Alastair Blaine, home on leave from India, and had married him.

Julia had not liked India. Alastair, a junior officer in an Indian Cavalry Regiment, knew too many people and had too many friends there, and Julia was jealous of anyone and anything that distracted his attention from her. It was there that she first tried out a gambit that was in time to wreck her peace of mind and all prospects of a happily married life. At any party, picnic, ball or social gathering where Alastair appeared to be enjoying himself, she would develop a headache or feel suddenly unwell, and ask to be taken home.

It became her way of demanding his attention and demonstrating her possession of him, and satisfied some hungry, jealous, grasping instinct in her that could not bear to see him entertained or interested by anything or anyone but herself. She loved him with a bitter, jealous love that drove her to almost pathological extremes of behaviour in order to prove to herself that she had at least the power to wound him, and which only served to drive him further from her. The nerves and ill-health that had at first been imaginary, she pandered to and coaxed into reality. And there had been no children to direct her energies and emotions into more normal channels. The plumpness which had been pleasing in youth had turned in her thirties to fat, and the uncharitable were quick to decide that it was only his wife's money that kept Alastair

Blaine from running off with some younger and more glamorous charmer. Not that gossip had ever been able to name one. Everyone liked Alastair, but despite his wife's unreasonable jealousy no one could accuse him of taking any particular interest in any other woman, and he had perhaps paid as much attention to Amanda Derington as he had ever been known to pay to anyone.

At the moment he was dancing with Persis Halliday, and Persis, slim and spectacular in flame-coloured chiffon, was flirting with him with a deliberate and malicious ostentation that was undoubtedly aimed at annoying his wife.

'I can only hope that Persis changes her mind about going to Cyprus,' murmured Amanda's aunt, watching Mrs Halliday with a troubled frown. 'Julia isn't going to like it a bit, and she really does need a holiday. The heat has been very trying and she is not at all fit.'

'You mean she's too fat,' said Amanda with the callousness of youth and a twenty-two-inch waist. 'If she took a bit more exercise, instead of sipping all that diluted lemon juice, she'd feel far better. Who are these people she and Alastair are staying with in Cyprus?'

'The Normans. He's Alastair's first cousin, and next in line to inherit Tetworth if Alastair doesn't come up with any children — which seems highly likely at this late date. I met them when I was over there last year. They have a fascinating house in Kyrenia. I rather think that Claire Norman is delicate — lungs probably — and that is why they have to live in a warm climate. They must have plenty of money, as George Norman does nothing. Julia tells me that they'll be crossing on the same boat as you are, as they've been staying with friends in Alex. You'll probably be seeing quite a lot of them.'

'I do *hope* not,' said Amanda feelingly. 'Not if it means seeing much more of Mrs Blaine. The proper place for her is flat on her back on some psychiatrist's couch being de-complexed. You can't blame Mrs Halliday for trying to take a rise out of her — she's been consistently rude all evening. That's no way to keep a husband!'

'When you have acquired one of your own, Mandy, you will be able to show us how it should be done,' said the Brigadier dryly.

Amanda laughed and made a face at him. 'If you really want to know, darling, I've decided to be a spinster.'

'What? Do you mean to say that in all this seething mob of males you see nothing that attracts your eye?'

'Only one,' said Amanda reflectively. 'Present company excepted, of course.'

'Ah!' said the Brigadier. 'That champagne you were referring to a moment or two ago. Don't tell me that young Toby has at last succeeded in making a dent in your affections? — where is he by the way?'

'He had to rush off and turn out a guard, or something equally martial,' said Amanda. 'He'll be back. No, Toby isn't my idea of champagne, poor lamb.'

'Not Andrew Carron I hope? — or is it young Haigh? or the Plumbly boy or — no it *can't* be Major Cotter! I won't believe it of you.'

'It isn't anyone you know,' said Amanda regretfully. 'In fact it isn't anyone I know either.'

She indicated by a brief gesture of the hand a lone gentleman who was lounging in a chair on the terrace just beyond the nearest door that led out of the ballroom, his long legs stretched out before him and his hands deep in the pockets of a pair of burnt-orange slacks of the type worn by Breton fishermen.

'Good God!' said the Brigadier, revolted. 'The *Artist?*'

'That's right,' agreed Amanda. 'Don't you think he looks rather intriguing?'

'No I do not. Needs a hair-cut! Where did you meet the feller?'

'I didn't. I mean I haven't. I've only seen him here and there. And as I'm off to Cyprus on Monday, I don't suppose I shall ever meet him now. A pity. He looks precisely my cup of tea.'

'You are mixing your drinks,' observed the Brigadier, hitching his chair round so as to obtain a better view. 'He probably wears sandals and manicures his toenails and thinks Picasso is terrific.'

'Well so do I, if it comes to that.'

'*Tacha!*' said the Brigadier. 'All you women are alike. Hand you a lot of nice clean-living normal chaps on a platter, and you won't look at 'em! But you fall over your feet at the sight of the first long-haired blighter who dabbles in art. What's he doing here anyway?'

'Painting the pyramids,' sighed Amanda's aunt. 'They will do it!' She turned an affectionate smile upon her niece: 'You are quite right, Mandy. Such a change from chlorinated drinking water or gin and lime. I must get to know him at once.'

'What on earth are you talking about?' demanded the Brigadier, bewildered.

'Champagne, of course,' said Amanda's aunt. 'So much more exciting and stimulating than — well, beer.' She rose to her feet in a swirl of grey draperies and turned towards the door.

'Muriel!' said the Brigadier, scandalized, 'even at your age you cannot go accosting strange men!'

'Watch me,' said Amanda's aunt, and left them.

It was perhaps half an hour later that her niece, leaving the ballroom for the cooler air of the terrace, was hailed by her aunt.

'Amanda dear, come over here. I want to introduce you to Steven Howard. Mr Howard — my niece, Amanda Derington.'

Mr Howard rose and Amanda held out her hand and found herself looking up into a pair of coolly observant hazel eyes that held a curious glint of speculative interest. There was no trace of admiration in that level gaze, or any recognition of the fact that Miss Derington was an exceptionally pretty girl. Only that oddly speculative interest.

Brown hair ... light brown eyes ... sun-browned face ... thirtyish; he isn't really good-looking, thought Amanda confusedly: his face is out of drawing. But that's what makes it so intriguing ...

A muscle twitched at the corner of Mr Howard's mouth and Amanda suddenly awoke to the fact that her hand was still in his and that she had been studying his face for a full minute. She snatched her hand away, blushed vividly, and was instantly furious with herself and — illogically — with Steven Howard.

'Mr Howard is an artist. He paints,' said Amanda's aunt helpfully. 'He is collecting material for an Exhibition in the autumn.'

'Oh,' said Amanda briefly.

Mr Howard said: 'I am afraid that your aunt gives me credit for more zeal than I possess. To tell the truth, I find art an admirable excuse for avoiding work and loafing around in the sun.' His voice was slow and pleasant and contained the hint of a laugh.

Amanda said: 'Really?' in the tone of one who is not amused, and the band launched into 'La Vie en Rose'.

'I'm sorry I can't ask you to dance,' said Mr Howard, 'but as you see, I am improperly dressed. Perhaps some other time——?'

'I shan't be here,' said Amanda flatly. 'I'm leaving on Monday. Toby, isn't this our dance?'

She turned abruptly away and left him, and when the dance was over and she and Toby returned to the terrace, he was gone.

'But I thought you wanted to meet him, Mandy!' said Amanda's aunt plaintively. 'Why did you snub the poor man after I'd gone to all that trouble?'

'I don't know,' admitted Amanda ruefully. 'Because I felt I'd make an exhibition of myself, I suppose. Or else because I don't like being laughed at. And he wasn't in the least snubbed. He was amused — and I don't think I like him at all.'

'Oh well,' said Amanda's aunt, 'I don't suppose you're ever likely to see him again.'

But in this she was entirely wrong. Amanda was to see him again not five minutes after Julia died.

2

The decks of the S.S. *Orantares*, which was due to leave Port Said for Limassol, were hot and crowded, and the party from Fayid had taken refuge in the lounge where they had turned on all the fans and ordered iced drinks.

They had been joined there by Mr and Mrs Norman, who had arrived from Alexandria earlier in the day.

Claire Norman was a petite, small-boned and magnolia-skinned woman who possessed a pair of wide grey eyes fringed with silky black lashes, and a cloud of short dark curls cut like a child's. She was not particularly pretty, but her lack of inches and look of slender delicacy somehow suggested the drooping fragility of a snowdrop bending before a harsh wind, and managed to make every other woman appear, by comparison, buxom and oversized. She owned in addition a sweet, soft little voice, and her beautifully cut dress of pale green linen, small white hat and the faint scent of lily-of-the-valley that clung about her, strongly emphasized the First-Flower-of-Spring motif.

Her husband, George Norman, appeared by contrast almost aggressively solid and beefy as he fussed about his tiny wife like some large and over-anxious St Bernard dog. His square, homely face was burnt brick-red by the sun and his thick brown hair was streaked with grey, and he looked completely out of place in the hot, garish and cosmopolitan setting of the crowded lounge. One felt instinctively that he would have been more at home wearing old tweeds and a hat with salmon flies stuck into the band, drinking draught beer at some English country pub, rather than wearing thin tropical duck and accepting an iced gin sling from a coffee-coloured gentleman in a red tarboosh.

'Oh, this heat!' sighed Claire Norman, 'I'm exhausted!'

'Claire tires so easily,' explained George Norman to the assembled company. 'Darling, don't you think you should go and lie down? It's probably a lot cooler in the cabin.'

'And leave dear Julia? — and Alastair — just when we've met? Of course not! Why I've been *longing* to see them again. It's been such *years!*'

'January,' said Julia blightingly. 'Six months.'

'So it is. But it *seems* like years. It's dreadful the way one misses one's real friends ...'

' ——and before that, September,' continued Julia as though Mrs Norman had not spoken.

'And now again. It's so wonderful to see you Julia — and you too Alastair ...' Claire Norman laid a small white hand caressingly on Alastair Blaine's lean brown one and Amanda saw him flush, and saw too that for a brief moment there was a queer, unreadable look on his face.

Julia put down her glass with a grimace of disgust and said: 'They've put sugar in it! Alastair, make that man get me another. I particularly said only lemon and water, *not* lemon squash. They don't listen!'

Major Blaine dutifully hailed a passing steward and Claire said: 'It's so good of you both to come and stay with us, Julia. I get so lonely in Cyprus — so far from home and friends.'

'Then why stay there?' demanded Julia.

Claire Norman drew a soft, quivering breath and smiled wistfully. 'The doctors,' she said gently. 'They tell me that I could never ... But don't let's talk about me. Let's talk about something more interesting. *You!* You're looking so well Julia darling. I only wish I could put on a little weight too. George makes me drink pints of cream and eat pounds of butter, but it's no good. I cannot seem to gain an ounce. Daddy always said I was a changeling — too small for a mortal.'

Persis choked into her gin and lime, dabbed her mouth with a vast chiffon handkerchief and muttered something into its folds that sounded suspiciously like *'Teeny weeny me!'* and Amanda's dimples were suddenly visible. She turned hurriedly away, and looking out of the window said: 'We must be going to sail. They seem to be getting the gangway in.'

There was a burst of shouting and invective from over the side as two more passengers, late arrivals who had almost succeeded in missing the boat, scrambled up the gangway and stood panting and breathless on the deck.

They were an ill-matched couple. The attractive, dark-haired woman in the pink linen suit was as smartly and expensively dressed as Persis, and her white shoes and gloves, despite the heat and the coal dust, were fresh and spotless. She carried a small white leather dressing case in one hand, and what appeared to be an easel in the other. Her companion, by contrast, appeared hot, grubby and dressed with deliberate carelessness. He wore a pair of exceedingly dirty blue linen slacks topped by an orange sports shirt that could also have done with a wash, and sported a scanty ginger beard and a black beret.

Artist, thought Amanda; and was suddenly reminded of Steven Howard. No one meeting Mr Howard for the first time could have typed him, she thought. He had, it is true, worn brightly coloured slacks; but then a good many members of the Sailing Club affected them too, and there was nothing else about him to suggest his profession. He might have been anything: *Tinker, tailor, soldier, sailor,* mused Amanda; and wondered why it was that she should remember everything about him, and every line of his face, so clearly?

The blatantly artistic gentleman on the deck dropped two suitcases and an untidy paper parcel containing canvases, and said crossly and as though continuing a previous conversation:

'Of course I declared them. What a country! Not a tube of usable paint in the place. Students' Water Colours — *Bah!* Put that down, you frightful coolie! Put it *down* — it's not dry yet! *God in heaven*—— *!*'

George Norman, his attention attracted by the howl of fury from the deck, stood up and peered through the window over Amanda's head.

'I thought so,' he said. 'It's that chap Potter.'

Claire turned quickly. 'Lumley? Why, whatever can he have been doing over here?'

'Painting the pyramids, I suppose,' said her husband in an unconscious echo of Amanda's aunt.

'Tell him to come in and join us,' said Claire. She turned to Major Blaine: 'You remember Lumley Potter, don't you Alastair? He has a studio-flat in Famagusta. You met him once or twice at our house when you and Julia were staying with us last year. I think I took you over to see his paintings.'

'You did,' said Julia. '*Lumley!* That wasn't what his mother christened him. I met a Mrs Deadon in Cairo last winter who knew *all* about Mr Potter. I'm not surprised that he decided to settle in Cyprus. As for his paintings, I could do as well with my eyes shut — better! If that's art——'

'But Julia darling, it *is* Art' — Claire pronounced it as though it had a capital A. 'You mustn't be conventional, darling. Lumley doesn't paint what ordinary, conventional people see. He paints the *soul* of a place — the spiritual aroma.'

'Spiritual garlic you mean!' snapped Julia. 'Don't be such a humbug, Claire! The man's a flop, a failure and a fake, and you know it. He can't paint well, so he dresses himself up in what is practically fancy dress, grows a beard, talks a lot of rubbish and paints as badly as he can in the hope of fooling a lot of credulous artistic snobs into thinking he's a genius. And so I told him!'

'Yes, I remember,' said Claire dryly. 'And lost him a great deal of money by doing so. That new-rich Australian couple had

25

practically bought eight of his canvases, but when they heard you they took fright and backed out. However Alastair at least did not agree with you. He bought one — "Sea Green Cypriots" — didn't you Alastair?'

'Only because he felt he had to, to make up for the Blaggs backing out of buying those dreadful daubs,' said Julia unpleasantly.

'Oh darling! You *do* misjudge Alastair so. He has a real, deep-down feeling for truth in Art.'

'I understand Alastair perfectly, thank you Claire,' said Julia acidly.

Alastair Blaine flushed uncomfortably and Persis rose with determination: 'Well, I don't know about you, but I guess I've had all that I can take of the ship's gin,' she remarked cheerfully. 'Alastair honey, how about leaving the girls to sort out your artistic sensibilities while you escort me on deck? I'd like to take a slant at the waterfront before we pull out. Will you spare him, Julia?'

Major Blaine rose with alacrity and assisted Persis to collect her handbag and gloves, while Claire Norman watched them with a sudden frown on her white forehead. After a moment she turned abruptly to her husband and said: 'George dear, I asked you to call Lumley.'

George Norman looked embarrassed and spoke with obvious hesitation: 'Er – well – I thought perhaps I had better not. He had someone with him.'

'Oh?' Claire Norman's soft voice sharpened a little. 'Who was it? Anyone we know?'

'Anita.'

'*Who?*' said Major Blaine, turning sharply. 'But I thought——'
He glanced at Amanda, but did not finish the sentence, for Persis took his arm and said: 'Let's go,' and they turned away together and disappeared through the doorway.

'Anita!' said Claire Norman. There were suddenly two bright

26

patches of colour in her pale cheeks. Her small mouth tightened into a hard narrow line, and for a moment it was as if the frail, pliant snowdrop had been transformed into something made of steel.

The impression was only a fleeting one, and then the corners of her small mouth drooped childishly and once more the sense of wistfulness and fragility was back, and Mrs Norman was saying in her soft, apologetic voice: 'I think after all that I will go and lie down for a while, George dear. I feel so tired. I'll see you at dinner Julia — if I feel strong enough.'

She bestowed a faint smile upon Amanda, directed another at Toby Gates, tucked her small hand confidingly through her husband's arm and moved gracefully away.

Julia Blaine sat staring after her in silence and Amanda saw with surprise that her face was colourless and her eyes wide and fixed and filled with something that looked uncommonly like fear. It was a disturbing expression, and Amanda tried to think of something light and casual to say that would break the spell of that uncomfortable silence. But before she could speak Mrs Blaine stood up, pushing her chair back so violently that it overturned on the thick carpet, and walked quickly out of the lounge.

The ship had sailed some ten minutes later, and Amanda and Toby had gone out on to the deck to watch the garish waterfront of Port Said with its blaze of flame trees slide past them, shimmering in the heat haze.

Feluccas with their squat prows and huge triangular sails drifted by among a clutter of shipping from almost every nation in the world: a British destroyer bound for Colombo and the Far East; oil tankers from England, America, Holland, France, Scandinavia; a P & O liner, white and glittering in the hot sunshine; a troopship returning from Singapore; a dhow from Dacca and a cargo boat from Brazil.

They passed the long stone mole where the statue of de Lesseps gazes out upon that narrow ribbon of water that is his memorial for all time. Beyond and far behind the green-bronze figure, a fleet of fishing boats lay motionless on the shallow waters that curve away towards Damietta and the Delta of the Nile, their sails ghostly in the haze. A cool breath of wind from the open sea blew gently across the sun-baked deck as the ship turned her bows towards Cyprus, and when the white roof-tops and garish domes of Port Said had vanished into the heat haze, Amanda went down to her cabin to wash off the dust of the journey from Fayid.

The long, white-painted ship's corridor was hot and airless and smelt strongly of food, disinfectant, engine oil and that curious all-pervading and entirely individual smell of shipboard. A small but voluble group of people were standing halfway down the corridor and Mrs Blaine's voice made itself heard above the babble:

'I don't care, you'll just have to find me another cabin. I didn't notice it before, or I would never have let you move my things in. I won't sleep in there, and that's all there is to it!'

Mrs Blaine, looking flushed and angry, pushed her way through the group and caught sight of Amanda.

'Really, these people are impossible!' she announced heatedly. 'There must be dozens of other cabins!'

'What's the matter?' inquired Amanda. 'Is there something wrong with yours?'

'Only the number,' said Julia bitterly. 'It's thirteen. I won't travel in it. I'd rather sleep on deck. It isn't even as if the ship were full. Why it's half empty! And it's no good just saying that I'm superstitious. I am. Not about some things — like cats and ladders — but I am about thirteen.'

'Well I'm not,' said Amanda cheerfully. 'I'll swop with you if you like. They've given me a two-berth cabin all to myself.'

'Would you? Would you really?'

'Of course. I haven't unpacked anything yet so it won't take a minute. Mine's fourteen — right next door to you.'

The stewardess, a cabin steward, a hovering Cypriot deck-hand

28

and a man who was evidently the purser, expressed voluble relief, and the transfer was accomplished in a matter of minutes.

'It's very good of you,' said Julia Blaine awkwardly, lingering in the doorway of her late cabin and speaking in a halting, difficult voice. 'I know it sounds silly to be so superstitious, but – well I've wanted to get away from the heat and – and Fayid so badly, and I – I do so want this leave to be a success. But when I saw that number on the door it – it seemed like a bad omen, and I ...' Her voice trailed away and stopped.

Amanda smiled sympathetically at her, but Julia Blaine did not return the smile. She was not looking at Amanda. She was staring instead at her own reflection in the narrow strip of looking-glass behind Amanda's head, and her plump, ageing face was once again white and frightened.

Amanda had tea in the lounge with Toby Gates, and when the sun had set in a blaze of gold and rose and amethyst and the sky was brilliant with stars, they had all dined in the saloon: Amanda, Toby, Julia and Alastair Blaine, the Normans and Persis Halliday.

The saloon was far from crowded and Amanda caught sight of the ginger-bearded painter of spiritual aromas dining at a small table with his companion of the afternoon, who had changed her linen suit for a short, strapless dinner dress of scarlet lace.

Amanda had exchanged one cotton frock for another, and Julia Blaine had not bothered to change at all. But Claire Norman was looking cool and ethereal in white chiffon and pearls, while Mrs Halliday, despite the heat, had elected to wear gold lamé and some astonishing emeralds. The glittering cloth brought out the gold lights in her copper hair and the emeralds turned her eyes to a clear, shining green. She looked stunning and knew it, and was amusing herself by flirting outrageously with George Norman.

Alastair Blaine was sitting next to Amanda, but Claire Norman, seated on his right, monopolized most of his attention, and for once Julia's acid tongue was silent. She was watching her husband and Claire Norman with a furtive and almost frightened intentness, but if Alastair was aware of this he certainly paid no attention to it. Major Blaine, for the first time since Amanda had known him, appeared to be the better — or worse — for drink. His face was unnaturally flushed and his blue eyes overbright, and he appeared to be slurring his words a little.

They were half-way through the meal when Claire leant across and spoke to Amanda:

'Alastair tells me that you've never been to Cyprus before, Amanda? — I may call you Amanda, mayn't I? Are you staying long?'

'Only ten days,' said Amanda regretfully. 'It doesn't seem nearly long enough. Ten days is such a little time.'

'Oh, but it's a very little Island. Where are you staying? In Kyrenia?'

'No, I'm afraid not. I'd much rather have stayed somewhere near the sea, but my uncle arranged for me to stay with some people in Nicosia.'

'Army people I suppose. They're nearly all stuck in Nicosia, poor things.'

Amanda shook her head. 'No. They're something to do with wine. People called Barton.'

'Barton! You can't mean *Glenn* Barton?'

'Yes, I think that must be it. Glennister Barton. Do you know them?'

'Yes, of course I know them; but you can't possibly be staying at the Villa Sosis. Why—— ' She stopped suddenly and bit her lip.

'But I am staying with them,' said Amanda with a laugh. 'Did you think they were away?'

'No. I mean—— ' Once more Claire Norman did not finish the sentence. She laughed instead; a light tinkling laugh that somehow gave Amanda the impression that she was both disturbed and angry. 'Oh well — we shall see. It will be very interesting. But personally I should have thought that Glenn would have had more respect for the convention. He is such a stickler for propriety.'

With which cryptic remark she turned her attention to Toby
Gates, and Amanda had no further opportunity of reopening the
subject, for it was at that point that the artistic Mr Potter and his
companion rose to leave the dining saloon and paused beside their
table. Amanda, looking round, saw the painter pull at the
woman's arm as though he would have hurried her past, but she
disengaged herself deliberately and spoke in a clear high voice:

'Hullo Claire. Hullo Mrs Blaine. Alastair! — fancy seeing you
here again!'

Alastair Blaine stood up quickly. He was swaying a little. 'Hullo
Anita. What are you doing here?'

'As if you didn't know!' mocked Mr Potter's companion. 'However if you don't, you soon will. Claire will see to that. Won't you,
Claire?'

Claire Norman stiffened where she sat. She turned slowly and
it seemed a full minute before she spoke:

'Hullo Anita. I'm not sure that I expected to see you here either.
I should have thought—— ' She broke off with a shrug of her
white shoulders and gave her tinkling little laugh: 'Oh well, it's no
concern of mine, is it? Hullo Lumley. You remember Major and
Mrs Blaine, don't you?'

She made no attempt to introduce the woman she had addressed
as Anita, but turned instead to the three men at her own table: 'Do
sit down, darlings. There's no need for you to stand around while
your food gets cold. They're just going.'

Mr Potter's face, which had acquired a fiery glow that reduced
his beard to luke-warm proportions, turned an even richer shade
of puce and he said hurriedly: 'Yes, we – we were going on deck.
Come on Anita.' He grabbed his companion's arm and almost
dragged her from the dining-room.

'Say, who was that dame?' inquired Persis, interested.

'Just someone we have the misfortune to know,' said Claire in
a small, cold voice, and instantly changed the subject.

Persis raised her eyebrows but did not press the question. And presently they left the table and went up to drink coffee in the lounge, and later someone turned on a gramophone and they danced on deck under a blaze of stars.

It was almost eleven o'clock by the time Amanda went down to bed, and except for a passing Cypriot deck-hand the long brightly lit corridor was silent and deserted. Her cabin was hot and stuffy after the cool night air on deck and she was pleasantly surprised to see that a thoughtful stewardess had placed a brimming frosted glass, with ice and a long strip of lemon peel floating in it, on a small stool near her berth. A moment or two later she realized that the drink must have been ordered by Julia, and placed in error in the cabin that Julia should have been occupying: she would have to take it in to her, but as she had already removed her dress it could wait until she was ready for bed. She put on a thin silk nightdress, washed in cold water and removing the pins from her hair, brushed out its long, shining length.

Amanda's hair — a deep golden brown with glints in it the colour of the first chestnuts in September — was a glorious anachronism. In the sunlight there were other colours in it too; purple and green and bronze; and it fell far below her slim waist in a rippling, glinting cloak that might well have rivalled Monte-zuma's fabled cloak of feathers. Yet as she brushed it she regretted — not for the first time since the advent of the hot weather — that she could not summon up the moral courage to defy her uncle and chop it off.

But Oswin Derington did not approve of short hair for women, and although Amanda was now of age and had demonstrated her independence in a drastic manner, the habit of years made her shrink from the prospect of Uncle Oswin's scandalized wrath should she cut off what he persisted in referring to as 'Woman's Crowning Glory'.

Amanda sighed and rummaged in her suitcase for a length of ribbon with which to tie it back, and she was pulling the bow tight when the door of the cabin burst open without any preliminary knock to disclose Julia Blaine, arrayed in a pink satin dressing-gown liberally trimmed with lace, a tight pink satin nightdress and feathered mules.

Mrs Blaine banged the door shut behind her and subsided heavily on the end of Amanda's berth. She was trembling violently and her teeth chattered as though she were cold.

'What's the matter?' demanded Amanda sharply; appalled by the sight of the older woman's ravaged face. 'Are you ill? Shall I call the stewardess?'

'No,' said Mrs Blaine hoarsely. 'It's – it's Alastair—— '

'Alastair? You mean he's ill?'

'No. But he hasn't come to bed. He – he was dancing to that gramophone, and I told him that I wasn't feeling well and would have to go to bed, but he wouldn't come with me. He wouldn't even come as far as the cabin with me! He said I could find the way myself. I waited and waited; and then I sent the stewardess to tell him to come as I was feeling very unwell, and he – he sent back to say that I'd better take an aspirin and that he couldn't come just now. Couldn't come . . .! It's that woman! I should have known it. I've always known that this would happen one day. Alastair . . . *Alastair . . .!*'

She broke into gulping, hysterical sobs.

'Mrs Blaine,' said Amanda gently, 'don't you think you'd better go back to your cabin and lie down? You shouldn't say these things to me — really you shouldn't. You'll feel quite differently about it in the morning. It's only because it's been a hot, tiring day that you're feeling upset. You don't really mean it. *Do* lie down.'

But Julia Blaine was beyond the reach of reason. She had to talk, and if it had not been to Amanda it would have been to someone else — anyone else — the stewardess, or a stranger.

She said violently: 'I shall say it! I do mean it! I shall tell everyone. *Everyone!* I've always known that he'd leave me one day. I've felt it; *here*—— '

She struck her billowing breasts with her clenched fists, while the tears poured down her plump, faded cheeks:

'Only he couldn't leave me! I had the money and he needed that. He might have managed in an Indian cavalry regiment, but when he had to transfer into a British one he had to have money. And I had more than the others. A lot more. There might have been prettier women, and younger and – and slimmer ones, like Anita, but they couldn't give him the horses and cars and comforts that I could. But now it's different. That American woman. She's rich. You saw those emeralds! They must have cost a fortune. And Claire — it isn't George's money. It's Claire's. That's why George has to stay in Cyprus. He hates it — he's always hated it. But if he left her he wouldn't have a penny, and he's grown used to doing nothing. When she got him to give up the Army she told him that they'd buy a farm in England. But she didn't; and he hadn't even qualified for a pension. She's got him where she wants him. But I didn't realize that she wanted Alastair. He can't do this to me! — he can't!'

She wept noisily, rocking her stout body to and fro, and Amanda sat down beside her and put her arms about the fat, satin-clad shoulders, wondering desperately what she could say to comfort this hysterical, despairing woman.

'I'm – I'm sure you must be imagining it,' said Amanda helplessly.

'I know him and you don't,' sobbed Julia, 'and I've never known him behave like this before. But she shan't have him! I'll kill myself first! I'd be better dead than having to go through all this – this awful agony.'

Amanda began to wonder if she ought not to ring the bell for the stewardess and ask for sedatives or the ship's doctor. She said anxiously: 'Wouldn't you like a – an aspirin or something?'

Mrs Blaine turned her head slowly and looked at Amanda as though she was awakening from a deep sleep or an anaesthetic. Her blotched and tear-disfigured face coloured a slow, ugly red and she jerked herself free of Amanda's arm and stood up abruptly:

'That's what Alastair said. He said to take some aspirin. The stewardess brought me some. The one who – who brought me the message.'

She opened her hot, plump hand to show two small white tablets that were already beginning to crumble.

Amanda said: 'You take those and get into bed. They'll make you sleep, and you'll feel much better in the morning.'

'Yes,' said Julia slowly. 'Perhaps it's the heat. I always feel so dreadful in the heat. It's horrible, having to live so much in the East. I've always hated Army life ... but Alastair likes it. Perhaps if I sleep ...'

She put the tablets into her mouth and reached out one plump beringed hand for the glass that stood beside the berth. The diamonds on her fingers winked and sparkled in the light of the ceiling bulbs as she lifted it to her lips and drank deeply.

She made a wry grimace and drank again, swaying a little as she stood, and presently said in a harsh whisper: 'I've been a fool. I should never have let him go back to Cyprus. But I never suspected ... Claire's too clever. We stayed with them last year, you know. And then they came and stayed with us, and we all spent Christmas and New Year together in Alex. He never seemed to pay any special attention to her. He – he always said that he didn't like little women. But tonight – tonight—— '

She swayed again and put up a hand, catching at the edge of the upper berth to steady herself. Holding it, she drew herself erect and said in a voice that was no longer trembling with hysteria but cold and venomous: 'Well he can't divorce me! And I'll never divorce him. *Never!* He knows that. I'd kill myself first — I'd kill myself!'

She clung to the edge of the berth, breathing stertorously and shivering, her eyes staring blindly across the small cabin. There were great beads of sweat on her forehead that trickled down and mingled with the tears that smeared her cheeks, and the silence in the cabin, broken only by the sound of her hoarse panting breath, began to grow oppressive.

Amanda watched her anxiously and presently said: '*Do* go to bed. You're only upsetting yourself. I'm sure your husband will be along soon.'

Julia Blaine looked at her as though she did not know who she was or could not focus her, and lifting the glass that she still held, drank again, thirstily.

A minute or two later she suddenly swayed and staggered and seemed to gasp for air, and releasing her hold on the berth, doubled up, retching; her face suffused and her eyes starting from her head.

The glass dropped from her hand and rolled on its side, spilling what little remained of its contents on to the floor in a scatter of melting ice, and Julia gave a curious, choking cry and fell forward to sprawl face downwards on the narrow cabin floor.

3

She's fainted, thought Amanda frantically. What on earth does one do for a faint? Oh, *bother* the woman!

She leapt for the bell and pressed it hard. The stewardess would know what to do.

Amanda bent and attempted to lift the limp body, but the task was beyond her. She managed to turn Mrs Blaine over. But at the sight of that contorted face her heart gave an odd lurch: Julia Blaine's mouth had fallen open and her eyes were wide and fixed and staring.

'It isn't a faint. She's had a fit,' said Amanda, unaware that she had spoken aloud. She reached for the unbroken glass, and filling it with water from the cold tap, splashed it over Mrs Blaine's face and neck: the water streamed over Julia's contorted features and across her staring eyeballs. But her eyelids did not close . . .

Amanda straightened up, cold and trembling. She sprang to the bell and pressed it again, frantically, and then seized by a sudden, shuddering horror, jerked open the door and ran out into the corridor. It stretched away on either side of her, blank, brightly lit and empty, and she had no idea at which end of it the stewardess had her cabin, or where to find her. But she must fetch help, and quickly.

Julia's own cabin was empty, and there was no one in No. 12, for it was a darkness and the door stood open. She turned in desperation to the one beyond it and hammered on the door.

'Who is it?' demanded a man's voice impatiently.

Amanda tried to speak and found that she could not. The next moment the door opened and Steven Howard, pyjama clad and sleepy, was staring down at her with a mixture of amusement and unqualified surprise.

'Well, well!' said Mr Howard cordially, his interested gaze missing no detail of her unorthodox attire. His eyes went to her white face and his own face changed abruptly, so that all at once it was an entirely different person who was standing there in the white, brightly lit corridor of the S.S. *Orantares*. His hand shot out and gripped Amanda's shoulder, steadying her:

'What is it?'

'It's Mrs Blaine,' said Amanda, shuddering. 'She's in my cabin. I – I think she's had a fit and I can't bring her round. And I rang and rang, but no one has answered the bell, and ... and ...'

Mr Howard said briskly: 'Just a minute.' He reached for a dressing-gown, put it on and said: 'Where is she?'

Amanda led the way to her cabin and stood back for him to enter, and he went quickly past her and dropped on one knee beside the sprawling figure whose pink satin attire was blotched and stained with water.

After a moment or two he lifted his head and said curtly: 'She's dead.'

He came to his feet rather slowly and looked at Amanda. It was a long, measuring look that held that same curious suggestion of speculation and intentness that she had seen in his eyes on the terrace of the Club at Fayid.

'No!' said Amanda in a whisper. 'Oh no! She can't be — she was talking to me! Why don't you get a doctor? Why don't you do something? If it's a heart attack a doctor—— '

Mr Howard cut her short: 'I'm not too sure that it was a heart attack.'

'What else could it *possibly* be?'

'Well, it could be suicide.'

'No,' said Amanda loudly and definitely. 'She wouldn't have

38

done that, because it would mean that he could—— ' She stopped abruptly.

'Mean that who could what?' inquired Steven Howard softly.

'Nothing,' said Amanda confusedly. 'I didn't mean ... it was just something that she said.'

Mr Howard reached across her and shut the cabin door.

'I think you'd better tell me just exactly what happened,' he said. 'Quickly, before anyone comes. If you rang for the stewardess she may be along at any moment, so let's have it.'

He spoke quite quietly, but with an unconscious note of authority which, for some reason, it did not occur to Amanda to question, and she found herself telling him exactly what Julia Blaine had said and done: repeating the substance of that hysterical outburst almost word for word.

Mr Howard said: 'Then you saw her take the tablets herself?'

'Yes. She put them in her mouth and then drank some lemon-water, and a little while later she seemed to feel ill, and then she fell down like – like she is now, only on her face.'

'Is that the glass?'

'Yes.' Amanda's teeth chattered a little and she clenched them on her lower lip.

Mr Howard reached out and picked it up, holding it by the extreme edge of the rim. He smelt it, put it down again and said: 'Where did all that water on her clothes come from? It didn't all come out of this glass, did it?'

'I filled it again at the basin and poured it over her. I thought it might bring her round.'

'I see.' He went down on his knees again and examined the contorted, staring face and then lifted the slack hands one after another. A few coarse grains of white powder clung damply to the palm of one hand. Steven Howard sniffed it, and rubbing the tip of his finger over it, touched it to his tongue with infinite caution, and frowned.

39

He sat back on his heels and looked around at the floor and presently said: 'What was the last thing she said again?'

'She said she'd kill herself. But I didn't think she meant it. I thought she was only – only—— '

'Quite,' said Mr Howard curtly. 'All the same it looks as though she may have meant it.'

He frowned thoughtfully down at the plump-fingered hands with their glittering rings and then stood up abruptly:

'It doesn't look as though anyone is going to answer that bell. You'd better see if you can find someone. See if you can rout out a steward or a stewardess; or grab the first ship's officer you see and tell him to send along a doctor.'

He looked Amanda over and added dryly: 'And if I were you, I'd put on a dressing-gown.'

An hour later Julia Blaine's body had been removed to the sick bay and the water had been mopped off Amanda's cabin floor. Amanda herself, having repeated her story — with several reservations — at least half a dozen times, was at last left in peace.

The ship's doctor had seemed puzzled by the cause of death and he too had suggested the possibility of suicide, but the stewardess had sworn with fervour and a touch of hysteria that she had given Mrs Blaine two aspirins and nothing else. She had produced the bottle in evidence, and the doctor had taken charge of it and after careful examination pronounced the tablets to be innocuous.

Alastair Blaine, white-faced and incredulous, had agreed that his wife had been in poor spirits of late; that she was highly strung and, though her health had not been of the best, there had never been any suggestion of heart trouble, and he did not know how she could have obtained poison.

'In the East, that is easy,' commented the Captain dryly. 'A little money, and the thing is done' — he had pantomimed a sly, expressive Oriental gesture.

Amanda, prompted by Steven Howard, had agreed that Mrs Blaine had talked of taking her life. And looking at Alastair

Blaine's haggard face, she had refrained from any mention of names or motives; allowing it to be inferred that a combination of nerves, ill-health and the heat had been responsible for Mrs Blaine's state of mind. She had not looked at Steven Howard, and to her relief he had failed to point out that this version differed considerably from the one that she had given him so short a time ago. He had, in fact, barely spoken. But Amanda had the odd impression that in some way that she could not define, he had directed the course of the inquiry and headed it away from dangerous ground. He had eventually, and still without appearing to do so, managed to get rid of the Captain, the First Officer, the doctor, the stewardess and sundry other spectators who had crowded in and asked questions and talked in unison. He had been the last to leave, and had stood in the doorway, his hands thrust into the pockets of his dressing-gown, frowning down at her.

'Are you sure you're all right? You wouldn't like me to knock up Mrs Halliday or get one of the stewardesses to sleep on that top berth?'

'No thank you,' said Amanda wearily. 'I'm all right. You wouldn't think that anyone could feel sleepy after all that, but I do. I feel very stupid and dopey.'

'Reaction from shock,' said Mr Howard. 'Well if anything scares you, don't wait for someone to answer that bell. Come out into the corridor and yell!'

'*Scares* me? What is there to be scared of?' asked Amanda, puzzled.

'I don't know,' said Steven Howard slowly. 'Nothing, I hope.'

He looked round the narrow cabin almost as though he were making certain that no one could be concealed there, and the frown line deepened between his brows. Then he shrugged his shoulders, smiled briefly, and was gone.

Amanda yawned. She felt unbelievably exhausted. She slipped out of her dressing-gown, leaving it in a heap on the floor, and climbing into her berth, switched off the light.

41

After a minute or two she became aware that there was a small hard lump either in or under her pillow, and she put up a sleepy and impatient hand to investigate.

And that was how she found the bottle.

It was a small bottle, and there was something in it that rattled. Amanda lay for a time in the semi-darkness, turning it over in her hand and wondering how it could have come there. Presently she reached out to switch on the light again, and sat up to look at it.

It was an ordinary glass bottle of the type that usually contains aspirins. There were three small tablets in it and it bore a bright red label with a single warning word printed blackly across it. POISON.

All at once Amanda was frightened. She had been shocked and horrified by Julia's collapse, and frightened by the staring, sightless eyes that had not blinked when the water splashed across them. But this was a different sort of fear. A cold, creeping fear that seemed to chill her blood and slow down the beat of her heart. For the bottle had not been there earlier that evening. She was quite sure of that. And for a very good reason.

She had sat down on the centre of the berth to read some letters before changing for dinner, and, reaching for the pillow, had tucked it between her shoulders and the back of the berth. There had been no bottle under it then.

That meant that someone had placed it there some time after eight o'clock. Julia? But Julia had not come near the pillow. She had sat on the foot of the berth and had not moved from there until she had stood up and put those tablets in her mouth and reached for the glass. Amanda had been between Julia Blaine and the pillow and it was quite out of the question that Mrs Blaine could have reached across her and put anything under it without her knowledge.

Who then? And why?

Quite suddenly an answer slipped into Amanda's head as though someone had whispered it very softly into her ear.

Julia Blaine had neither died of a heart attack nor killed herself. She had been murdered. And that small bottle with the poison label proved it——!

The tablets that Julia had put into her mouth had been aspirin tablets given to her by the stewardess. The poison had been in the glass. In that innocent iced drink whose unsweetened tartness would serve to disguise any additional acidity.

Someone who knew that Julia Blaine drank lemon juice and water, but who did not realize that she had changed cabins with Amanda, had laid that deadly trap for her. Julia should have drunk from that glass in her own cabin, and she would have been found there, dead. And presently the bottle would have been found under her pillow, to ensure a verdict of suicide.

Fate had been on the murderer's side, for chance had brought Julia to her former cabin and she had, after all, drunk from the glass and died. But it was Amanda who had found the bottle. And its presence under the wrong pillow was no longer a pointer to suicide, but proof of murder.

'No!' said Amanda, speaking aloud in the hot, silent little cabin. *'No!'*

Almost without realizing what she meant to do, she slipped out of bed. The carpet was still damp and faintly sticky under her bare feet, and she groped for her dressing-gown and putting it on rang the bell. This time it was answered promptly.

Amanda could hear the stewardess rustling down the corridor, her stiff, starched uniform sounding brisk and reassuring.

'What is it, dear? Can't you sleep?' The stewardess was stout, middle-aged, motherly and, by some miracle, English.

Amanda said: 'Did you – did you put a glass of water and lemon juice in here for Mrs Blaine, by mistake?'

The stewardess looked bewildered. 'A lemon squash dear? No. Would you like one?'

'No thank you. But there was one here. It was on that stool when I came in. Did you put it there?'

'Me? Oh no, dear. We don't provide drinks for the passengers unless they ask for them. But you'd only have to ring.'

'*Did* Mrs Blaine ask for one? This was her cabin before, and I – I thought perhaps it was put in here by mistake.'

'She didn't ask me for one, poor lady. And no one who has to do with the cabins would have made such a mistake, I assure you. They were all aware of the exchange. So it must have been put there by one of your friends. Now what is it that you want, dear?'

'Nothing,' said Amanda, white-faced. 'I – I only wondered ... You see when she — Mrs Blaine — swallowed those tablets she drank out of a glass that was on that stool; and I – I wondered who had put it there.'

'I'll tell you what's the matter with you, dear,' said the stewardess kindly. 'You're sufferin' from shock. That's what it is. You mustn't let it worry you. The poor lady must have bin out of her mind. Now just you try and forget all about it and go to sleep. I expect she had a drink out of that tooth glass over there.'

'No she didn't,' said Amanda. 'It was another glass.'

'Then where is it now?'

Amanda turned and looked about her, but the glass had gone. It was nowhere in the cabin.

'There now!' said the stewardess cosily. 'You're lettin' your nerves run away with you, dearie. An' no wonder! I'll fetch you a nice cup of hot milk, and you'll soon be asleep.'

'No thank you,' said Amanda in a small unsteady voice. 'It's very kind of you, but I don't want anything. I'm sorry to have bothered you.'

'That's all right,' said the stewardess. 'Now you get back into bed, and I'll turn the light out, and if you should want me you only have to ring.'

She tucked Amanda into her berth and went out, switching off the light and closing the door behind her. Her starched skirts rustled crisply away down the passage, and from somewhere nearby a door latch clicked softly.

A faint light from the passage outside filtered in through a narrow open grill above the door and thinned the darkness of the small cabin, and beyond the open porthole the sky was bright with moonlight.

Except for the soothing swish of the sea and the muffled, rhythmic throb of the engines, the night was still and silent and Amanda had heard no sound of footsteps. But suddenly her cabin door opened and closed again. And someone was there, standing beside her; a dark shape against the faint light from the transom.

Amanda's heart seemed to jerk and turn over sickeningly. She sat up, shrinking back against the head of the berth, and tried to scream — and could not, because her throat was dry and constricted with terror; and because there was a hand across her mouth.

A voice spoke in a whisper: 'Don't make a noise. It's I — Steve Howard.'

Amanda crumpled up in a small sobbing heap against him, and he put an arm about her, holding her hard, and sat down on the berth.

'I'm sorry. I didn't mean to frighten you' — his voice was barely a breath against her ear. 'But I had to talk to you. Come on, dear — take a pull on yourself.'

Amanda lifted her head from his shoulder and said in a sobbing furious whisper: *'Get out of my cabin!'*

'That's more like it,' approved Mr Howard. He produced a handkerchief and dried her eyes. Amanda snatched it from him, and having completed the operation for herself, reached for the electric light switch.

Steve Howard's hand shot out and caught her wrist. 'No! Don't turn on the light. I don't want the stewardess coming in here to find out why you're still awake. What were you telling her about

45

a glass? I heard you talking to her. Your door was open. What about that glass, Amanda?'

Amanda shivered and her teeth made a small chattering sound in the silence. She said in a halting whisper: 'There was a glass of water in here – with – with lemon in it, when I came to bed. Mrs Blaine always drinks – drank – lemon and water. She did it to make her thin. And she changed cabins with me.'

'When was that?' the whisper was suddenly sharp. 'Why did you change cabins?'

'This afternoon. Just before tea. This was her cabin. But she wouldn't go into it when she saw the number. It's thirteen, and she was superstitious about thirteen. So I told her that she could have mine.'

'Who knew about it?'

'I don't know. The stewardess said that – that the ship's people would all know. But I don't suppose anyone else would. Except Alastair of course — her husband. The – the stewardess said that it must have been one of the passengers who put that glass there.'

'Yes I know. I heard her. What made you ask her about it?'

'I – I was frightened. Mrs Blaine drank out of it. And now it's gone. Someone must have taken it.'

'I did,' said Steven Howard softly.

'You! But why? I don't understand.'

'Don't you? Why were you frightened because Mrs Blaine drank out of it?'

'Because of the bottle,' breathed Amanda tremulously. 'There was a bottle hidden under my pillow, and I thought——'

'What's that!' The whispered question cracked like a whip in the silence.

Amanda turned and thrust a shaking hand under the pillow, found the bottle and held it out.

Mr Howard took the bottle from her gingerly, holding it with extreme care, and turned to face the light that filtered in through the grill above the door. The little cabin that had seemed so dark

46

when the light had first been switched off no longer appeared dark now that Amanda's eyes had grown accustomed to the dim light, and the single word printed across the red label was clearly readable.

He turned back to her and said: 'How did you come to find it?'

'I told you. It was under my pillow. But it hadn't been there before.' She told him about that, and why she knew that it had not been there before eight o'clock.

'You don't think Mrs Blaine could have put it there while she was talking to you.' The words were less a query than an assertion.

'I know she didn't.'

'Then what *do* you think?'

Amanda did not answer him. She stared down instead at the small bottle that he held so carefully with a corner of his hand-kerchief.

'Why were you frightened, Amanda?'

Amanda's eyes lifted slowly to his face. His back was to the light from the passage and his face was in deep shadow, but she could see the gleam of his eyes and the line of his mouth and jaw.

She said: 'You know, don't you? That's why you took the glass.'

'*Ssh!* Quietly. Yes I know. You don't think that she died from a heart attack. Or that she killed herself either. That's it, isn't it?'

'What else can I think?' said Amanda shivering. 'If – if it was something in the glass and not the tablets in her hand, then it must have been – have been—— '

'Murder,' finished Steven Howard softly. 'Of course. And I think you're right. Mrs Blaine took two tablets of aspirin. The stuff that killed her was in that glass.'

'How – how can you know?' demanded Amanda in a shaking whisper.

'There are only two sets of finger-prints on the glass, and both of them are quite clear.'

Amanda said: 'But of course there are only two! Only two people touched it. Myself and Mrs Blaine. Oh, and you.'

Mr Howard shook his head. 'I lifted it by the rim. Those marks are there too. But what about the person who brought it here in the first place? There should have been at least three sets of prints on it.'

Amanda put her hands to her throat. It seemed oddly constricted. 'Then she *was* murdered. No! No, it can't be true!'

Her voice rose and Steven Howard's hand was instantly over her mouth. Amanda twisted her head away and said in a shuddering whisper: 'But – but don't you see, that would mean that it was someone she knew. Someone *I* know! — Persis or Toby—— No, it can't be. It couldn't possibly be!'

'It must be. Unless—— '

He stopped, and Amanda said breathlessly: 'Unless what?'

Mr Howard did not answer her. His eyes had not moved from her face, but he appeared to be listening intently and his hand closed warningly about her wrist.

There was someone in the passage outside. Amanda did not know how she knew it, or how Steven Howard had known it, for her ear had caught no sound of approaching footsteps. Perhaps someone had brushed against the door in passing, or a shadow had flickered briefly across the white wall of the passage.

Steve Howard sat between her and the door so that she could only see the edge of it. The door did not quite fit and there was a thin sliver of light where age had warped the wood. But even as she looked, the slit of light vanished.

Steve saw her eyes widen, and for a brief moment his fingers tightened on her wrist. He turned his head and drew something out of the pocket of his dressing-gown, moving with infinite caution. Amanda saw the light from the transom glint on the barrel of the gun he held, and thought with a stunned illogicality, 'He's left-handed.'

48

Booted feet clattered noisily down a companion-way at the far end of the passage and instantly the thin sliver of light reappeared at the edge of the door. Whoever had paused outside Amanda's cabin had gone as silently as they had come.

Someone, a ship's officer by the sound, passed quickly down the passage, and a distant door banged shut. Mr Howard slid the small gun into his pocket and sighed.

'I was afraid of that,' he said softly.

'Of what?' breathed Amanda.

Mr Howard turned to look at her. 'Without wishing to be an alarmist,' he said, 'I think you would be advised to walk extremely warily for the next few days. In fact I would suggest that you send yourself an urgent telegram and take the next available plane for England?'

'Why?' said Amanda. 'I don't understand——'

'Don't you? I should have thought it was obvious. It looks as though somebody planned a murder that was to pass as suicide. That someone has either realized already, or will shortly realize, that the thing has blown a fuse, in that you and not Mrs Blaine are occupying Cabin No. 13, and that you will therefore be in a position to know — or at least suspect — that Mrs Blaine was murdered. That being so, whoever planted that bottle may go to considerable lengths to get it back.'

'Then what are you going to do with it?' demanded Amanda in a dry whisper.

'Dispose of it.'

'But you can't! The Captain must see it — the police. If you don't tell them, I shall!'

Mr Howard stood up. 'I wouldn't do that if I were you,' he said quietly. 'Not unless you want to find yourself under arrest.'

Amanda shrank back against the pillow, her breath coming short. 'What do you mean?'

He stood looking down at her, his hands in his pockets, and

49

after a moment he said softly and very deliberately: 'You see, there is always the possibility that you might have worked the whole thing yourself.'

There was a long silence in the little cabin. A silence that seemed to stretch out into interminable minutes. Outside that silence the quiet night was once again full of sounds: the rustling wash of water along the sides of the ship, the monotonous throb of the engines and the hundred and one tiny creaks and squeaks and rattles that the shudder of the screw set up in the fabric of the ship.

Amanda spoke at last. 'You can't believe that. You can't!'

'Perhaps not. But there'll have to be a post-mortem, and the police may — if this turns out to be a case of murder. You see, they would have only your own word for what happened in this cabin, and of how you came to be in possession of that bottle. If it turns out to contain the same poison that killed Mrs Blaine, they may even think that you invited her in to talk to you. And since her husband presumably inherits anything she had to leave, Major Blaine will now be an exceedingly eligible widower — and you saw quite a lot of him in Fayid, didn't you?'

Amanda caught her breath in a hard gasp. She said in a furious whisper: '*Get out!* Get out of my cabin before I call someone to put you out!'

'Don't be silly, Amanda;' Steven Howard had not raised his voice, but the words held a cutting edge that was as effective as a slap in the face. 'You are in no position to behave stupidly. You have no idea at all what it would be like to get yourself involved in a police inquiry out here. It's no joke anywhere. With this set-up it would be hell. If you have any sense in that charming head you will keep your mouth shut about that bottle and the glass and let it be supposed that Mrs Blaine committed suicide. Any other course is likely to prove very sticky for you, if not downright dangerous. And you are in a sticky enough position already, without that.'

Amanda said: '*Who are you?*'

Mr Howard grinned unexpectedly. 'The name is Howard. Steve to my friends. I paint indifferent pictures and have a passion for meddling in other people's affairs. Anything else you'd like to know?'

'Yes,' said Amanda. 'Who are you really? Why do you carry a gun? What are you doing in all this? Don't tell me that you're just out here to paint pictures, because I don't believe a word of it!'

Mr Howard laughed. 'All right. Let's say that I happen, for reasons of my own, to be interested in one or two people who are on this boat.'

'Are you in the police?' demanded Amanda abruptly.

'No.'

'Then why are you taking a hand in this?'

Steve Howard grinned. 'Pure knight-errantry. Or mere meddling — take your choice. And now I think you'd better get some sleep, if you think you can manage it. There's a bolt on that door. I suggest you use it. Goodnight Amarantha.'

The door closed softly behind him.

4

Amanda shot the bolt on the inside of her cabin door with unsteady fingers, and returned to her berth to sit rigidly upright with her arms about her knees, straining to listen and starting at every unidentified sound.

The full import of Steven Howard's statement that sooner or later someone must inevitably realize that Amanda, as the present occupant of cabin number thirteen, was bound to obtain possession of evidence that pointed to murder, had only just come home to her. It was a singularly unpleasant thought; and even more unpleasant was the sudden realization that but for Julia's arrival, she would have carried that glass into Julia's cabin. Her fingerprints would have been found upon it, and there would only have been her own word for why she had handed a glass of poison to Alastair Blaine's wife.

Alastair's wife ... Was that the key to this cruel murder? Had Alastair—— ? But no, that was absurd! It could not be Alastair because he at least would know of the exchange of cabins. Who then? Someone who knew Julia well enough to be aware of her lemon-and-water slimming fad, and who had made a note of the number of her cabin but had not realized that she had subsequently moved into Amanda's. Mrs Norman—— ? George Norman? Persis? Toby? No, it could not be! There must be some mistake. Julia must either have had a heart attack or committed suicide after all, and there must be some other explanation for that bottle. There *must* be!

Why, oh why, thought Amanda desperately, had she ever

offered to exchange cabins with Julia Blaine? But for that, no one need ever have suspected that there had been a murder. No one would ever have known. Yet because she had made that exchange, she knew — and someone else must suspect that she knew — that Julia's death was not suicide, but a carefully planned murder.

The sky was paling to the dawn, and the swish of hoses and a thump of holystones betokened the arrival of a new day before Amanda fell at last into an exhausted sleep, from which she was eventually awakened by a loud knocking on her door. Starting up with her heart in her mouth, she found the cabin full of reflected sunlight, and the stewardess demanding entrance with a lukewarm cup of tea.

In the gay morning sunlight Amanda could not remember for a moment why she should have been frightened. Her first impression was that she must have had a particularly vivid and unpleasant dream. But this was quickly dispelled by the stewardess, who on being admitted, announced with relish that the police were already on board and that the captain wished to see Miss Derington in his cabin as soon as possible.

Amanda was suddenly aware that the sea was no longer swishing past the ship and that the engines were silent.

'Have we arrived?'

'Half an hour or more ago,' said the stewardess. 'We're at Limassol. I would have woken you before, but the gentleman in number eleven said to let you sleep. *Such* a nice man! So thoughtful. It's not many that are these days. Shall I get you some breakfast, dear? You looked a bit peaked — an' no wonder.'

'No thank you,' said Amanda. 'Just coffee, if you would. What does the captain want to see me about?'

'I'm sure I don't know, dear. I expect they just want you to tell the police what happened last night — just as a matter of form as you might say — before they bury the poor lady. Very cut up her husband is. Looks like a ghost he does. As for the little lady in 31, she came over all queer when she heard the news. The dead lady

53

and her husband were going to stay with her. Fancy! Cousins or something. Very delicate she is — Mrs Norman, that is. The sensitive kind I should say. *Dreadfully* upset she was. "Why, Mrs Norman," I said——'

A knock on the door mercifully stemmed the flow and Toby Gates' voice inquired anxiously if Amanda was all right and wasn't it ghastly?

Amanda replied in the affirmative to both, adding that she would be out in five minutes; and while the stewardess went in search of coffee she dressed hurriedly, plaiting her hair into two thick braids and pinning it swiftly about her head instead of coiling it into the heavy knot at the nape of her neck that took considerably more time and care to achieve.

The yellow cotton frock that she had worn on the previous day seemed too gay a garment in which to attend an inquiry into sudden death (she would not say the word 'murder' even to herself), and she rummaged hastily in her suitcase and found a silver-grey poplin with a narrow white belt. Gulping down the coffee that the stewardess had brought, she slipped her feet into white sandals and found Toby Gates waiting for her at the end of the passage.

'They want to see all of us,' said Toby, taking her arm and hurrying her up the stairs. 'Those of us who knew her. She must have had a brain-storm. I always thought she was a spot peculiar. Rotten for Alastair, poor devil; utter hell I should think.'

Amanda said anxiously: 'What do they want to see us for, Toby?'

'Oh, just to give them some sort of a picture of the whole thing I suppose. Matter of form an' all that. They've already had poor old Alastair answering questions for the odd half-hour or so. Jolly kick-off to a holiday for all of us, I must say!'

The ship was anchored near a town whose white-walled houses were set among green trees and the silver-grey of olives, against a backdrop of low, barren hills. The sun blazed down from a cloudless sky and glittered on the dancing water, and the blue shallow sea was streaked with bars of vivid emerald, clear cerulean and a soft, milky jade. There was an exhilaration and a sparkle in the air and once again Amanda found that it was impossible to believe that any of the events of the past night had really occurred, or that Julia Blaine was dead.

Toby said: 'Up this ladder. Left turn. Here we are.'

The captain's cabin appeared to be filled to overflowing. Besides the captain, the first officer, the doctor, purser and stewardess, there were three unidentified men in uniform, presumably police officers, one of whom, at least, was British. Alastair Blaine, the Normans and Persis Halliday were also present, and Steve Howard was standing at the far side of the room, leaning on the window-sill and looking out across the sunlit deck towards the little town of Limassol. He glanced round as Amanda and Toby Gates entered, but he did not speak and presently returned to his idle contemplation of the view.

Alastair Blaine was looking drawn and grey. He appeared to have aged ten years, and the merciless morning sunlight showed unexpected traces of silver among his thick blond hair.

Persis Halliday, looking, as ever, as if she had that moment been unpacked from an expensive bandbox, was sitting on the arm of a chintz-covered chair swinging one silken foot in a neat alligator shoe and fidgeting with an unlighted cigarette. She looked up as Amanda came in and said: ''Lo, honey. This is a pretty set up, I'll say! Did you sleep at all?'

Claire Norman said: 'Sleep? I am sure none of us did! How *could* we? Poor Julia! I shall never forgive myself. Never! Dancing, while she was dying . . .!'

Her voice was tragic and quivering and she had managed to find among her suitcases a deceptively simple and most becoming frock in black linen that made her appear smaller and whiter and more fragile than ever.

George Norman patted her shoulder with awkward tenderness

and Persis, turning to face her, said: 'So you knew about it last night? Now that's very interesting. I didn't get in on it until the stewardess spilt the beans this morning. How did you hear about it?'

For a brief moment two small patches of colour appeared in Claire Norman's ivory cheeks, and she was all at once very still; her grey eyes no longer limpid with tragedy but curiously alert and guarded. She did not answer Mrs Halliday's question and it was George Norman who broke the brief silence:

'We didn't hear until this morning,' he said. 'Claire was only speaking figuratively. She's a little upset.'

The rigidity went out of Claire Norman's small body. She did not contradict her husband's statement, and there was no further chance for conversation, for the captain, clearly impatient to be done with the whole affair, was introducing the police officers and hurrying on with the business in hand. This proved to be merely a repetition of last night's questions and answers, with the sole difference that four of the late Mrs Blaine's friends and acquaintances were also present, each of whom gave their individual opinion as to her state of nerves and mind.

Amanda was asked to repeat her story, and did so; making the same reservations that she had made the night before. Mrs Blaine, said Amanda, had been overwrought and hysterical. She felt the heat badly, had complained of the East and Army life in general and had talked of taking her own life. She had been holding some tablets in her hand — no, Amanda could not say how many — and had eventually swallowed them——

Amanda's voice wavered suddenly, and looking beyond the captain's shoulder she encountered Steve Howard's deceptively lazy gaze. He shook his head very slightly. It was only a fractional gesture but in the circumstances plainly readable. Amanda turned her eyes away and looked at the ring of silent faces — the red, impatient face of the captain; the avid gaze of the stewardess; the weary resignation on the face of the ship's doctor and the alert

56

concentrated gaze of the three police officers — and closed her lips without mentioning the glass in her cabin. She did not look at Steven Howard again but she had the impression that he had relaxed.

The police were courteous and sympathetic and the captain only too eager to wash his hands of the lot of them, and after leaving their names and addresses and completing various other formalities, the passengers were hustled out of the cabin and told that they could now go ashore.

It was perhaps twenty minutes later that they descended the gangway and were rowed away from the ship over water so crystal clear that as they neared the shore every rock and pebble and shell on the sea floor was clearly visible, and they could see the shell markings on the back of a huge turtle that flippered its way lazily through the water beneath them.

There was a man waiting on the water steps by the quay; hatless and presumably British, since he wore a thin, well-cut and very English tweed coat. He was a slim man in the late thirties, of medium height and with a face so deeply tanned by sun and wind as to make his eyes and his crisp, sunbleached and slightly greying hair seem light by contrast. But despite its brownness it gave an impression of being pale under the tan. A paleness that gave a curious greyish tint to the shadows on his face. It was a thin, pleasant face that would have been handsome except that just now it looked desperately tired and was scored with lines of weariness and anxiety.

'There's Glenn,' said George Norman. 'Do you suppose he's—— ' He checked suddenly and coughed in an embarrassed manner. The prow grated upon stone and a moment later the passengers were on shore and Claire Norman was holding out a small white hand to the man in the tweed coat:

'Glenn. How nice to see you! I suppose you are here to meet Miss Derington. Or did you come to meet ... someone else?'

There was the faintest pause before the last two words, and Mr

Glennister Barton's pleasant tanned face flushed deeply and the muscles about his mouth tightened. Claire Norman said: 'Amanda, this is Glenn Barton. Your host in Cyprus.'

Amanda held out her hand and found herself looking into a pair of grey eyes that were unmistakably desperate and unhappy. And she was suddenly unreasonably angry with Mrs Norman, who had said something which, though meaningless to Amanda, had undoubtedly possessed a hidden and hurtful meaning for this pleasant, rather diffident man.

Glenn Barton barely touched her hand, was introduced to her companions and exchanged a few civilities. He inquired after her Uncle Oswin and, having taken charge of her luggage and seen her through the customs, led the way to a long grey saloon car that was parked near the customs' shed. Amanda had expected to see Mrs Barton, but there was no sign of any other woman, and Glenn Barton, having piled Amanda's suitcases on to the back seat held open the front door of the car for her.

Persis called out: 'See you in Kyrenia, honey!' and Toby Gates, looking like a spaniel puppy that is being left behind from a walk, said in an urgent undertone: 'You *will* let me come over and see you, won't you?'

Amanda glanced over his shoulder, but Steve Howard, his back to her, was leaning lazily against a pillar with his hands in his pockets, talking to Claire Norman. Amanda got into the car feeling unaccountably annoyed and said: 'Why, of course, Toby,' with unnecessary cordiality and emphasis, and a moment later Glenn Barton released the clutch and the car slid out of shadow into the bright sunlight of the road to Nicosia.

The countryside, once they had left the coast and the incredible sapphire, turquoise and jade of the shallow waters that fringed it, was bleached and colourless in the hot sun. The earth was brown and stony and dotted with small shrubs, and except for an occasional olive grove there was little green and almost no shade as the road wound and twisted through barren hills and past dried-up watercourses where the heat haze shimmered on the stones and boulders.

It was all new and strange and different to Amanda, and she might well have found it fascinating but for the fact that her host was strangely silent and was driving much too fast. She wondered if he were shy or if there was something in that seemingly innocent remark of Claire Norman's that had goaded him to this silence and speed? The big car was moving with dangerous velocity, shaving corners with a screech of tortured tyres and singing down the straight stretches of road with the speed of a steel-shafted arrow, while Amanda, who was not normally of a nervous disposition, found herself unconsciously clutching at the edge of her seat with rigid fingers and watching the flickering needle of the speedometer with fixed and apprehensive eyes.

She turned her head away with an effort and covertly studied her prospective host. He was sitting hunched forward a little, as a man will sit who steadies a nervous horse at the approach of a dangerous fence, and there was a look of nervous strain and tension in every line of his brown face and slim body. His hands were gripping the wheel so tightly that the knuckles stood out white against the tanned skin and there was a deep crease between his brows. Amanda thought that she had never seen anyone look so unhappy, and she looked away quickly, embarrassed and disturbed.

The needle of the speedometer wavered on ninety and she tightened her clutch on the seat, shut her eyes briefly and swallowed hard. Making a valiant effort she attempted a few polite observations on the scenery, to which Mr Barton returned equally polite but brief replies. The car whipped between an ox cart and a bus load of Cypriot peasants on their way to market, avoiding both by a hair's breadth; flashed past a string of camels on to a narrow bridge, and missed a small boy on a donkey by a matter of millimetres.

Amanda shut her eyes again and Mr Barton inquired if she had had a pleasant trip from Fayid.

'No,' said Amanda with feeling. 'It was perfectly beastly!' She found herself telling him about Julia Blaine's death, and Mr Barton expressed concern but no surprise.

Amanda said: 'Did you know about it then?'

'Yes. You see we ship a good bit of our wine from Limassol, so there are always several of our people on those boats or at the docks and most of them had heard. There was a lot of talk about it. The Blaines were over here for a couple of weeks last year, staying with Claire and George Norman. They're related I believe. I was away on business at the time so I didn't meet them myself, but my — wife knew them slightly.' He was silent for a moment or two and then said apologetically: 'Of course I had no idea that Mrs Blaine had died in your cabin, or I should not have asked such a stupid question. It must have been a most unpleasant experience. I'm sorry that you should have had such a horrible introduction to Cyprus. I wish I could do something to make up for it.'

He turned to look at her and his tired, unhappy face broke into a smile. It was an extraordinarily pleasant smile and Amanda found herself returning it with frank friendliness.

He's nice, she thought. But he's got something on his mind. He's tired and badgered and worried sick about something — and then he has to come and meet me and put me up and look after me!

She said quickly: 'It's very kind of you and your wife to have me to stay. I do hope it hasn't been an awful nuisance. I feel rather bad about it — inflicting myself on you like this. I don't imagine that Uncle Oswin gave you much choice, did he?'

'Well — no,' said Glenn Barton with a rueful smile and a return of the anxious crease between his brows. 'But—— '

He slowed the car down and said abruptly: 'Look, would you like something to eat? There's an inn just ahead. We could get some bread and cheese and olives and some goat's milk if you'd like it.'

'I'd love it!' said Amanda, suddenly remembering that she had had no breakfast. Mr Barton removed his foot from the accelerator and brought the car to a stop before a small shabby building half hidden by trees.

The little inn consisted of one large room furnished with rough wooden chairs and tables and decorated with portraits of the King and Queen of the Hellenes, torn from some illustrated paper and tacked against the walls. The charming, elfin face of Fredricka smiled out from a wreath of green leaves, reminding Amanda that this was an island where many of the inhabitants resented the British occupation and were demanding union with Greece.

The room was crowded with black-haired, dark-eyed Cypriots and redolent with garlic and the spilled lees of wine, but the proprietress, a buxom red-cheeked woman who seemed to know Mr Barton well and addressed him in rapid Greek, found them a table and fetched coarse bread, grapes, figs and lumps of cheese made from goat's milk. At Mr Barton's request she added a bottle of some colourless liquid that appeared to be gin, a carafe of water and two glasses.

Amanda ate the simple food with relish and Glenn Barton poured a small portion of the liquid into each glass and added water, whereupon the mixture turned a cloudy white.

'What is it?' demanded Amanda, intrigued.

'*Ouzo*. The national drink. Do you see that old man over there by the door?' Amanda turned and observed an ancient and decrepit greybeard who appeared to be dozing comfortably in his chair. 'He's our hostess's husband. He used to be a tough upstanding chap when I first came to Cyprus, but he took to drinking his *ouzo* straight. If you drink enough of it it's supposed to send you off your head. But it's quite harmless in small quantities. Try it.'

Amanda picked up the nearest glass, sniffed at it and wrinkled her nose expressively. Glenn Barton laughed. 'It smells pretty pungent, doesn't it? Aniseed. Don't you like it?'

'No,' said Amanda frankly, 'I've always detested the smell of aniseed ever since my kindergarten days when there was a small

61

boy who used to sit next to me in class and suck aniseed balls. I hated him — and them.'

'It tastes better than it smells,' said Glenn Barton. He raised his glass to her. 'Here's to your first visit to Cyprus. May it be a very pleasant one.'

'Thank you,' said Amanda, and smiled at him.

Mr Barton drank and pushed away his glass. The frown was suddenly back in his forehead and Amanda saw that his hands were not quite steady and that there was a tinge of whiteness about his mouth. He offered her a cigarette, and when she refused, lit one himself and said in a jerky and difficult voice: 'I – I'm afraid that I – we – shall not be able to put you up after all. You see – my wife is not well, and I couldn't ask you to stay in the house while – while——'

He stopped and pushed his hands through his hair in a gesture that was somehow boyish and despairing.

'But of course you can't!' said Amanda, moved by a sudden warm feeling of compassion. 'Don't give it another thought — please. I'm terribly sorry to hear about your wife. Are you sure that there is nothing I can do to help?'

'No, nothing,' said Glenn Barton wretchedly. 'It's very good of you to take it like this. I feel pretty terrible about it — saying that we'd put you up, and then letting you get here and failing you like this.'

'Nonsense!' said Amanda cheerfully. 'It doesn't matter a bit. I can easily go to a hotel.'

'Oh no. I couldn't let you do that!' Glenn Barton lifted his eyes from the table and looked at her earnestly. 'I've arranged all that. A friend of mind in Kyrenia, a Miss Moon, is going to put you up instead. She's a bit eccentric, but very kind. I know you'll like her.'

'But I can't go sponging on your friends,' said Amanda dismayed. 'It was quite bad enough Uncle Oswin pushing me on to you like this, but——'

'Please!' interrupted Glenn Barton with a twisted smile. 'You're being kind and letting me down gently, but I'd be very grateful if you'd add to your kindness by agreeing to stay with Miss Moon. I'd feel much better about it. Besides, she's expecting you. She's a dear and is delighted at the idea of having you. She likes young people — specially pretty ones.'

His smile pointed the compliment and Amanda laughed and capitulated. She had been disappointed at the prospect of staying in Nicosia instead of on the coast, and Persis and Toby would be in Kyrenia. She would have preferred to be independent and stay at a hotel, but she could hardly treat Mr Barton's arrangements in a cavalier fashion.

Mr Barton said: 'Then that's fixed. We'll have to stop in at the office in Nicosia just for a minute or two I'm afraid, but we should be in Kyrenia in time for lunch. If you really won't try the *ouzo* we'd better be getting along.'

5

The buxom proprietress of the inn presented the bill and embarked on an animated conversation with Mr Barton that, judging from her laughing glance, referred to Amanda.

'What is she saying?' asked Amanda.

'She was asking where you'd come from, and she says that you are a very beautiful young lady and wishes to know if you can sit on your hair when it is unbound,' said Glenn Barton with a smile.

Amanda laughed. 'Tell her, only just!'

'You come on *Orantares*, yes? From Port Said?' said the woman in halting English. 'My man too. Is fine ship.'

She smiled broadly at Amanda, swept up the handful of small coins that Mr Barton had counted out onto the table, and hurried away to deal with an impatient patron.

'Are all the people here as friendly and cheerful as that?' asked Amanda.

'A good many of them. Why? You sound surprised.'

'I suppose I am,' admitted Amanda. 'The only things that ever get into the papers about Cyprus are articles about how discontented they are with the whole set-up.'

Glenn Barton smiled and said: 'I think you'll find them cheerful enough.'

He dropped the end of his cigarette into Amanda's glass, where it hissed out and disintegrated slowly, and sat watching it abstractedly for a moment or two with his own face anything but cheerful. Presently he gave a sharp sigh and stood up.

'Let's go, shall we?'

They walked out into the bright sunlight to the car and continued their journey towards Nicosia; but at a less dangerous speed. The interlude at the inn appeared to have lessened Glenn Barton's nervous tension, and he was more talkative and at ease; but he did not refer again to his wife's illness and it was obvious that he did not wish to discuss it.

Amanda found herself wondering what Mrs Barton was like, and if she would meet her — and passed from that to wondering whether she would meet Steven Howard again, and why it should be a matter of concern to her whether she did or not? Mr Howard had been brusque and arbitrary and rude, and had had the incredible effrontery to hint that she might have planned the murder of Julia Blaine as the result of an intrigue with Julia's husband Alastair. True, he had said nothing to suggest that he himself believed it. But that such an idea could even enter his head, infuriated and frightened her. She ought by rights to be thankful that she need have no more to do with him and could put him out of her mind and forget him.

But she found that she could not stop thinking about him. Who was he? Why had he been on the *Orantares*? What had he been doing in Fayid and who was it that he had followed to Cyprus?

The road twisted downwards through the sun-bleached hills and ran out upon the wide, flat, dusty central plain of Cyprus, and it was midday by the time they came in sight of the green trees, jostling rooftops, Byzantine churches and Gothic mosques of Nicosia.

The heat danced in the narrow, crowded streets; on minarets and domes and fretted balconies, the concrete walls and roofs of innumerable newly built suburban-style houses, petrol pumps, jeeps, Army lorries and creaking carts drawn by oxen.

Presently the car turned in between white-washed gateposts shaded by flamboyants and oleanders, and drew up before a small bungalow.

'This is our Nicosia office,' explained Glenn Barton. 'Would you like to come in? I won't be more than a few minutes.'

The office walls were bare and white-washed. There was coarse matting on the floor, and green wooden jalousies over the windows kept out the midday heat and made the rooms cool and dim. A woman who had been seated at a littered desk rose quickly as they entered and Glenn Barton said: 'This is Miss Ford — my secretary. Monica, this is Miss Derington.'

Miss Ford was plain, solidly built and verging on middle age. She had slightly protruding teeth and her hair — of that indeterminate shade that is usually described as 'mouse' — was drawn loosely back from her forehead and confined in a small hard bun at the nape of her neck.

Glenn Barton said: 'I didn't think you'd be here today, Monica. Sure you're all right? You needn't have come you know.' There was concern in his voice and he put a hand on the thick shoulder and pressed it affectionately, and turning to Amanda said: 'Monica's not only my secretary. She's my right hand — and my left one! I don't know what I'd do without her. She practically runs the business.'

Miss Ford's sallow face flushed with pleasure and for a moment she looked almost girlish. 'That's nonsense, of course,' she said to Amanda. 'Glenn works far too hard. I'm always telling him that he'll have a breakdown if he doesn't let up a bit. How is your uncle, Miss Derington? I haven't seen him for over a year. He got me this post you know. I used to work in his London office.'

'Uncle Oswin is fine,' said Amanda. 'He's ramping round the Middle East putting the fear of Derington into Deringtons, which is his idea of bliss.'

Glenn Barton laughed. 'Then we can consider ourselves very lucky that he has sent us such a charming representative instead of paying us a personal visit.'

'Oh, I'm not a representative,' said Amanda, smiling back at him. 'I'm merely having a holiday on my own. Uncle Oswin would

66

have come himself if he could have fitted it in, but he couldn't, and once he's worked out a programme nothing will induce him to alter it by an hour — let alone a day. So he decided that you would have to get along without a personal pep-talk for another year or so.'

'It's a pity he couldn't come,' said Glenn Barton with a sigh. 'We have a lot of problems to contend with that I don't think your uncle fully understands. They lose a lot of force when they are reduced to official reports, but a few days on the ground would have brought them home to him. Perhaps you could persuade him to come over on his way back?'

'I'm afraid not,' said Amanda lightly. 'He'll be in Kenya now, and he flies to Tripoli for a few days this week-end, and goes back to London from there for a conference. I don't believe he'd alter a schedule for the H Bomb. That is, not unless you could think up something that would really lure him; like flagrant immorality among the staff! Uncle Oswin is very hot on the Purity of Deringtons. It's his hobby.'

Amanda laughed, but there was no answering smile on the faces of her two companions. It was, on the contrary, instantly and painfully obvious that she had made an exceedingly tactless remark, for once again there was a white line about Glenn Barton's mouth while Miss Ford's sallow face had flushed a dull and unbecoming shade of red.

There was a brief uncomfortable silence and then Miss Ford turned hurriedly to Mr Barton:

'Kostos is here, Glenn. He arrived just before you did. I don't know why he didn't see you in Limassol and save himself the journey. These people never think.'

'He couldn't,' said Mr Barton. 'They had a bit of trouble on the ship. One of the passengers died, and things got a bit held up. I'll see him now. Will you look after Miss Derington?'

'Yes, of course. Wouldn't you like a wash, Miss Derington? I – I know how dusty that road is. And what about some orange juice

67

or sherry or something? Or there's some iced coffee if you'd prefer that? Glenn will be here about ten or fifteen minutes; there are some invoices he'll have to look at.'

'Iced coffee sounds wonderful,' said Amanda gratefully. 'And so does a wash. I'm stiff with dust and parched with thirst.'

Glenn Barton said: 'I'll be as quick as I can,' and Monica Ford led Amanda away. 'Come on to the verandah when you're ready,' she said. 'It's through that door over there. I'll have the coffee ready for you.'

The verandah was wide and shady but it seemed intolerably bright after the cool dimness of the shuttered rooms. Monica Ford had set out two chairs and was pouring out iced coffee from a frosted jug.

'Lovely!' said Amanda, drinking thirstily. 'I needed that!'

She smiled gratefully at Miss Ford and noticed that in the full light of the verandah the sallow, sensible face looked older, and somewhat ill. There were dark shadows under Miss Ford's eyes that the wide pink plastic rims of her glasses failed to hide, and Amanda suspected that she had been crying. The square, plain face with its pale blue eyes, sandy lashes and entire absence of make-up, looked sensible and efficient. An impression that was somewhat belied by Miss Ford's choice of costume, for she wore a gaily coloured and full-skirted cotton frock which did nothing to improve either her thick waist or her unadorned complexion. To this she had added as a final incongruous touch a necklace and ear-rings of large plastic flowers and a liberal application of some cheap scent that smelt like violet hair oil.

Amanda suspected that the ear-rings at least were a recent and unusual adornment, for Monica Ford could not keep her hands from them. She kept touching them while she talked, as though they worried her; loosening the screws and tightening them again; her strong, square-fingered, sensible hands with their short un-varnished nails providing a sharp contrast to the glittering transparent petals of the plastic flowers.

She had arrived in Cyprus less than a year ago, she told Amanda, at the instigation of Mr Oswin Derington in whose office she had previously worked for over five years: 'He thought that Mr Barton needed someone to help him,' explained Miss Ford. 'Things were not going so well at first, and these little local typists are often worse than useless. There was a great deal of work. You've no idea what Glenn has had to contend with. Labour troubles and customs troubles and local prejudice, and no one to give him any help or encouragement. It's been an uphill fight. He ought to go on leave, but he won't. He works himself until he drops. He doesn't know how to spare himself. Some men are like that — Bobby was like that too ...'

Her voice suddenly broke and stopped and Amanda saw to her horror that the pale eyes had filled with tears.

Miss Ford fumbled in one of the large pockets that ornamented her skirt and producing a damp handkerchief blew her nose fiercely. 'Do forgive me. I – I'm not quite myself today. I – Hay fever you know—— '

'How horrid for you,' said Amanda politely. 'But I'm not surprised, with all these gorgeous flowers around.'

'They are lovely, aren't they?' said Miss Ford recovering herself. 'It's odd to think that I didn't want to come out to Cyprus at all.'

'Then you like it here?'

'Oh *yes!*' said Monica Ford clasping her hands together in a sudden convulsive gesture. 'It's – it's a beautiful island. I couldn't bear to leave! I won't leave! – I *won't* – I—— '

She stopped abruptly and the colour flamed up into her sallow cheeks. There was a brief embarrassed pause and Amanda said sympathetically: 'I suppose Uncle Oswin is trying to drag you back to London or Liverpool or somewhere? He is an old bully, isn't he? Pay no attention to him! I was scared stiff of him for years and then one day I suddenly realized that I wasn't a schoolgirl any longer, and I staged a token strike and got away with it. All you've got to do is to stand up to him.'

Monica Ford smiled uncertainly and said: 'Have some more coffee?'

'I'd love some.' Amanda held out her glass and said: 'I'm sorry to hear that Mrs Barton is ill. What's the matter with her? I didn't like to ask her husband; he seemed rather upset about it. Is she really bad?'

Inexplicably the hot colour deepened in Monica Ford's plain face and she fumbled with the jug so that the coffee spilt in a pale brown stream down the skirt of her gaily patterned cotton frock. She sprang up hurriedly, her face crimson, and said in a muffled voice: 'Oh dear! — and it stains so! Excuse me just a minute——' and fled.

Amanda looked after her in considerable surprise. What *was* the matter with Mrs Barton? Had she perhaps gone off her head? Or contracted some illness like poliomyelitis that the authorities wished to hush up for fear of creating a panic? It was all rather mysterious and Amanda was suddenly intensely sorry for Glenn Barton. What with work and worry, a wife who was ill — or worse — and a secretary who was quite obviously suffering from nerves (Amanda did not believe the hay fever story) her own arrival at this juncture must have seemed to him like the proverbial last straw.

A door at the far end of the verandah opened and Mr Barton himself walked quickly towards her.

'I'm sorry to have kept you waiting. I hope that Monica kept you entertained. Where is she?'

'She spilt some coffee down her frock and she's gone to mop it off,' said Amanda, rising. 'I don't think she's feeling very well.'

A shadow crossed Glenn Barton's pleasant face and he glanced towards the door and lowered his voice:

'I know. Poor Monica. She's had a ghastly shock, but she's taking it splendidly. She's got lots of guts. She only heard yesterday that her brother was shot by Mau Mau terrorists in Kenya. He had a farm out there, and they attacked the place and wiped

70

it out. He was all the family she had. There don't seem to be any other relations, and she was devoted to him.'

'I *am* sorry!' said Amanda, smitten. 'How dreadful for her. No wonder she seemed so upset.'

She turned to look out across the sun-drenched garden with its blaze of flowers, and all at once, in that hot, quiet verandah, she shivered as though she were cold.

'What is it?' asked Glenn Barton, his voice suddenly gentle.

'Nothing. I – I was only thinking that – that it's such a lovely day, and it doesn't seem possible that awful, tragic things can happen to people. And yet they do. To ordinary, nice people like Alastair Blaine — and Miss Ford——'

'I shouldn't have told you about it,' said Glenn Barton contritely. 'I'm sorry. You've had quite enough to upset you already. Tragedy is not for the young. Forget it and enjoy yourself. It *is* a lovely day!'

He held out a hand to her: 'Come on, or you will be late for luncheon and Miss Moon will never forgive me.'

6

The road from Nicosia to Kyrenia runs for a few miles across the plain and then begins to climb the long narrow barrier of the Kyrenia range that forms a rampart between the plain and the north coast of the Island.

The car topped the pass and began to descend, swinging and turning to the curves of the winding road, and there below them lay the sea — an impossible cerulean blue streaked with sapphire and viridian, with the white, beautiful coastline fading away into the heat haze until sky and sea and coast seemed to merge and melt into one.

Olive groves, the tree trunks so gnarled and twisted with age that some of them must surely have seen the Crusaders come and go, stood dark against the glittering expanse of blue, and below them the little white town of Kyrenia lay basking in the noonday sun like a handful of pearls and white pebbles washed up by the sea.

They drove down a long road that wound and curved between olive, carob, cypress, mulberry and mountain fir, and which finally ran straight from the foot of the hills to the sea.

A quarter of a mile short of the harbour the car turned off into a side road and drew up before a large, square, two-storeyed house that was separated from the road by a white wall, a line of cypress trees and a tangle of oleanders.

'Here we are,' said Glenn Barton. 'This is the Villa Oleander. Andreas will bring in your suitcases.'

The house was high and old, weather-worn and beautiful. Its walls had been colour-washed a flaking and discoloured pink that had bleached to a warm, uneven shade of apricot, and the wrought-iron balconies and wooden shutters at the windows were a soft, faded, dusty emerald green. The roof tiles had probably come from the South of France, for they were not red, but a deep beautiful pink, each one curved and marked with the outline of a heart.

A short, flagged walk and six shallow stone steps led up to a massive front door whose heavy bronze knocker was green with age, and the garden was a neglected tangle of orange and lemon trees, figs, plum trees, oleanders, roses, and cascades of yellow and white jasmine. A vine grew along the wrought-iron of a balcony to the right of the front door, and water trickled from the mouth of a bronze dolphin into a deep pool full of lily pads and reeds; the sound of its fall providing a tinkling counterpoint to the cooing of pigeons from among the warm shadows of a gnarled olive tree.

Amanda stood with her hands on the gate and looked about her with a feeling of awe. It was all so right. So exactly right — the quintessence of serenity and enchantment.

Glenn Barton, watching her, said a little anxiously: 'I'm afraid it's a bit neglected. But Miss Moon says that she can't be bothered with keeping up the garden and that she likes it like this.'

'So do I,' said Amanda on a breath of rapture. 'It's beautiful! It's just exactly like a picture I've always had in my mind of what a house on a Mediterranean island should look like, but I've always been afraid that it wouldn't. It's like a dream!'

Glenn Barton looked relieved but uncomprehending, and it was obvious that he himself saw little to admire in the shabby house and neglected overgrown garden. He led the way up the short flight of stone steps to the front door and banged on the knocker. There was a sound of quick footsteps and the door swung open on well-oiled hinges to show a stout black-eyed woman who wore a voluminous and rather dirty apron and a brightly coloured cotton handkerchief tied over her abundant greying hair.

'Ah! Kyrie Barton! Kalossorisis. Ti habaria. Kopiase messa!'

'This is Euridice,' said Glenn Barton turning to Amanda. 'She's the cook and housekeeper and housemaid and everything rolled into one.'

Amanda smiled at her, and the woman beamed back and breaking into a flood of unintelligible speech, led the way across a wide hall into a large dim drawing-room full of old, beautiful furniture and dusty curio cabinets, where the shutters had been closed against the hot sunlight.

'Can't she speak English?' whispered Amanda apprehensively.

'Quite a lot. You'll find that she speaks enough to manage on. But Miss Moon has always refused flatly to speak to her in Greek, so Euridice, who has been with her for over thirty years, refuses to admit to any English. It's a point of honour with both of them.'

'How do they manage?'

'They both speak to each other very slowly and at the tops of their voices in their own languages. Here, I think, is your hostess——'

High heels clicked rapidly on the hall staircase: there was a jingle of jewellery and a strong scent of heliotrope, and Miss Moon was with them.

Miss Moon was small and bony and birdlike, and somehow managed to suggest a homely British sparrow that has gone to a fancy dress ball dressed as a peacock. Her thin hair, which she had thought fit to dye an improbable shade of scarlet, was dressed in innumerable frizzy curls and decorated with a bow of violet gauze. Her dress, also in shades of violet and mauve, was of the type known to an earlier generation as a 'tea gown', and she had confined it at the waist by a wide belt of silver filigree adorned by an enamel buckle in a design of irises. She wore a number of necklaces and bracelets of silver filigree, amethysts and opals, and a pair of amethyst ear-rings of rococo splendour.

'Glenn! Dear boy. How it warms me to see you! And this is Amanda? Let me look at you, child. Beautiful! You refresh my eyes. How *good* of you to come and stay with me. So few young people care to do a kindness to the old these days, alas! It will be delightful to have you in the house. Quite delightful — it needs cheering up, and so do I. You are looking at my dress. Not *quite* the thing to welcome a guest in. It should have been pink for that. Pink for joy! But it's Tuesday you know, and so it had to be mauve. I always wear mauve on Tuesdays. Monday is my pink day. I do so resent it when people speak of *black* Monday. Why, Monday is a new start! A fresh week — anything might happen! And so, of course, I always wear pink. In welcome. I think that colours are *so* important, do not you? But here I am keeping you talking when you must be quite famished! Glenn, dear boy, will you not change your mind and stay to luncheon?'

'I'm afraid I can't. Nothing I would have liked better, but I have to meet Gavriledes at the Dome. He's giving me lunch and we can get through our business at the same time.'

'Oh dear. How disappointing. You know, of course, that Lumley Potter has taken the top floor of one of the houses on the harbour, don't you? He arrives today.'

'Potter — who told you?' Glenn Barton's face was suddenly white.

'So you did *not* know! I think Anita should have told you. So awkward if you met. Lady Cooper-Foot told me. The flat — if you can call it that — belongs to her cook's second cousin. Mr Potter intends to set up a studio.'

'But – but I thought he was staying on in Famagusta.'

'He wishes to paint in Kyrenia. Famagusta has not enough spiritual essence. I could have told him that.'

Glenn Barton's eyes were wide and blank. He turned to Amanda as though he were about to say something, and checked. After a moment he said instead, in an uncertain, rather formal voice: 'I must go now, I hope to see you again soon. If you are by any chance writing to your uncle, let me have the letter and I will see that it is sent with the office mail. It will go quicker that way. I will see that someone calls every day in case you should want to send anything. I am sure Miss Moon will look after you well. I won't say good-bye. Only *au revoir*.'

He took Miss Moon's withered, be-ringed hand and kissed it in an affectionate gesture that was entirely without affectation, and went quickly away.

Miss Moon drew a gusty sigh. 'Poor boy! How that woman *can*—— But I must not stay gossiping here all day, must I? I will show you your room. Andreas will have taken up your luggage. And then we will have luncheon and hear all about each other. So stimulating!'

She led the way back through the high, dark hall and up a wide, shallow stepped staircase. 'This is the bathroom, dear, and there is a lavatory. That is my room, and here is yours—— '

She opened a door and Amanda found herself in a large, high-ceilinged room that was painted a soft green and carpeted with coarse matting. There were flowers in tall jars and the furniture, like that in the drawing-room, was old and beautiful and dusty from neglect. A portrait of a girl in a green satin dress of the Restoration period hung on one wall, while on another a vast silvery looking glass, spotted with age and wreathed with garlands, ribbons and cupids of tarnished gilt, hung above a small painted French bureau that served as a dressing-table. A graceful Venetian glass chandelier, not entirely innocent of cobwebs, hung from the ceiling, and only the bed struck an incongruous note. It was a narrow cheap iron bedstead that supported, on four poles of varying size that had been lashed to it with string, a somewhat darned mosquito net. The shutters were closed against the heat of the day and the room was dim and green and smelt of lilies and syringa, dry rot and dust.

Amanda turned to her hostess with shining eyes:

'It is so good of you to have me. This is the most *beautiful* house!'

'Oh, I *am* so glad that you should feel like that!' said Miss Moon, suddenly embracing her. 'I knew the moment I saw you that you were *right*, and that the house would like you. So many people are wrong. Such a pity! It is indeed beautiful — the whole island. I came here with dear Papa forty-three years ago. That is a very long time, is it not? I cannot have been much older than you are now. He died here, and I meant to go back to Norfolk. But somehow I never did. I had walked through the looking-glass like Alice, and I could not get back. The enchantment had got me. I bought this house and I have been here ever since. And when I die I shall be buried among the lemon trees and the oleanders in the garden. I have it all arranged. Ah, Kyrenia——! The very name sings, does it not? Like a warm wind through the olive trees. How delightful that you should feel it too. Are you ready, dear? Euridice will be waiting to serve luncheon.'

The dining-room looked out across a froth of lemon trees to an old stone wall with deep, arched embrasures, crumbling into ruin, in which fantailed pigeons strutted and cooed, and the meal began with fruit. Purple and green figs, melons, oranges, grapes, and tiny plums like balls of blue velvet: ice-cold and piled in careless, colourful profusion on shallow dishes of Venetian glass. There were tall green glasses flecked with gold, also Venetian, into one of which Miss Moon poured a white wine of local manufacture:

'It is quite harmless, dear. A child could drink it. Glenn lets me have it. The firm exports it in bottles, but bottling seems to spoil the flavour, and it is never so good afterwards. This is straight from the cask, and really very pleasant. Or so I am told. I myself never take anything but barley water. Euridice makes it for me after breakfast, fresh every day.'

Amanda said: 'You know, I think I am going to be very grateful to Mrs Barton for being ill.'

'Ill?' said Miss Moon sharply. 'Who told you that she was ill?'

'Mr Barton. That's why I'm here. I was to have stayed with the Bartons in Nicosia. My uncle arranged it. But they couldn't have me after all because Mrs Barton was ill. Didn't he tell you?'

'Yes he did, now that you mention it, dear. But I never thought that he would really do it. Pretend that she was ill, I mean. So *much* better to stick to the truth, however unpleasant. I cannot see why Glenn should try and shield his wife at his own expense. He did ask me not to tell you, but now that they will actually be here in Kyrenia of course you are bound to find out.'

'Find out what?' inquired Amanda, puzzled. 'Isn't Mrs Barton ill?'

'She most certainly is not!' said Miss Moon with an indignant clash of bracelets. 'On the contrary, it is her poor husband who appears to be heading for a nervous breakdown. I cannot understand it — she seemed such a nice girl. But in my young days there was a good old-fashioned word for people who behaved as Anita Barton is behaving. We called them trollops.'

'Anita?' — the name struck a sudden chord of memory.

'That is her name,' said Miss Moon, and sighed. 'I should never have thought it of her. But I suppose that she found Glenn dull. He has been sadly overworked. And she is so good looking. Perhaps she felt the need for more excitement and attention and admiration than he could offer. No, she is not ill. She has merely left Glenn and run away with a painting person who calls himself Lumley Potter. She has not even left the Island. They are living together quite brazenly, and she has attempted to justify her flagrantly immoral behaviour by spreading scandal about her husband and his secretary, Miss Ford.

'*Oh!*' gasped Amanda, her eyes wide with horrified dismay. 'So *that* was why——' She was remembering her light-hearted remark of that morning on the subject of Uncle Oswin and flagrant immorality. Could they possibly have imagined that she had said anything so cruel and unkind on purpose? A hot wave of colour mounted to her cheeks at the very thought.

'What is it, dear?'

'Nothing,' said Amanda hastily. 'I was just thinking of – of something I said to Miss Ford.'

'You have met her then?'

'Yes. We stopped at the office on our way through Nicosia.'

'Then you will know what I mean when I say that Anita must have taken leave of her senses. If she felt that it was necessary to slander Glenn in order to justify her own quite unjustifiable behaviour, she should have picked on a more plausible story. Monica Ford is a nice, sensible woman and a most efficient secretary — and she worships Glenn. But speaking entirely without malice, she possesses no feminine charm whatsoever. There are plenty of pretty girls in Cyprus, and if that was what Glenn Barton was after he could have taken his pick. But Monica Ford——!'

Amanda was suddenly reminded of Julia Blaine and her equally senseless suspicions, but she pushed the thought quickly from her, and said lightly: 'She isn't exactly glamorous.'

'Glamorous! The poor girl is *Plain!* If she had even been ugly she might have stood more chance. Ugliness is at least arresting. The trouble with Glenn Barton is that he is too *soft.* You need to be hard if you marry a girl like Anita — as hard or harder than she is. She has accused him of carrying on with all sorts of people. Claire Norman for one. I would put nothing past Claire, and I am well aware that she cast a handkerchief in Glenn's direction — oh very discreetly of course; Claire is always discreet — and that she is not likely to forgive him for not picking it up. Dear me! What a lot of scandal I have been talking. *So* stimulating! You know, dear, there are a great many people — women of course — who will assure you that they *never* gossip, and that in fact they detest and abominate gossip. It is hardly ever true (the ones who say that are *always* the worst I find!) but if it *were* true, what a lot they must miss! Just think how much we should *all* have missed if people like Somerset Maugham had refused to listen to gossip? What would you like to do this afternoon, dear?'

'Sleep,' said Amanda promptly. 'I know that sounds very dull of me, but I feel as if I could sleep for hours. So much has happened, and – and I didn't get much sleep last night.'

'Not a rough crossing, I hope?'

'No,' said Amanda slowly; and for the third time that day told, with reservations, the story of Julia.

'You poor, *poor* child!' exclaimed Miss Moon in horrified sympathy. 'But how terrible! How too shocking. How fortunate that it should be a Tuesday. I should never have forgiven myself if I had been wearing orange or yellow when you arrived. So upsetting for you. Blue perhaps — blue is so soothing. But *not* orange. Certainly you must sleep. So sensible.'

She accompanied Amanda to her room at the conclusion of the meal. 'Just come down whenever you wake up,' urged Miss Moon. 'We pay no attention to the clock in this house. Time is our servant here, Amanda. We are not the servants of Time. *Amanda!* such a pretty name. So unusual. Amanda — "worthy to be loved".'

Amanda said abruptly, following a sudden train of thought: 'Did you ever hear of anyone called Amarantha?'

'Now I wonder who has been calling you that!' said Miss Moon, beaming. 'A man, of course. And one with a very pretty taste in compliments. Not Glennister Barton; he is *lamentably* unread. Amarantha was the subject of a charming poem by a cavalier named Richard Lovelace. He addressed some verses *To Amarantha, that she would dishevel her hair*. I am not sure that I remember them aright. My memory is *not* what it was, alas. Let me see — "*Amarantha sweet and fair, braid no more that shining hair. As my curious hand or eye hovering round thee, let it fly——*" something like that. Ah, I see that you are blushing! *Such* a charming accomplishment. You must tell me all about him when you wake up.'

Miss Moon withdrew, leaving behind her a scent of heliotrope to mingle with that of the lilies, the syringa, the dry rot and the dust. And Amanda, barely pausing to remove her dress and kick off her shoes, wriggled in under the mosquito net and was instantly and deeply asleep.

7

Amanda had awakened too late to be able to see anything of Kyrenia that day, but shortly after breakfast on the following morning Toby Gates called at the Villa Oleander.

'I heard you were here,' he told Amanda. 'Mrs Norman told us. They asked us all to dinner at their house last night; those of us who were on the boat; and she'd heard that you were staying here. We came here from Limassol in their car. The hotel had a car laid on for us, but a jeep ran into it just outside Nicosia, so we all piled into the Normans' car.'

'Who's "we"?' asked Amanda, sniffing ecstatically at a foaming torrent of jasmine that tumbled over the edge of the verandah rail outside the french windows of the drawing-room.

'Claire and Persis and Howard and myself. Claire — Mrs Norman — said that she was sure you wouldn't be staying at the Bartons' house, because Mrs Barton has run off with that painter chap and you couldn't very well stay in the house with just Barton there. Funny that we should have seen them on the boat.'

So Steve Howard was staying in Kyrenia! Amanda said quickly: 'What happened to Mr Norman? Or did he have to come by bus?'

'Oh he stayed behind to help out Alastair Blaine. They didn't get in until late last night. I gather the body was taken to a hospital in Nicosia for a post-mortem, and he'll have to go over there this afternoon for some sort of an inquest. But they had the funeral yesterday evening.'

'So soon?' said Amanda, startled and distressed. Somehow, although she could have not explained why, Julia had not seemed

81

really dead until this moment. Now that she was buried — hidden under six feet of foreign soil in an alien country — the fact and the finality of her death came home to Amanda with a renewed sense of shock.

'It's a hot country,' said Toby uncomfortably. 'You have to bury people pretty quickly in this sort of climate.'

'What is he going to do? Alastair, I mean.'

'He's staying on with the Normans. No point in his doing anything else, really. He and Norman got in about ten o'clock and he went straight off to bed. Claire met Barton in the town yesterday afternoon and he told her you were here, so we rang up to ask you to join us, but the Moon woman said that you were asleep, and she wouldn't wake you. I say—— ' Toby sank his voice to a conspiratorial whisper — 'she's a bit peculiar, isn't she? She told me that I shouldn't be wearing a blue shirt because it was Wednesday. Do you suppose she's all there?'

'She's not dangerous, if that's what you mean,' said Amanda laughing. 'She just has a theory about wearing different colours on different days. If you'd turned up in cerise you'd have been dead right.'

Toby looked relieved. 'Oh I see. I thought the old girl was bats. She asked me if I had called to see Aramathea — sounded rather Biblical to me — must be one of her servant girls I suppose. I said no, as a matter of fact I'd called to see Miss Derington, and she said "Ah, I thought not. You do not look at all the sort of man who could quote loveless to the point." I began to think I'd got into the local looney bin. What on *earth* do you suppose she meant?'

'I haven't an idea,' said Amanda shamelessly.

'By the way,' said Toby diffidently, 'I - er - asked her if she'd mind if I took you out to luncheon and she said not at all. So would you come? It's not really just me — I wish it were — I mean, we arranged last night to have luncheon together at the Dome. Claire — Mrs Norman — thought it would cheer Alastair up, and it's

82

their cook's day off. I said I'd like to ask you along too, and——
You will come, won't you?'

'I'd love to.'

'That's marvellous,' said Toby enthusiastically. 'Let's go now!'

'It isn't ten yet,' pointed out Amanda, 'and there are lots of things I want to do this morning. I want to prowl around and explore.'

'I'll come with you. I must get hold of a car. Howard's hired one. A pound a day and you drive yourself; something like that. You know he's really an astonishingly good type, for an artist.'

'What do you mean — for an artist?' demanded Amanda, unaccountably annoyed.

'Oh I don't know. So many of them look like that bearded blighter in sandals; the one Barton's wife ran away with. Well I mean to say! if you're any good, surely you don't have to go about practically in fancy dress just to show what you are?'

'Nonsense!' said Amanda briskly. 'Look at you when you're on duty. You wear a weird khaki outfit with pips here and badges there and a peculiar hat with feathers that would make a man laugh his head off if he saw his wife wearing it. If you can go around in fancy dress just to show what you are, why can't he? It's the same idea. Which reminds me — wait while I get a sun-hat and I'll be with you!'

They spent the morning exploring Kyrenia, and towards twelve o'clock came down to the little harbour where the pastel-coloured houses, the ancient, glowing walls of Kyrenia castle, the minaret of a mosque and the white walls of the Greek Orthodox Church reflect themselves in the clear, luminous greens and blues of the harbour water and look as though they had been designed by an inspired artist as a Mediterranean mural.

A voice hailed Amanda from one of the small tables outside a café on the quay, and there was Persis, as decorative as the morning.

'Hi there, honey! I hear you're parked right here in Kyrenia after all? Nice work. I thought nothing of Nicosia from what little we saw of it. Nothing *at* all. Now this! — this is quite a town, and I shall write a romance that will go into half a dozen editions in as many months. Why, it's just made for love! I must get me a beau.'

'Won't your imagination do?' inquired Toby solicitously.

'No, honey. My imagination is Grade A plus, but when it comes to Love, I like 'em over six foot and solid.'

'What about me?' offered Toby.

'That's just sweet of you, honey, but I prefer my beaus to keep both eyes on their work; and if you watch Amanda over my shoulder I can't see myself getting really in the mood. Still, there's a lot of talent lying around; as well as some pretty stiff competition.'

'Meaning me?' inquired Amanda showing her dimples.

'Of course, honey. Who else? Though to tell you the truth I was casting a mental eye over Mrs Norman. That gal is a smooth worker. I am no amateur myself, and Lord knows I count my calories. But when she's around I feel just a shade like Sophie Tucker's twin sister; and say what you like, that is lowering to the morale. Besides, she has the edge on outside operators. It's her own ground and it kinda looks as though she's worked it well. Remember that guy with the beard and an outfit like sunset in technicolor?'

'Lumley Potter,' said Amanda, recognizing the description.

'That's the boy. The one who beat it with your pal Barton's ball and chain. Well, who do you suppose was whispering to him on the boat deck at two o'clock in the morning the other night? Lil' Claire, no less.'

Toby said sharply: 'That's impossible! I mean — how can you know?'

'How? By using my great big eyes, Grandma. That two-by-four cabin of mine was as hot as Broadway in a heatwave, and I slid out for a breath of air. I passed No. 31 — that was the Normans' cabin — on my way. George was snoring fit to shift the deck plates and I spared a sympathetic sigh for his life partner. I need not have wasted my sympathy. The little woman was on the boat deck — taking, we must suppose, an intelligent interest in Art. She's quite a gal!'

'But he's run off with Barton's wife!' said Toby indignantly.

'Maybe the guy's a Mormon.'

Amanda said slowly: 'So *that's* how she knew——— '

'About Julia? I guess so. The Potter had probably gotten the dirt from the first officer or the doctor or someone by that time. I imagine that there must have been quite a ruckus going on about it, and most of those who were out and about probably got an ear full. Yes, little Claire is certainly stiff competition. I shall have to brush up on my technique.'

'Who are you thinking of starting on?' inquired Toby, interested.

'Well there's always Major Blaine; and though it may be bad taste to pursue a bereaved widower, we heard plenty last night from his hostess about not letting the poor boy mope, so I guess I may as well try my hand at a little light consolation. And then there's Steve Howard. He's quite a guy. Plenty of looks and charm — and has he got that certain something! Claire seems to have noticed it too.'

'He's *not* good looking!' said Amanda with something of a snap. 'His face is out of drawing.'

'Well as far as I'm concerned, honey, it can stay that way. I never could draw anyway.'

Toby said: 'Persis darling, I never remember you sounding so aggressively American when I knew you in the States. Or did you always talk that way?'

'Not when I'm back home,' said Persis placidly. 'I keep it for foreign travel. It amuses the natives.'

Toby laughed. 'You're just a highly coloured fake and I adore you!'

Persis gave him an odd, slanting look and said: 'Do you, honey?

Well maybe you did once. Or maybe you're like this guy Potter — or any other guy for that matter! — just a Mormon at heart.'

For a moment there was an unexpected tinge of bitterness in Persis Halliday's clear incisive tones and Toby said quickly: 'What's that stuff you're drinking? It looks like ammonia.'

'Maybe it is, at that. The boy with the dinky white apron calls it *oozoo* or *ouzo* — and is it filthy! Still, I'm all for trying anything once. Drag up a chair and join me.'

'Do you mean to tell me that you're knocking back drinks alone and unprotected?' demanded Toby, astounded.

'Not quite. I am not entirely lost to all sense of what is due to me. My escort is in back — trying to get something under the counter if you ask me. Ah, here he is. Okay, George?'

George Norman appeared from the interior of the café bearing a bottle of beer. 'Got it!' he announced triumphantly. 'I knew they had some stored away. Good morning, Miss Derington. 'Morning, Gates. I'm showing Mrs Halliday the sights.'

Toby said: 'Is your wife here?'

'She'll be along in a minute. Alastair had to send off some cables and she went along to the Post Office with him. Here they are now.'

Claire Norman, still in black and wearing a wide-brimmed black hat that shaded her small face in a most becoming manner, appeared round the corner of the quay, her hand through Alastair Blaine's arm. Major Blaine looked tired and grim and as though he had had remarkably little sleep, if any, during the last forty-eight hours.

'Why — Amanda,' said Claire in her soft, light voice. 'How nice to see you. And Toby. Have you two been exploring the harbour?'

'No,' said Amanda. 'We've been exploring the town. I'm going to look at the harbour now, from the sea wall.'

'I'll come with you,' said Toby.

'I don't want you, Toby,' said Amanda perversely. 'I just want to sit and look at it and not talk. I'll be back.' She turned on her heel and walked quickly away.

Toby made a move as though to follow her, but Claire Norman laid a small hand on his arm and asked him prettily to fetch a chair for her, and by the time he had done so Amanda had gone.

A long stone wall with a small lighthouse on the end of it protected the tiny horseshoe-shaped harbour of Kyrenia from the seaward side, and walking along it Amanda looked across the translucent harbour water to the towering walls of the old Crusader castle, golden in the sunlight, and the beautiful curving coastline that faded into the shimmering heat haze beyond the age-old buttresses.

There were several other people on the sea wall, one of whom, a man who was sitting on the edge of the wall at the harbour side with his legs dangling above the water, was surrounded by an interested crowd of children. He was sketching swiftly with quick, bold strokes of a conté pencil on a large loose-leaf drawing block, and Amanda paused involuntarily, attracted by a burst of childish laughter.

The man spoke without turning his head: 'Good morning, Amarantha.'

'How did you know I was here?' demanded Amanda, startled.

Steve turned about and grinned up at her. 'I have eyes in the back of my head. Or perhaps I'm like that chap in *Maud* whose "*heart would hear her and beat, were it never so airy a tread*".'

Amanda flushed and turned away. Mr Howard spoke one quick sentence in Greek and instantly Amanda found her way barred by half a dozen laughing children, while three more laid hold of her arms and the belt of her grey linen frock. Amanda's sense of humour got the better of her and she laughed.

'Is this a hold-up?'

'It is. Now come off your high horse, Amarantha, and sit down and relax. I want to talk to you. You can sit on this—— '

He ripped off a sheet of cartridge paper from the drawing block and laid it on the edge of the harbour wall. Amanda, surrendering to curiosity and *force majeur*, sat down beside him, and looking downwards at the clear harbour water beneath her dangling feet, saw her own reflection and that of the group of children behind her.

'So much for the eyes in the back of your head. You saw my reflection.'

'I did,' admitted Steve.

Amanda turned to look at him and her gaze fell on the drawing block in his hands. The page was covered, surprisingly enough, with quick, vivid sketches of elephants, tigers, a sailor in bell-bottomed trousers, a witch on a broomstick, a horrific dragon, a sea serpent and a pirate brandishing a cutlass.

Mr Howard had the grace to look abashed. 'Not what you would call a hard morning's work,' he remarked, 'but popular with my public.'

Amanda said in a voice of blank amazement: 'So you *can* draw!'

'Why this unflattering incredulity? Or do I look like a painter of Spiritual Aromas, like my brother-of-the-brush, that dashing home-breaker, Mr Potter?'

Amanda flushed and bit her lip. 'I thought——' she began, and stopped.

'You thought it was merely an act,' concluded Steve. 'But no one should put on an act unless they can also put it across.'

He turned over to a fresh page and idly sketched in the outline of a girl's face and figure that turned suddenly into Amanda as she had looked in the cabin of the *Orantares*. Amanda in a nightdress with her long hair falling below her waist and her eyes wide and frightened.

There was a murmur of admiring recognition from the audience of children, and Amanda reached out, and snatching the pencil from his hand, said abruptly: 'What did you want to talk to me about?'

Steve turned his head and spoke briefly to his youthful audience, and received what appeared to be a chorus of assent.

Amanda said: 'What did you say to them? And how is it that you speak this language so well?'

'There is no end to my accomplishments,' said Mr Howard airily. 'And if you really want to know, I told them that I wished to declare my love to this so beautiful lady, and should any of the English approach I relied on them to give me due warning. The gang are with me to a man, so we can now relax and talk without fear of being overheard.'

'Oh,' said Amanda in a small voice.

Steve laughed. 'Don't worry. I only make love by moonlight. At the moment I merely propose to discuss crime.'

He retrieved the pencil and turning over another page began to sketch the houses on the far side of the harbour, but he was no longer smiling and his voice when he spoke again was terse and low pitched.

'The results of the post-mortem show that Mrs Blaine took poison. And I was right about that glass in your cabin. There are only two sets of finger-prints on it: yours and Mrs Blaine's. The bottle has only one set — yours. Which means that it was polished very carefully before it was put there, and probably handled with gloves. And the tablets in it were the same stuff that was in the glass: pilocarpine nitrate.'

'But – but you can't be sure that there was anything more than just lemon juice and water in that glass,' said Amanda, forcing the words past an uncomfortable constriction in her throat. 'I filled it again with water from the tap — to throw over her.'

'I know. But the remains of the original stuff had spilt and soaked into the carpet. I mopped it up with a handkerchief. There wasn't much of it, but with that bit of peel it was enough. The analysis shows that it contained a solution of pilocarpine nitrate which was probably sufficient to kill a dozen people. A single mouthful would have been enough to kill Mrs Blaine, though it would have taken a good bit longer.'

Amanda said: 'But the bottle! No, it can't be true, because don't you see, if Julia hadn't changed cabins with me, there wouldn't have been *any* finger-prints on the bottle and someone would have noticed it.'

'I wonder. How did you find it?'

'I felt it when I lay down. It made a hard lump.'

'So that you found it almost as soon as your head touched the pillow. The chances are that Mrs Blaine would have done the same, and would have touched it, as you did, and probably thought that some previous occupant of the cabin had left it behind by mistake. It only meant something to you because you had seen Mrs Blaine die of poison. Even if she had not found it, it is an even bet that several people would have handled it before it occurred to anyone to see if it had her finger-prints on it. Now let's have your story again. Right from the beginning this time. Anything that you knew or noticed about these people when you were in Fayid, and why they — and you — are in Cyprus, and as much as you can remember of what they did and said in Fayid and on the way to Port Said and on the boat. In fact the whole works.'

Amanda turned her head and looked at him, but his entire attention appeared to be concentrated on the drawing that was taking shape under the leisurely, unerring strokes of the conté pencil.

She said uncertainly: 'Then you *are—— '*

Steve Howard threw a brief glance in the direction of the café on the quay where Persis Halliday, the Normans, Major Blaine and Toby Gates were seated about a small table in the shade, and said curtly: 'Quickly, Amanda!'

There was not much to tell, and what there was seemed to date back to the evening at the Club in Fayid when her aunt had introduced her to Steven Howard. And yet Amanda had a queer feeling that it went farther back than that, and that Steve himself had been in Fayid for some specific purpose that was entirely unconnected with art, and that his presence at the Officers' Club that night had not been accidental.

She told him what she knew, thinking as she did so that it all sounded very trivial and unimportant. But he questioned her exhaustively on a number of points, and seemed interested to hear that Toby had met Persis in the States while visiting a married sister whose husband was attached to the Embassy Staff in Washington. She re-told yet again how she had come to occupy the cabin that had been allotted to Julia, and everything that she could remember of that last hysterical scene.

Steve said: 'What time did she go down to her cabin? Was she still on deck when you left?'

'No. She went quite early. About ten I think. Someone put on a gramophone record and people started dancing. Alastair danced with Mrs Norman, and I think Julia must have left about then. She started making rather a fuss about having a headache, and went off to her cabin.'

'When did you go down to yours?'

'Just about eleven. I remember the time, because I wound up my watch when I took it off to wash.'

'And Mrs Blaine came into your cabin around five or ten minutes later. Is that right?'

'Yes.'

Steve was silent for a moment or two, and then he said: 'Did all of you know that she made a habit of drinking unsweetened lemon juice?'

'Yes. She used to make rather a virtue of it. She took it to take down her weight. People always seem to advertise their dieting fads. She'd never touch a sweet drink, yet she'd eat ice creams and sticky puddings and chocolates by the ton.'

Steve said: 'Are you quite sure that you've told me everything you know?'

'Quite. Oh there is one other thing, but it can't possibly have anything to do with all this.'

'Never mind; let's have it.'

'Persis says that she went on deck much later that night, because her cabin was hot, and that she saw Mrs Norman and Lumley Potter together on the boat deck.'

Steve made no comment, but his pencil checked and he sat quite still, staring across the lovely harbour with eyes that did not appear to see the charm of the scene that lay before him.

After a moment or two he shrugged his shoulders and returned to his work, and presently one of the children called out something in a shrill piping tone, and he looked round.

'I rather think that a search party is about to be sent after you,' he observed, 'so let us talk of other things in a bright and audible manner. What are you doing in Kyrenia, for instance?'

'You know quite well why I'm here,' said Amanda accusingly. 'You were dining at Mrs Norman's house last night, and she seems to have broadcast the whole story.'

'Oh yes — of course. You couldn't stay unchaperoned with the manager of your uncle's Cyprus venture, so this man Barton has parked you instead *chez* Moon. His loss is our gain. Did you have an entertaining journey from Limassol?'

Amanda embarked on an account of her drive, her stop at Nicosia and her arrival at Miss Moon's, and was still talking when a shadow fell across them and Claire Norman's soft fluting voice said: 'Why, *Steve!* I'd no idea it was you who were monopolizing Amanda. We wondered what was keeping her. Have you been here all morning? You're supposed to be meeting us at the hotel at one o'clock, you know, and it's five past now.'

Steve closed his sketch book, pocketed the pencil and stood up:

'Hullo, Mrs Norman. 'Morning, Gates. Yes, I have been pursuing my vocation in an industrious manner. Miss Derington has been offering advice.'

He leant down and pulled Amanda to her feet.

'Do let me see,' begged Claire Norman. 'If you only knew how I envy people who are *really* creative! Do show us what you have been doing.'

92

Steve held up the sketch book to display the drawing of the harbour and Toby Gates said involuntarily: 'Why that's damned good! I suppose you make a packet out of this sort of thing?'

'Alas, no,' sighed Mr Howard regretfully. 'I shall never make a fortune from my art. It contains a fatal flaw: anyone can instantly recognize what it is intended to represent. One can only make a packet nowadays if one's creative efforts are of the type that the purchasing committee can hang upside down without anyone — including the artist — spotting the error.'

A sudden and unexpected breath of wind ruffled the quiet water of the harbour and lifted the sheet of paper, disclosing the page that lay beneath it. It was only for a brief moment, but quite long enough for both Claire Norman and Toby Gates to see and recognize that quick, brilliant sketch of a girl with unbound hair.

Tony Gates said in a thunderstruck voice: 'But that's Amanda! How on earth—— ' He stopped, red-faced and scowling, and Claire Norman laughed her light, tinkling laugh and said: 'Why, Steve! How secretive you are! I had no idea that you and Amanda knew each other so well.'

Steve closed the sketch book and tucked it under his arm. He smiled down at Claire with lazy pleasantness, but Amanda was suddenly and vividly aware, without knowing why she should know it, that he was angry.

'I am afraid,' said Steve gently, 'that that was merely an example of what is known as artist's licence. I do not know Miss Derington well. But that, fortunately, is an error that can be remedied. And now what about some food?'

Claire Norman's glance went swiftly from Mr Howard's smiling face to Amanda's entirely blank one and Captain Gates' scowling countenance, and she laughed again: a laugh that this time was not quite so sweet and tinkling:

'Yes, let's!' she said. 'I'm famished.'

She slipped one small hand through Steve Howard's arm and

93

laid the other on Toby's sleeve, and they walked away towards the Dome Hotel, four abreast in the bright glittering sunlight, their shadows foreshortened on the hot stones at their feet.

8

The dining-room of the Dome Hotel was long, spacious and cool, and a little breeze blew in from the line of windows that opened on to the burning blue of sea and sky.

Amanda looked about her with interest and decided that most of the guests were tourists, with a sprinkling of permanent residents. The Normans and Alastair Blaine were seated at a small table just beyond the one occupied by Persis, Steve Howard, Toby and herself: Claire Norman having suddenly decided that owing to Alastair's recent and dramatic bereavement, it might cause comment if he were to appear as one of a large and cheerful luncheon party at the hotel.

Amanda wondered why, in the circumstances, Claire could not have managed to give him a meal in the privacy of her own home? But Claire was a law unto herself, and Alastair, silent and stunned, was in the mood to do anything he was told without question.

Amanda's gaze, wandering farther, stopped at a strapless and backless white sunsuit printed with several huge scarlet roses and apparently remaining in position upon its wearer by faith alone. She was puzzling over the mechanics of this arresting garment when she became suddenly aware of the identity of the owner. The lady in the sunsuit was none other than Mr Glennister Barton's errant wife, while her companion, temporarily hidden from Amanda's view by an attentive waiter, was presumably her partner in guilt, the improbable Mr Potter.

Amanda was both interested and surprised. Somehow she had not expected Anita Barton to flaunt her liaison in such a public spot as the dining-room of the Dome Hotel. The attentive waiter removed himself, giving Amanda an uninterrupted view, and she studied the couple with considerable interest.

Lumley Potter, she decided, was not enjoying himself. He was looking morose, sulky and more than a little apprehensive, and kept darting anxious glances in the direction of the Normans' table. Anita Barton, however, appeared to be entirely at ease. She was laughing and talking — perhaps a shade too loudly.

Mrs Barton was a dark-haired woman of about twenty-five, with an excellent figure and striking good looks that owed much of their impact to a lavish and theatrical use of make-up. Altogether an unexpected wife, thought Amanda, for someone as quiet and fine-drawn as Glenn Barton.

As though she had felt Amanda's interested gaze, Anita Barton turned full face towards her. Her dark, over-bright eyes looked Amanda over with cool and deliberate insolence and her wide scarlet mouth curved in a mocking smile. She made some remark to her companion and shrugged one bare, sunburnt shoulder. And then all at once her eyes became fixed and hard and her red mouth tightened into a thin line. But she was no longer looking at Amanda. She was looking at someone immediately behind her, and, involuntarily, Amanda turned.

Glenn Barton was standing in the doorway, searching the room with anxious eyes. He did not see his wife, but he saw Amanda and came quickly towards her, threading his way between the tables.

'Glenn!' Claire Norman's voice arrested him as he was about to pass their table, and he paused beside her. She looked up at him with large, luminous eyes and said reproachfully: 'Glenn, you've been overworking again. You look as if you've had no sleep for weeks. You don't know Major Blaine, do you? I think you were over in the Lebanon on business when they were here last year, weren't you?'

'No, we haven't met. But of course I heard about you from——'

96

Glenn checked suddenly and Claire said: 'Stay and have something to eat. We've only just started.'

'I'm afraid I can't. I've a lot to do.'

'Then what about tea? Drop in at the house on your way back.'

'I will if I can,' said Mr Barton hesitantly.

'We shall expect you,' said Claire, smiling up at him.

He nodded absently and made his way across to Amanda. Claire's smile faded and her wide childlike eyes were suddenly narrowed and speculative.

Amanda turned in her chair: 'Hullo, Mr Barton. Were you looking for me? Persis, this is Mr Barton. He very kindly collected me at Limassol.'

'Yes. We met,' said Persis, producing her most dazzling smile. 'But I'm just delighted to meet you again, Mr Barton. Any friend of Amanda's is a friend of ours. Say, why not get a chair and join us?'

Mr Barton blinked and his drawn face relaxed in a smile:

'I – I'd like to very much. But I'm afraid I can't just now.'

'Some other time then,' said Persis warmly.

As one angle of the local triangular scandal, Glenn Barton represented copy; and Persis, whose interest had been aroused by the story, had been determined to make his closer acquaintance; though it is doubtful if her interest would have been so great had he proved to be a less personable man.

'Thank you,' said Glenn Barton. He turned rather abruptly to Amanda and said: 'I really came to ask you if you'd be in this afternoon. At the Villa Oleander I mean. Could you spare me half an hour of your time if I came in about three? I—— ' he hesitated a moment and glanced at her three openly listening companions. 'I have had a letter from your uncle. He has some messages that he wishes me to give you.'

'Of course,' said Amanda. 'I'll expect you about three o'clock.'

'I'll try not to keep you waiting.'

Persis said: 'Say, Mr Barton, I hear you run a wine business.

Vineyards and vats and pretty girls treading out the grapes and all the rest of it.'

'He does,' said Amanda. 'Miss Moon gave me some of his wine yesterday. It was delicious.'

Glenn Barton laughed. 'I'm glad you liked it. You were lucky not to get barley water. I thought that was the only thing that she drank.'

'It is. But thank goodness, she doesn't expect her guests to drink the stuff. It always tastes to me like water in which someone has stewed up half a lemon and three yards of flannel.'

Persis said: 'To get back to your vineyards, Mr Barton. I'm just crazy to see the whole works. Would you take pity on a poor foreigner and show me round one day?'

'I'd be delighted to.'

'Then how about tomorrow?'

'You can't go looking at vines and vats tomorrow, Persis,' said Toby Gates firmly. 'We're all going for a picnic to St Hilarion. Amanda's coming too. You know you arranged the whole thing with George Norman only this morning.'

'So we did. I'll tell you what, Mr Barton — suppose you join the picnic? Then we can get together and fix a day for the vines. Tomorrow at two-thirty. You can give me a lift to Hilarion. Is that a date?'

'I ought not to,' said Glenn Barton with a rueful smile, 'I'm rather busy just now, but — all right. I'd like to come. But I shan't be able to give you a lift I'm afraid. I can't get off as early as that. I could be at Hilarion about four o'clock if that's all right?'

'Sure. That's okay by me. Be seeing you then.'

Glenn Barton smiled at her, turned away and then stopped suddenly, his face rigid, and Amanda, following the direction of his fixed gaze, saw that he was staring at his wife. It was obvious that he had not noticed her until then, and highly unlikely that he would in any case have expected to see her lunching openly at the Dome with Lumley Potter.

Anita Barton had turned in her chair so that she faced him directly. Her eyes were bright and defiant and her painted mouth was hard and ugly. The room was noisy with chatter and the chink of glasses and cutlery, but the four at Amanda's table and the three at Claire's were suddenly silent with the silence of embarrassment and curiosity.

There was a queer grey look about Glenn Barton's thin, tanned face, and his mouth had shut hard. A muscle twitched at the corner of his jaw and his hands had clenched so tightly that the knuckles stood out bone white.

He stood there for perhaps a full minute, and then suddenly swung about and walked quickly and unsteadily from the room.

'Well, what do you know!' remarked Persis into the silence. 'Did you see that guy's face? If I had a dollar for every time I've written "*he turned white under his tan*" I'd buy the Koh-i-noor. But, so help me, I've never seen it happen until now. Fiction is certainly no improvement on nature.'

Steve said: 'Tell me, Mrs Halliday, are all American women as ruthless as you are?'

'Persis to you, Steve honey. And why ruthless? Why, I was *charming* to the poor guy.'

'That's what I meant,' said Steve with a grin. 'But what are you going to do with him when you've got him? Gaff him, or throw him back into the pool?'

'Steve *daaarling!* All I want is to get to know him. Can't you see what divine copy he is?'

'I see all right. You're a ruthless vamp and should be kept under lock and key. And don't bat your eyelashes at me — I suffer from extreme susceptibility.'

'But that's just *wonderful*,' said Persis warmly. 'I can see that you and I have a lot in common. You can drive me to Hilarion.'

'It's a date,' said Mr Howard.

Toby escorted Amanda back to Miss Moon's after luncheon and she dismissed him at the gate. She was feeling unsettled and restless and on edge, and the feeling of enchantment that she had experienced on her arrival at the Villa Oleander had vanished. Miss Moon peered over the landing rail as she closed the front door behind her.

'Ah, you're back, dear. Glenn Barton was asking for you. I told him that I thought you were taking luncheon at the Dome.'

'Yes I saw him, thank you, Miss Moon. He's coming to see me this afternoon. I hope that's all right? My uncle has been writing to fuss him about me.'

'Quite all right, dear. I usually rest in the afternoon, so you will have the drawing-room to yourselves. I shall be down to tea about four o'clock. Ask Glenn to stay. He'll let himself in. Euridice is out for an hour.'

She disappeared and Amanda heard her bedroom door shut. A clock in the hall struck three mellow notes, and almost before the echo had died away in the quiet house there was a sound of quick footsteps on the stone-flagged path and Glenn Barton was there, breathing a little quickly as though he had been hurrying.

'I haven't kept you waiting, have I?' he asked anxiously.

'About two seconds,' said Amanda with a laugh. She led the way into the drawing-room and sat down in a straight-backed chair, carved and gilded and upholstered in faded green velvet. Glenn Barton stood looking down at her with a deep crease between his brows and did not speak.

Amanda said: 'Do sit down. What is it? Has Uncle Oswin been devilling you about me?'

Glenn Barton sat down on the sofa and pushed his hands through his hair in the same boyish and despairing gesture that Amanda had seen him use on the previous day.

He said jerkily: 'I haven't heard from your uncle. That was just an excuse; I had to say something.'

He raised his eyes and looked at her wretchedly.

Glennister Barton must have been at least fifteen years Amanda's senior, and his hair was already flecked with grey at the

100

temples. But all at once Amanda felt as maternal as though she were twice his age and he was a small boy in trouble.

She said quickly and warmly: 'What is it? What's the matter?'

'I had to tell you——' his voice had a ragged edge to it — 'I had to. About Anita — my wife. You see I didn't know that she would be here. I hoped that you wouldn't find out. So I — well I said she was ill. It was a lie of course.'

'Look, Glenn,' said Amanda, unconsciously using his name, 'it doesn't matter. You were only covering up for her. You couldn't have done anything else. I do understand, so don't worry about it — please!'

Glenn dropped his head into his hands and said in a low, uneven voice: 'It's all such a mess. Such a ghastly mess! I didn't believe that it could happen. But it did. I didn't mind what other people said or thought, but this involves the good name of the firm, and you are a Derington. I wanted to hush it up, but I see now that it isn't possible. I – I did what I could.'

'Of course you did,' comforted Amanda, distressed. 'But it's no good trying to cover up for your wife if she doesn't care what people say.'

'I don't understand it,' said Glenn tiredly. 'I don't know why she should behave like this. Perhaps it's some sort of defence mechanism. She's such a child really. A spoilt child who is trying to cover up its own naughtiness by accusing other people of worse things.'

'You mean those stories about Miss Ford?' said Amanda.

Glenn looked up, his face haggard. 'So you've heard about that already!'

'Miss Moon told me. But you don't have to worry, Glenn. She says that no one believes it.'

'How can she know?' said Glenn bitterly. 'There are people who will believe anything.'

He dropped his head on his hands again and after a moment spoke in an almost inaudible voice, as though he had forgotten about Amanda and was finding some relief in speaking his troubled thoughts aloud:

'Anita doesn't like Monica — she never has. Monica is efficient and she has brains, but she's not very tactful. Anita is so gay, and so careless about money and housekeeping and things like that. She likes expensive clothes and parties and late nights, and admiration. She's young; it's only natural. And I suppose I was a bit dull — there was always so much work. Monica used to drop hints; very heavy ones I imagine — and it annoyed Anita. Then one day she lost her temper and they had a quarrel. A silly, rather childish quarrel—— '

Glenn sighed and pushed his hands through his hair again: 'Anita told me that either Monica went or she would. She wouldn't see that I *could* not sack Monica — she was Mr Derington's personal nominee for the post, and until she arrived things were in a bit of a mess in the office. Monica got the whole thing into shape and worked like a demon. I couldn't replace her without damaging the firm's interests. I told Anita that she need never see her or speak to her — I would have seen to that — but that I had to keep her. I *had* to. I can't deal with all the stuff she copes with, as well as my own work; it isn't possible. But Anita wouldn't see it. She just went on saying that if I didn't sack Monica immediately she'd go. I – I didn't think she could mean it. But she did. And now that she's gone she's too proud — and too young — to admit the truth, so she has spread it about that she was forced to leave me because I was having an affair with the woman. An *affair!* With Monica Ford of all people! *Monica!* Oh God, if it wasn't so tragic it would be damnably funny!'

Amanda, looking at him with an aching pity beyond her years, was once again reminded of Julia. Julia whose jealous love of her husband had prompted her to accuse him of entirely imaginary affairs with any and every woman he paid the smallest attention to. Was Mrs Barton only another Julia? Did she really love her husband with the selfish, jealous love that Julia had had for

Alastair? and had he, because of his work, neglected her and so driven her to much the same hysterical extremes of behaviour that Julia had indulged in? Could love really do such dreadful things to people? Drive them so mercilessly?

She said quickly: '*Don't*, Glenn! I don't want to sound catty, but anyone who has ever met Miss Ford will know that it's all nonsense. No one would believe it.'

Glenn lifted his head from his hands and looked at her.

'No,' he said with a wry smile. 'I don't suppose they would. But there are a good many people who have not met her, and it makes an unsavoury story. God knows I can't spare her from the office just now, but for her own sake I've tried to make her go. I can't let her name be spattered with mud by every gossip in the Island. It isn't fair on her. I have got some sort of duty towards the woman — and to your uncle for that matter. But she won't go. She says that if she went now it might look like an admission of guilt, and that anyway she will not be forced to leave by an entirely baseless scandal. I've done my best to persuade her, but it's no use.'

'She's quite right,' said Amanda warmly. 'If you wouldn't sack her because she had a row with your wife, I don't see why she should lose her job now, just because your wife is telling everyone that she was your——' She stopped abruptly and flushed.

'Mistress,' finished Glenn Barton wryly. 'I suppose not. But she is the only one I worry about. The others can not only take care of themselves, but give as good as they get.'

'What others?' asked Amanda, puzzled.

'Didn't Miss Moon tell you that too?' inquired Glenn Barton bitterly. 'Monica is not the only one I am supposed to have carried on with. Anita has been very generous with her accusations. I am supposed to have made love to half a dozen women — Mrs Norman for one. In fact it seems that no woman is safe from me. You wouldn't think it to look at me, would you?'

He laughed again. A short, harsh laugh that was entirely devoid of amusement.

'Why don't you strangle her!' demanded Amanda indignantly.
'Anita?'

'Yes. It sounds to me as if it would be justifiable homicide!'

Glenn smiled a curious, twisted smile. 'You don't understand.
You see she doesn't really mean it. She's just a spoilt kid who has
found that the party isn't as much fun as she thought it would be.
She drinks a little too much, and that doesn't help. She's only
hitting about her because she's bored and disappointed — with me
and marriage and Cyprus.'

'She sounds to me,' said Amanda candidly, 'as if she needed a
dozen with a good solid slipper. It's a pity you didn't try it.'

'Perhaps,' said Glenn wryly. 'But it's too late for that now. She
wants me to divorce her.'

Amanda said: 'Of course you're going to?'

Glenn Barton got up suddenly and walked over to the open
french windows that gave out onto a small covered verandah
shadowed with jasmine and climbing roses. He stood with his back
to Amanda and his hands in his pockets and spoke without turning
his head.

'I *can't!*'

'Why, Glenn? Do you mean because of your job? I know that
Uncle Oswin is pretty rabid on the subject of divorce, but it's not
your fault.'

'It isn't the job,' said Glenn Barton, still without turning. 'I
don't care a *damn* about the job. It's Anita. You see I – I love her
so much.'

He swung round suddenly to face Amanda and said harshly, 'I
suppose you find that difficult to believe? It's absurd, isn't it, to
go on loving someone who can do that to you, and to be unable
to stop? I know it doesn't make sense, but it's true all the same.
I want her back — on any terms. I don't believe that she loves
Lumley Potter. It's only a silly escapade, and if I don't divorce her
she'll get over it one day and – and come back to me.'

He looked appealingly at Amanda; his tired, desperate eyes

104

pleading with her to agree with him; to reassure him. Amanda got up swiftly and went to him, gripping his arm:

'Don't look like that, Glenn! Please don't. I'm sure it will all come right in the end. Oh, Glenn, I am so sorry! Isn't there anything I could do? Perhaps if I saw her? — talked to her?'

A sudden light leapt into Glenn's grey eyes and for a moment his whole face seemed to change and the lines in it to alter; the avid, incredulous look of a cornered animal who is suddenly presented with an avenue of escape. It faded as quickly as it had come and his eyes fell.

'No. No, I couldn't possibly ask you to. I shouldn't have talked to you like this. I didn't mean to — honestly I didn't. I only thought that you should know something about it because — well because you're a Derington, and because I'd lied to you. I apologize. It was unforgivable of me to go to pieces and bore you with my sordid private affairs. Will you forgive me and – and try and forget about it?'

He covered her hands with one of his own, and despite the warmth of the hot Mediterranean day she could feel that it was cold and quivering.

'Now you're being silly,' said Amanda with a light laugh. 'You know very well that you don't have to apologize for anything. I'm the one who should do that. Here you are, in the thick of a perfectly beastly crisis in your life, and on top of everything else Uncle Oswin orders you, practically at pistol point, to put me up and show me round. You must have wanted to murder me!'

Glenn's cold fingers tightened convulsively on hers and he said quickly: 'Don't talk like that. You weren't to know. If I'd had any guts I'd have written and explained the whole thing, but – but I couldn't believe that she wouldn't come back. I couldn't think about anything else. My brain seemed to have stopped working, and if it hadn't been for Monica Ford I'd probably be without a job by now as well as without a wife. You've helped me quite enough by letting me talk to you, and I can't let you get involved

105

any further in an affair like this. There's a proverb about touching pitch, and I won't have you touching it.'

'What nonsense!' said Amanda warmly. 'You told me yourself that this involved the good name of the firm. Well, I am a Derington, so you can't keep me out of it. If you'd like me to see your wife, I will.'

Glenn dropped his hand and turned away to stare once more at the sunlit garden beyond the shadowy verandah.

He said slowly: 'I don't know. I simply do not know. You see she refuses to see me, and I don't think she even reads my letters. She says that until I agree to a divorce she has nothing to say to me. If I could only talk to her! — but perhaps she might talk to you.'

'It's worth trying anyway,' said Amanda. 'At the worst she can only show me the door, and after being brought up by Uncle Oswin I am practically immune to snubs!'

Glenn Barton turned quickly and took her hands in a brief hard grasp:

'You're a brick, Amanda. I can't thank you enough. I know I shouldn't let you do this, and probably no good will come of it, but I've reached the stage where I feel I'd try almost anything!'

'Then that's settled,' said Amanda. 'When would be the best time to see her? Now?'

'A good bit later I should think. She's sure to be out bathing or watching Lumley paint during most of the afternoon and evening. Lumley's the snag, of course. He'll be there.'

'I'll go down after supper tonight,' decided Amanda, 'and just walk in. And you're right about Mr Potter. He's going to be terribly in the way. Couldn't we think up some method of getting rid of him, just for an hour?'

Glenn Barton frowned thoughtfully. 'Yes,' he said hesitantly. 'I think it might be done. I could send him a message or something.'

'That's it!' said Amanda with enthusiasm. 'We'll pretend that

106

someone at the hotel wants to see his pictures with the idea of buying one. That's sure to fetch him. I'll get Toby to do it.'

Glenn Barton said uncertainly: 'I think I'd better do it myself. I don't quite feel like explaining this whole sordid set-up to anyone else.'

'We don't need to. But Mr Potter probably wouldn't come for you, and I shall merely tell Toby Gates that I have a date with your wife and as I do not want Lumley Potter around, will he be an angel and decoy him away for an hour? I know he'll do it if I ask him. How do I find the house?'

'It's on the harbour,' said Glenn Barton; and gave directions in detail.

'I'll go down about half past nine,' said Amanda, 'and wait until I see Mr Potter leave, and then go straight up. And as Toby is far too rich for his own good, it won't hurt him at all if he finds that he has to end up by buying a genuine Potter Masterpiece.'

The tense lines around Glenn Barton's mouth relaxed and he laughed.

'How nice to hear you laugh again,' said an approving voice from the doorway. They had not heard Miss Moon's approach and they turned, startled and looking a little guilty.

'I see that dear Amanda has been cheering you up,' said Miss Moon cosily. She was wearing today a linen skirt patterned in shades of cerise, with a blouse of cerise organdie copiously orna-mented with narrow frills of lace. Her improbable hair was adorned with a gay bow of tulle in the same shade, while a scarf composed of several yards of the same material encircled her thin neck and floated behind her. The amethysts and opals of yesterday had been replaced by a set of garnets that did not tone well with the prevailing colour scheme, but the chains of silver filigree were the same and the scent of heliotrope accompanied her in an almost visible wave.

She reached up and patted Glenn Barton's thin, tanned cheek with a be-ringed hand: 'Dear boy! It does me good to see you in spirits. Amanda dear, I trust that you will insist on Glenn showing you some of our beauty spots. He should get about more.'

'He's going to,' said Amanda. 'He's coming on a picnic to St Hilarion tomorrow. But I can't take the credit for that, I'm afraid. He was shanghaied into it by a glamorous American authoress. We're all going. Come with us Miss Moon — do!'

'You're a dear child,' said Miss Moon approvingly. 'I wish I could. Although I must admit that I have never enjoyed picnicking. Ants, you know. Not to mention wasps. But I shall be out tomorrow. Lady Cooper-Foot is giving a small afternoon bridge party and tea. Three o'clock to six-thirty. Rather a nuisance, as Andreas and Euridice will both be out for most of the day, though they have promised to be back by seven-thirty at the latest. There is some festival or fête at Aiyos Epiktitos that they wish to attend. There is always some fête somewhere that they cannot miss. Very trying. Though why should they not be gay? So it is probably just as well, now I come to think of it, that we shall both be out for the afternoon. Here is Euridice with the tea. Glenn dear, you will stay and have tea with us, will you not?'

'I'm afraid I can't. I have to get back to the office. Monica has one or two things on the files that have to be dealt with before the post goes tomorrow. Any letters I can post for you, Amanda?'

'I haven't had time to write any yet,' confessed Amanda with a laugh.

Mr Barton bent to kiss Miss Moon's hand — evidently an established ritual that pleased the old lady enormously — and Amanda accompanied him to the front door.

'I'll hunt up Toby after tea and explain about Lumley Potter,' she said in a conspiratorial whisper.

'Bless you!' said Glenn Barton with a catch in his voice.

He turned and ran quickly down the steps and a moment later the front gate clanged behind him and Amanda heard his car start up and purr away up the long rising road that led to Nicosia.

9

It was close on half-past nine when Amanda walked quietly down one of the narrow lanes that led to the harbour, and paused in a patch of deep shadow near the quay.

The warm night was milky with moonlight and the air smelt richly of dust and garlic and fishing nets, and fragrantly of flowers. The streets and the quay were full of idlers and no one turned a head to see Amanda pass. Her short, full-skirted frock of coffee-coloured poplin blended equally well with the white moonlight and the dark patches of shadow, and she had tied a scarf of matching chiffon loosely about her head, peasant-wise, that helped to conceal her face.

She did not expect to meet anyone she knew in the narrow lanes at that hour, but she preferred to be on the safe side as she did not in the least wish to explain her mission to any of her friends or acquaintances.

Alastair Blaine had passed her as she crossed the main road. He was hatless and walking very slowly, his hands in his pockets, and the light from a street lamp had glittered for a moment on his blond hair. But Amanda did not think that he had seen her, for his eyes had been blank and unobservant and he had passed her without pausing.

Thanks to Glenn Barton's directions she had no difficulty in locating the house on the harbour where Lumley Potter had rented a studio flat, and she waited in the shadows of an alleyway, sniffing the spicy air and revelling in the warm beauty of the moonlit night.

Presently she was aware of muffled footsteps clattering on a wooden stair near-by. A door creaked and a moment later Lumley Potter hurried past clutching a large portfolio under one arm, his ginger-coloured beard looking grey in the moonlight.

Dear Toby! thought Amanda gratefully. She waited until Mr Potter turned the corner of the quay, and then left the shadowed alleyway and walked quickly up to the door that Lumley had left open behind him.

A single oil lamp dimly illuminated a narrow hall with flaking plaster walls and a long flight of rickety wooden stairs that led up into darkness. Amanda squared her slim shoulders and started upward.

She passed several landings giving on to rooms that appeared to be unoccupied, for no chink of light showed from under any door and their sole illumination came from the moonlight beyond the grimy landing windows. Glenn had said the top floor. Then this must be the Potter Love-Nest . . .

A strip of light showed from under an ill-fitting door, and a single guttering candle, in a ship's lantern hanging from an iron bracket on the wall, provided a faint, flickering illumination. On the other side of the door a gramophone or a wireless was playing dance music, and Amanda took a deep breath and knocked on the door. She did not wait for an answer but turned the handle and walked in.

The big oblong room was ablaze with light, and Amanda blinked, momentarily dazzled by the contrast from the dimness of the landing and the dark flights of stairs outside.

The room had been colour-washed a vivid shade of salmon pink and there were thick white hand-woven curtains by the open windows. The floor was covered with rust-red matting, and enormous canvases, presumably the work of Mr Potter, hung against the salmon-pink distemper or were stacked in rows against the walls. Mr Potter evidently believed in Paint, and applied it by the pound with the aid of a palette knife or possibly a small trowel. He also, apparently, believed in Gloom and Prussian blue.

A voice said '*Pios ine?*' and Amanda turned quickly and saw Anita Barton.

Mrs Barton presented an incongruous picture in that setting. She was lying face downwards and at full length on a large divan, putting records on a gramophone that stood on the floor beside her. She turned over lazily, and seeing Amanda, came suddenly to her feet.

She was wearing a subtle, clinging dress of black chiffon that breathed Paris in every line, and there were pearls in her ears and at her throat. Her dark hair was cut short and brushed back in smooth shining waves and she looked like a professional fashion model waiting for the photographer.

She stood quite still and stared at Amanda while the record on the gramophone ground to a stop.

'Well I'm damned!' said Anita Barton loudly. 'What are you doing here? Who let you in?'

'I let myself in,' said Amanda apologetically. 'I do hope you don't mind. The downstairs door was open; and I wanted to meet you.'

'I suppose Glenn sent you,' said Mrs Barton, her voice suddenly strident. 'Well in that case you can just turn round and walk right out again!'

'No one sent me,' said Amanda composedly. 'It was my own idea. May I sit down?'

'It's a free country,' said Mrs Barton. She sat down herself with some suddenness on the divan, and Amanda realized with a sharp stab of dismay that she had been drinking and was not entirely sober.

'Well, what is it?' demanded Anita Barton. 'Sob stuff? or Good-Name -of-the-Firm? And where do you come in on this — that's what I'd like to know.'

Amanda said abruptly: 'Are you in love with Mr Potter?'

It was not at all what she had intended to say and the moment the words were out she would have given much to recall them, for

111

Anita Barton flung her head back and went off into a peal of laughter.

'With *Lumley!*' Mrs Barton controlled herself and looked at Amanda with frowning brows:

'Listen — you look a good kid. I don't know what you're after, but whatever it is I bet Glenn's behind it. Have a drink — come on, have one.'

She filled a glass and handed it to Amanda. 'Ouzo. Local poison. Go on, drink it. It won't kill you. They say it's an acquired taste. Well now's your time to acquire it.'

Amanda sipped it with repugnance and suppressed a shudder of distaste.

'What were we talking about?' demanded her hostess, refilling her own glass. 'Lumley! So we were. Dear Lumley. No one could love Lumley unlesh – unless – it were his mother. And do you know what *she* christened him? Well I'll tell you: Alfred! Alf Potts. He didn't think that was dish – distinguished enough, so he changed it to "Lumley Potter". Shall I tell you why he let me run away with him? Two re – reasons. To annoy Claire, and because he wanted to show off. The "Free Life" — t'hell with the conventions! The Creative Artist is above the laws that g – govern the uncreative herd. Long live the Revolution!'

Mrs Barton described an airy circle with her glass, splashed a generous proportion of its contents on the floor and drank the remainder.

'No,' she said, scowling. 'I don't love Lumley. Lumley loves Claire. Claire de la lune! They all love Claire — or that's what *she* thinks. And what a surprise she's going to get one day!'

She dropped her empty glass on to the floor where it rolled in a circle on the matting, and for an appreciable interval she sat staring at it with fixed unseeing eyes, and at last she said in a half whisper: 'But I had to run away with someone. I had to get away from Glenn. You don't know what it was like. You don't know! I want to *live*. I must get away. Right away from this narrow

112

deadly little island — escape. I'd have divorced him if I could, but there wasn't any evidence. What's the good of telling people things? It hurts him and he hates it like hell, but it isn't evidence in court. So I have to make him divorce me. He'll do it. He *must*. I sh – shall make such an exhibition of myself that in the end he'll have to do it f' his own sake' — she appeared to have forgotten Amanda — 'I've got to get away. Right away—— '

Amanda said tentatively: 'If you hate the life here so much couldn't you persuade him to get a job somewhere else? Wherever you *would* like to live? I'm sure he could get a transfer. If you went back to him I'm sure he'd try. He said that he only wanted you back — on any terms.'

Anita Barton lifted her head and stared at Amanda. She said loudly and harshly: 'You don't understand. I don't want to be dead and buried. I want to live! I want to have fun. I want to laugh and enjoy myself; and I will – I will! If I had to go back to Glenn I should die. Thash what — die! Nice, quiet, hard-working, dull, *deadly* little Glenn—— !'

With a sudden violent gesture she picked up the fallen glass and hurled it at the wall, where it smashed against one of Mr Potter's eccentric canvases and fell in a shower of broken fragments on to the rust-red matting.

'And now,' said Mrs Barton, rising unsteadily, 'I think you'd better go. So nice of you to call. Good-bye.'

Amanda rose. There seemed to be no point in prolonging the interview, as Mrs Barton was obviously in no condition to listen to reasoned arguments that night. But the interview had at least produced some interesting information, even if it had done little towards helping Glenn Barton. She said good-bye and left.

The candle in the ship's lantern had evidently burned out, for the landing was in darkness and she wavered, wondering if she should turn back and ask Anita Barton to lend her a torch or a box of matches. But Mrs Barton had put another record on the gramophone and Amanda could not face a return to that room.

She lingered on the landing for a moment or two, waiting until her eyes should accustom themselves to the gloom, and aware of an inexplicable reluctance to return down that narrow dark staircase.

Presently she walked cautiously forward, and groping for the stair-rail began to move downwards, feeling for each step.

The moonlight beyond the small window on the landing below provided a faint light, but Amanda, peering down the well of the staircase in expectation of seeing the glow of the oil lamp in the hall, could see nothing but blackness below her. Had the hall light too burned out, or had someone blown it out? Or were there three more landings between her and the hall? She could not remember.

Amanda hesitated at the top of the next flight of stairs. Above her she could hear a voice from Mrs Barton's gramophone singing a familiar, lilting French song. *La Mer: 'Voyez — ces oiseaux blancs — et ces maisons rouillées ...'*

It should have been a friendly and encouraging sound, but somehow it was not, and quite suddenly and for no reason Amanda found that she was shivering, and that her heart was beating in queer uneven jerks as though she had been running. She looked quickly over her shoulder, but beyond the faint square of moonlight the landing stretched away into dusty blackness, and if there had been anyone there she could not have seen them. But of course there was no one there! It was absurd to imagine such a thing. She was being ridiculous and childish — afraid of walking down a staircase in the dark!

There was nothing to be frightened of, for she had only to keep one hand on the stair-rail and walk straight down, and in less than a minute she would be out on the open quayside in the bright moonlight. Amanda straightened her shoulders and gripping the flimsy rail, felt for the top step and moved downwards once more into blackness.

She began to count the steps — *four — five — six — seven*. Then all at once she stopped, and stood frozen and still.

There was someone on the stairs behind her. She was quite sure of it. She listened intently, every nerve strained and alert, but she could only hear the muffled music of the gramophone two floors above her. There *could* not be anyone on the stairs behind her! It had only been an echo — or imagination. She must go on — *eight — nine — ten*——

'. . . *La Mer — a bercé mon coeur — pour la vi-e* . . .' The music stopped on a last, long note, and in the silence she heard the stairs above her creak to the soft footsteps of someone who was following her down.

Amanda fought down a rush of blind panic. How many steps to the next landing? *Was* there a next landing? Surely there should be a window? The footsteps behind her had stopped when she stopped, and the house was deathly quiet. But in that stillness she could hear someone breathing in the blackness above her. Or was it only her own frightened breathing?

From somewhere outside the house someone approaching along the quay was singing the tenor part of the love duet from *Butterfly* in a loud and tuneful voice that somehow conveyed the impression that the singer, if not exactly intoxicated, was somewhat elevated by liquor. Amanda took courage from the sound. There were people out there on the quay. Nothing could harm her. She had only to reach the quay——

She went on again, quickly; stumbling in the dark. And instantly those other soft, furtive footsteps followed her. They were quicker now, and closer; and it was not her own frightened breathing that she could hear, but the short hard breathing of someone who followed her. Someone who breathed as an animal breathes, avid and panting, and who, in another moment, would reach out and clutch her——

Amanda stumbled and came hard against the turn of the stair, and turning, pressed frantically back into the angle of the wall, trying not to breathe. She heard a groping hand brush against the rough plaster within a foot of her head . . . and then suddenly, in

115

the hall below her, the heavy door was flung wide and the bright glow of a torch showed in the well of the stairs.

Amanda heard a short hard gasp above her, and then the quick pad of running footsteps that retreated into the darkness.

She turned swiftly, but the stairs above her were empty, and whoever had entered the hall below was coming up the staircase towards her, humming softly. It was, oddly enough, the same song that Anita Barton's gramophone had played so short a time ago:

'. . . *Et d'une chanson d'amour — La Mer — a bercé mon coeur——*'

The beam of a torch fell full on her face, blinding her, and the song stopped short.

'Amarantha! — well, well! And who has been dishevelling your hair this time?'

Amanda spoke in a breathless, sobbing whisper: 'There – there was someone on the stairs! Behind me. I—— '

Steve caught her wrists in a painful grip that spoke as clearly as any words.

He raised his voice a little and said: 'I suppose you've been visiting the Potter studio? Then you can introduce me. Met a fellow at one of these cafés who says that Potter is a newer and bigger and better Picasso — and how! I told him that Potter was probably a mere painter of pot-boilers, but as a brother of the brush' — Mr Howard was slurring his words a little — 'it behoved me to prove his worth before presuming to criticize. I say, that's pretty good, isn't it? Let's go up and see him. There is no time like the present — Napoleon said that. Or was it Josephine?'

'He's out,' said Amanda, still breathless.

'Out? Then don't let's waste our time on the chap. Probably can't paint for pineapples. Let's go out and paint the town instead!'

'But—— '

'*Shut up!*' said Steve softly and savagely.

He pulled her arm through his own, and holding it hard against

116

him, turned and went back down the stairs, singing *'Dolce notte! Quante stella'* in a loud and cheerful voice.

The door banged behind them and Mr Howard, still retaining his hold on Amanda's arm, walked rapidly away along the quay and continued to sing.

He did not turn towards the town, however, but swung instead down the sea wall of the harbour, dragging Amanda with him. The loiterers whom she had observed earlier that evening were gone and the wall was deserted. Half-way along it he stopped and jerked her round to face him. She saw his gaze search the length of the wall, the open sea on one side and the dark harbour water on the other. But there was no boat anchored near them and the wall itself lay white and empty in the brilliant moonlight.

Steve drew a quick breath of relief and his voice when he spoke was no longer either loud or slurred, but low pitched and incisive:

'At least we can't be overheard here; which is more than I can say of any other spot in this damned town! However just in case anyone has a pair of night glasses and is curious, I propose to convey the impression that conversation is not what is on my mind. Stand still!'

The next minute his arms were about Amanda and his cheek was against her hair: 'And now,' said Steve tersely, his voice hard and curt and entirely devoid of any emotional content, 'perhaps you'll tell me what the hell you were doing in that house! Toby Gates told me that you'd gone to see Mrs Barton, and I got down there as quick as I could. What were you doing there?'

His shoulder was warm and firm and smelt comfortingly of shaving soap, clean linen and Turkish cigarettes, and Amanda struggled with a childish desire to turn her head against it and burst into tears. It is possible that Mr Howard was aware of this, for he said sharply: 'Take a pull on yourself, Amanda!'

Amanda steadied herself with an effort and said: 'It was Glenn——'

'*Glenn?* You mean Barton? Was he there?'

'No. He came to tell me about her — Anita. Because he'd pretended that she was ill, and when he heard that she was in Kyrenia he knew that I'd find out ...'

She told him the story as Glenn had told it to her that afternoon, and how she had offered to see Anita Barton and had arranged with Toby Gates to get Lumley Potter safely off the premises.

'And what happened when you got there?' demanded Steve brusquely.

He listened without interruption to her account of that unsatisfactory and abortive interview with Anita Barton, and when she had finished he said:

'What was that about someone on the stairs?'

'There *was* someone,' whispered Amanda, and shivered.

'Steve's arms tightened about her momentarily and he said: 'Go on. Tell me.'

She told him of that brief, ugly, terrifying interlude on the dark rickety staircase, and when she had done he said curtly: 'Quite sure you didn't imagine it?'

'Quite sure,' said Amanda, and shivered again.

'Any idea who it was?'

'No.'

'Could it have been Mrs Barton?'

'No,' said Amanda again, entirely positive.

'What makes you so sure?'

'She had the gramophone on. If she had opened the door it would have sounded louder at once.'

'H'mm. Maybe. On the other hand there is probably another door.'

He brooded for a moment or two, absently rubbing his cheek against her hair, and then said abruptly: 'Who knew that you were going there?'

'No one. Only Glenn — Mr Barton. And Toby of course. No one else.'

'And Toby told me — choosing a nice public spot to do it in

118

— and probably half a dozen other people as well. So that's not much help to us.'

Amanda said with a quaver in her voice: 'What's wrong with that house?'

She was aware of a brief, fractional tension of Steve's body, but he only said: 'Nothing that I know of.'

'Then why did you come there as soon as Toby told you where I was?'

'Because,' said Mr Howard with commendable restraint, 'I do not consider it healthy for you to wander around alone after dark. I warned you once that you'd have to watch your step. Well I meant it. In case you're not aware of it, this afternoon, in the absence of any other evidence, a verdict that amounted to "suicide while of an unsound mind" was returned on Mrs Blaine.'

'But — that means it's all over!' said Amanda. 'If the police think it was suicide, then no one would want to—— '

'Can't you understand?' interrupted Steve roughly. 'Mrs Blaine was murdered; and as far as the murderer knows, you are the only person who may be aware of it. If you had talked — if you talk now — that verdict would not stand. Use your head, Amanda!'

'Then you think that – that someone in that house meant to stop me talking by—— ' Amanda's voice died in her throat.

'I don't know about that. You can't say that because you heard someone coming down a staircase behind you it was necessarily someone who meant to harm you. Or, for that matter, that he or she even knew who you were. It is just on the cards that another visitor may have been expected to pay a call on Mrs Barton tonight, and that in the dark you were mistaken for someone else.'

'For – for someone who . . . somebody meant to kill? You mean another murder? Oh no!'

'It's possible. An attempt at one, shall we say?'

'I don't believe it. Why? Why should there be?'

'I'm not sure yet. It's just a theory. But it might account for that incident on the staircase. There are, of course, various other

119

possibilities—— ' There was an odd inflection in Steve Howard's voice.

'I know,' interrupted Amanda bitterly. 'One of which is that I might really have murdered Julia Blaine, and then invented a story of someone on the stairs just to make it look as though it couldn't possibly have been me!'

'Yes,' agreed Steve thoughtfully. 'There is always that of course. I hadn't lost sight of it.'

He heard Amanda's quick gasp of rage and continued reflectively: 'Poison, you see, is a woman's weapon. Women do not as a rule use a gun, and hardly ever a knife. They don't like noise or blood. They prefer poison or pushing someone off a cliff — something which produces death, but death at arm's length so to speak. Men don't mind the bang, or the blood getting on their hands.'

'You – you—— ' words appeared to fail Amanda. 'You dare to think that I—— ' She attempted to wrench herself free and Steve tightened his hold.

'There's no need to fly off the handle, Amarantha. One has to look at every angle. It's a possibility. There are, as I said, others.'

Amanda pulled back against his arms and stared up at him; but the moon was behind him and his face was only a dark shadow against the pale sky and the silver sea. She said in a breathless, furious whisper:

'There's something I haven't lost sight of either! *You* told me not to tell about that bottle. And *you* took it away — *and* the glass! How do I know that you didn't do that because your own fingerprints were on both? I don't believe that you were in Fayid, or on the ship, just because you paint. You were there for a reason. Something to do with Julia — or Toby, or Persis, or someone who was on that ship. There's something horrible going on, and you're mixed up in it!'

She stopped, breathless and trembling, and Steve said reflec-

120

tively: 'You look charming when you're angry. Like an infuriated kitten.'

Amanda made another ineffectual attempt to free herself, but the arms about her were suddenly like a vice, hard and painful, and there was no longer any trace of levity in Steven Howard's voice. He said harshly: 'Keep out of this, Amanda! I mean that. Murder is a diabolical thing. You can't risk taking an interest in the private affairs of anyone who was on that boat. It isn't safe.'

'Why?' asked Amanda uncertainly.

'Because it's essential that you avoid any appearance of suspicion or meddling. It's no secret that you were with Julia Blaine when she died, and someone knows that there was a small bottle containing the poison she died of under the pillow in that cabin. That someone is bound to wonder what you thought when you found it, and why you never mentioned it, and what you have done with it. Remember that a murderer always has a guilty conscience, and that a killer knows quite well that even if he kills a dozen people — or twenty — he himself can only hang once.'

Amanda said in a choking whisper: 'But I don't know anything — I don't want to!'

'You know about the bottle,' said Steve grimly. 'You also questioned the stewardess about that glass. I heard you, so the chances are that several other people did as well. And because of that, someone may be interested enough — or scared enough — to keep a pretty wary eye on you and to get unpleasantly upset when you behave as you did tonight.'

'But I only called on Mrs Barton. There's nothing suspicious in that!'

'No? Not when you tell Toby Gates to lure Mr Potter out of the house? Not when you slip out after dark and — I am willing to bet — sneak along in the shadows with a veil half over your face and lurk in some alleyway until Potter has left, and then steal into the house like a stage conspirator in Act II about to plant the time bomb in the Prime Minister's portfolio? You did, didn't you?'

121

'Well—— ' began Amanda defensively, and stopped.

'I thought as much,' said Mr Howard, resigned. 'Listen to me, Amanda — and I'm not going to tell you this again. You are in the unfortunate position of being able to produce evidence that what has scraped past as suicide was, in reality, murder. If, on top of that, you start paying elaborately furtive visits to a woman whom you have never met before, but who was a fellow passenger on board the *Orantares*, someone with a guilty conscience and a single-track mind may begin to ask themselves why all this First Conspirator stuff, if your visit to Mrs Barton is just a social call? — or could it be that you are beginning to make discreet inquiries among the passengers, and if so, what are you after? On the other hand, provided you behave in a perfectly normal manner, whoever was responsible for the murder of Mrs Blaine may be led to believe that you made nothing of that bottle after all, but merely threw it out of the porthole and dismissed the incident — maybe! Now do you get the idea?'

'Yes,' said Amanda with a shudder.

'Good. Keep thinking of it. And keep out of it!'

Amanda said haltingly: 'But – but Julia — If somebody killed her it isn't right that they should get away with it just because I – I hadn't the courage to tell.'

'Don't worry; they won't,' said Steve grimly. 'I promise you that. And it wasn't a question of your not having the courage to tell. You'd have told all right, if I hadn't stopped you.'

'Why did you?'

'Because it was too late to do anything for Mrs Blaine by then, and I had an idea or two of my own that I preferred to follow up without the issue being confused by a cat among the pigeons.'

'Ideas about what?'

'Limes, Times and Temperature,' said Steve lightly. 'And now, as I am beginning to get cramp, I think that the sooner we terminate this tender interlude, the better. Look at me!'

Amanda looked up, startled, and Steve bent his head and kissed her.

It was, as Persis would have said, quite a kiss, and indicated if nothing else that Mr Howard must have had plenty of experience in such matters. Amanda, who owing to a strict policy of chaperonage enforced until recently by Uncle Oswin, had not, had the oddest conviction that the ground under her feet was no longer solid and that for a long moment the moon and stars were describing circles about her head.

'That,' said Mr Howard, releasing her, 'was just for the record.'

'Was it?' said Amanda breathlessly. 'Then this is just for——'

Steve caught her hand a fraction of a second before it reached its mark.

'That would have hurt you much more than it hurt me,' he remarked reprovingly. 'Another time use your fist instead of your palm, and go for the point of the jaw. Like to have another shot?'

'Yes!' said Amanda, breathing stormily. 'With a flatiron!'

'Very wifely,' commented Mr Howard. He looked down at her and laughed.

'I apologize — there! But it was quite irresistible. Don't quarrel with me, Amarantha.' He kissed her hand lightly and tucked it under his arm. 'Come on; it's quite time you got back, or Miss Moon will begin to wonder if you really are a nice girl after all.'

He turned her about and walked her back along the sea wall and up through the moonlit town to the gates of the Villa Oleander.

10

Amanda avoided the harbour on the following morning. In the hot, brilliant sunlight that streamed through the open windows of the Villa Oleander and filled the dusty, gracious rooms with sunbeams, the events of the past night seemed unbelievable and unreal, and even faintly ridiculous. Amanda was almost tempted to wonder if she had not, after all, imagined the sound of those furtive feet on the stairs. Had they perhaps been only an echo of her own footsteps, or a trick played upon her nerves by darkness and an unfamiliar and empty house?

There was only one thing about the happenings of the past night that was entirely real. The fact that Steve Howard had kissed her.

Amanda, standing in the hot sunlight of the garden and remembering that kiss with a return of the curious sensation of dizziness that had accompanied it, was inclined to discount all that Steve Howard had told her, and to suspect that it had merely amused him to see how long he could keep her standing in a close embrace in the moonlight. Hadn't he made some flippant remark on the previous morning about only making love by moonlight?

'I wouldn't put it past him to have done it for a bet!' thought Amanda with sudden bitterness. 'He probably makes a habit of it, and I expect he has kissed Persis already!'

The reflection annoyed her unreasonably, and she did not realize that in the process of brooding over Steve Howard's outrageous behaviour she had very nearly lost sight of the terrifying and infinitely more important fact that she had been indirectly involved in what was almost certainly murder, and that she had entirely forgotten to be frightened. An end that Mr Howard may possibly have had in view when he had terminated their macabre conversation on the harbour wall in that particular manner.

Amanda stood among the freckled shadows of the lemon trees, with the pigeons cooing and fluttering in the deep stone arches of the ruined wall behind her and the scent of roses and syringa and sunbaked dust sweet on the windless air, and thought exclusively of Steven Howard and not at all of Julia Blaine ...

Miss Moon, a blaze of emerald green, appeared upon the creeper-covered verandah outside the drawing-room windows and called down to say that Captain Gates was on the telephone asking if Amanda would go bathing with him.

'Tell him I've gone out!' begged Amanda.

'Certainly, dear. Where to?'

'Just out,' said Amanda, seized with an urgent desire for solitude and a feeling of inability to cope with the conversation of Toby Gates or anyone else — with one possible exception.

She ran across the garden and out into the road, and taking the first turning that offered, presently found herself leaving the town behind her.

The houses became fewer and the road wandered between olive groves, dark pointed cypress trees and stony sun-baked fields where goats grazed among the coarse grasses, weeds and asphodel. An ox cart creaked towards her and a black-haired, black-eyed, bare-footed urchin riding a donkey flourished a branch of oleander and grinned at Amanda as he ambled past. The road was hot and white under her feet and she began to wish that she had thought to bring a hat.

A car swept past, covering her with dust. It drew up abruptly some distance ahead, and reversed until it drew level with her.

'Amanda!' said Alastair Blaine, leaning out over the door. 'What do you think you're doing?'

'Walking,' said Amanda. 'Hullo, Persis. Where are you two off to?'

'We are doing our duty as self-respecting tourists,' said Persis. 'According to the Guide Book, we should not fail to see the Abbey of Bellapais. We are not failing.'

'Come on Amanda,' said Alastair Blaine, leaning out to open the back door. 'Get in. You'll get heat-stroke or a peeling nose or both if you wander around the countryside in this sun, and as you'll have to do the sights some time you may as well do this one now.'

Amanda looked back down the hot dusty road and capitulated. She said: 'You will get me back by one o'clock, won't you?'

'Of course. Half an hour is about my limit for looking at ruins. Hop in.' He slammed the door behind her and changed gear.

Persis had not seconded the invitation and Amanda had the sudden and uncomfortable impression that she was not too pleased at the addition of a third person to the party. But it was too late now, for the car was already moving again.

The white road ran parallel to the sea and the long, narrow barrier of the Kyrenia range that lay between the coast and the central plain. The mountains were blue in the hot sunlight; a clear transparent blue that made them look as though they had been fashioned out of Lalique glass, and their pale serrated peaks, shimmering in the heat haze, had the strange beauty of those distant ranges that Leonardo da Vinci has painted as a background to the Mona Lisa and the Madonna of the Rocks.

A light breeze blew in from the sea, turning the olive trees to silver, and Amanda relaxed into a day dream and made no attempt to talk. Even Persis Halliday's clear and incisive voice had softened and slowed as though the warm peace of the morning was also having its effect on her, and she conducted a low-toned conversation with Alastair Blaine to which Amanda, occupied with her own thoughts, paid no heed.

The car changed gear as the road wound up through a village perched on a low hill. A village of white-walled, pink-roofed houses, bell towers and minarets, encircled with olive groves, silver in the wind, and spiked with the sharp dark green of cypress trees.

Persis said: 'Say, isn't this the cutest place you ever saw! Where's that map? . . . Aiyos Epiktitos. That'll be it. Do stop, Alastair, I want to take a photograph.'

Major Blaine looked at his watch and said, resigned: 'I'll give you five minutes. And no wandering round the place if you want to see the Abbey and get back by one.'

The streets were full of people in holiday attire and gay with a flutter of paper flags and green branches, and Amanda suddenly caught sight of a familiar face. It was Euridice, the prop and stay of the Villa Oleander, and Amanda remembered that Miss Moon had mentioned a fête at Aiyos Epiktitos that both Euridice and her nephew Andreas, the odd-job man, were to attend that day.

Euridice, however, appeared to be in anything but a festive mood. She was talking to a small group of black-clad women, one of whom was wailing aloud, and her normally cheerful face was full of woe. She looked up and, seeing Amanda, hurried over to the car.

This meeting, it was providential! declared Euridice. Her English was strangely scrambled and interlarded with whole sentences in her native tongue, but Amanda gathered from her flood of agitated speech that neither she nor Andreas would be able to return to the Villa Oleander that day, and that she wished Amanda to convey this information and her apologies to Miss Moon.

'Tomorrow morning, for the breakfast I come,' said Euridice. 'Today, no.' A relative had died, she explained; the husband of a cousin who kept a Taverna on the road beyond Nicosia. Apparently the cousin's husband had got into some bar-room brawl in Nicosia and had ended up in a culvert with a knife in his back.

Ah, these seafaring men! said Euridice, throwing up her hands.

On the ships they would work like oxen at the plough, but on shore they pursued pleasure and conducted themselves in a truculent manner. The poor Almena! — Euridice mopped her eyes — what sadness to lose a husband thus! This had been her home village before her marriage, and her family, together with Euridice and Andreas, were to leave shortly by bus for Nicosia to attend the funeral, and would not be back that night.

Amanda offered her condolences and promised to inform Miss Moon. Euridice thanked her tearfully and departed.

'Who was your lady friend?' demanded Persis, returning. Amanda explained the circumstances as Alastair Blaine restarted the car and they continued on their way.

The ruined Abbey of Bellapais lay on the knees of the hills, its pale stone walls, arches and tall campanile rising up out of a silvery sea of olives so graciously, so softly opalescent, that it seemed more like a mirage than something built by men, and as though a breath could blow it away.

Beyond and above and below the pale gold walls and empty archways lay a wash of blue; the intense cobalt blue of the distant sea, the cloudless blue of the sky and the soft blue barrier of the Kyrenia range.

Major Blaine braked the car in a patch of shade and Amanda said suddenly: 'I don't think I'm coming in. I'd rather look at it from the hillside. If I go inside there's sure to be a guide and instructive notices, and I couldn't bear to turn it from a dream into a string of dates. I shall sit under one of those olive trees and just stare at it.'

Persis laughed. 'You know what, honey? You are too romantic for your own good — or else you must be in love. Well I guess I won't dissuade you. We're only young once. But speaking for myself I do not intend to miss a trick. I've come to Cyprus to see the sights, and I'll see 'em if it kills me. Where's that dam' guide book? Alastair honey, if you think you're going to lie on your back under any olive tree and go to sleep, you have assessed the situation incorrectly. You were taking me on a conducted tour — remember? You start conducting right here. Lead on!'

They passed under the shadow of a stone archway and Amanda, left alone, turned away and climbed the slope above the road, and presently settled herself in the shade of an ilex with her back against the rough bark and gave herself up to a fascinated contemplation of the view.

I should like to live here, thought Amanda dreamily; and remembered what Miss Moon had said about Time ... that in the Villa Oleander, Time was their servant, and not they the servants of Time. Perhaps that was true of all Cyprus. Certainly this shimmering blue day held a timeless and dream-like quality. But it was a deceptive quality, for Time must move on here as relentlessly as it did in colder and harsher countries, and it was only a pleasant illusion that here it drifted slowly and lazily. One day the world would catch up with Cyprus. One day politicians and greedy, frightened, quarrelling factions would engulf the sleepy, enchanted island — as they had engulfed so many other lazy, beautiful places — in a wave of Progress, reinforced concrete and Town Planning.

The sun moved slowly across the sky and the shadow of the ilex moved with it. The bark of the tree trunk began to feel unpleasantly hard through the thin green cotton of Amanda's frock and there was an ant crawling down her back and several more investigating her ankles.

She rose reluctantly and made her way back to the car. There was still no sign of Persis and Alastair, and abandoning her decision not to enter the Abbey, she paid over the small entrance fee to the drowsy custodian at the entrance and walked into the Abbey grounds.

Only the shell of the gracious building remained. But the old stone cloisters were cool and quiet and the ruined arches gave on to soft blue distances and the grey-green of olives on the hillside below. Bellapais — The Abbey of Peace. It had been well named.

Amanda wandered across a square of emerald green turf surrounded by shadowed cloisters. There was a rose bush growing at one side of it and a single tall cypress tree. The close-cut turf looked more comfortable than the stony hillside, and she lay face down on it, stretched out at full length on the warm grass in the small patch of shade thrown by the scented sprays of the roses that curved above her. Amanda pulled a grass stem and chewed it reflectively, and presently, feeling pleasantly drowsy, closed her eyes ...

She was aroused by a sound of voices from under the arch of the cloisters on the far side of the rose bush. It was Alastair Blaine who was speaking, though it did not seem like his voice, for its slow, pleasant drawl was entirely missing and the words had a sharp, ragged sound:

'My dear, don't! Not now. You don't understand—— '

Persis Halliday answered him, and her voice too was almost the voice of a stranger: hurt and uneven and somehow vulnerable.

'I think I do. Cyprus isn't London, this isn't last year, and Time Marches On. That's it, isn't it? You've changed — and I haven't. Once I thought that you might almost walk out on everything — Julia, your career, everything, anything — for me. Almost — not quite.'

'Persis, you knew it wasn't possible.'

'Because you hadn't a penny beyond your pay and the money was all Julia's? But it's different now, Alastair. She's dead, and it's all yours.'

'You don't understand,' said Alastair tiredly.

'What don't I understand? I came out to Egypt because I had to see you. And her. To see what she was like. I knew the minute I saw you together that you didn't even care for her. But you didn't care any more for me either. Who is she, Alastair?'

'She? I don't know who you are talking about.'

'Neither do I. But I feel that there is someone. Is it Claire? You stopped off here, after that fortnight in London, to stay with the

130

Normans. Oh yes, I know that Julia was here too, and that when you were flown home to London for that conference I had a fair field because she couldn't come with you. But a little thing like having your wife around wouldn't stop Claire!'

'Oh God,' said Alastair Blaine. 'You too!'

Persis said: 'Don't fool yourself, darling — it isn't you she wants. She likes men around, but it's George she really relies on. George, who puts up with all her whims and whimsies and provides her with a nice safe respectable background and fetches and carries for her. Things no one else would do. Is it Claire?'

'I don't know what you're talking about,' said Alastair wearily. 'I have no interest in Claire Norman, and George is my first cousin. In fact now that Julia's dead he's my next of kin, so is it likely that I'd even think of — Oh, leave it!'

'Now you're angry. But if it isn't Claire, who is it? Is it Amanda? Have you fallen for those big grey eyes and that wonderful hair, like Toby Gates? You and Toby! And just over a year ago he was tagging round after me like Mary's little lamb. Oh well, who can blame him. She's a sweet kid, and worth anyone's while for half an hour in the moonlight.'

'Don't be ridiculous!' Alastair's voice was both angry and exasperated.

'Then who?'

'There isn't anyone, I tell you. Can't you see that after Julia——'

Persis cut across the sentence sharply and cruelly: 'You didn't give a dam' for Julia! I know. I've seen you look at her. The best turn she ever did you was to kill herself! That's true, isn't it?'

'Yes,' said Alastair Blaine heavily. 'It's true. But – but you can't shrug off death, Persis. She was my wife, and — oh I don't want to talk about it. I don't want to *think* about it. Can't you see that all I want is a little peace and quiet? I've had nothing but scenes for years. Scenes and tears and hysteria, and nagging, senseless, silly accusations. God! I'm sick of it!'

131

'Alastair, darling——'

'Don't darling me!' Alastair's voice was suddenly ragged with exhaustion and rage. 'All right, you asked for it and you shall have it! I did make love to you in London last year. Would you like to know why? Because you wanted me to. You shouted for it like a spoilt kid banging the table with a spoon. And you were attractive and amusing and you treated the whole thing as a joke. And because I knew — I knew so damnably well! — that when I got back to Julia she would accuse me of having had an affair with some woman, even if I'd spent the entire bloody fortnight locked in the cell of a monastery!'

'But Alastair——'

'Shut up! I'm talking now. I've never had affairs with women. Do you realize that? Julia was the first woman I ever fell in love with, and I married her. In all the years of our marriage I had never been unfaithful to her — never once! Do you know why? Because I'm not built that way. I cannot be rude or curt to women who put themselves out to be pleasant to me, but I don't want to make love to them. And believe me, they don't want it either! But Julia would never believe that. She preferred to imagine that I was some frightful Lothario, instead of a perfectly ordinary, dull sort of chap without an ounce of sex appeal. And now you! — it's too much! I'd put up with Julia's senseless, endless, *futile* suspicions for years, and I suppose there was bound to be a breaking point one day, and——'

'And I was it,' finished Persis quietly.

'Yes! Oh it wasn't you—— No, I don't mean it like that. But it was knowing so well that as soon as I saw her again I should have to listen to the same old sordid accusations. I suddenly felt that I couldn't take it any more.'

'So you said to yourself "What the hell? If I'm going to be accused of playing around anyway, okay, I'll play around!"'

'Yes!'

'And that's really all there was to it? Just – just a ten-day

132

flirtation with someone who was attractive and amusing and who treated it all as a joke?'

'I'm sorry. I didn't imagine for a moment that you—— '

Persis' voice interrupted him before he could finish the sentence:

'Don't, dear! You don't have to say any more. And so there isn't even anyone else!'

She laughed; a little bitter laugh. Alastair did not answer and there was silence for a moment or two. Presently their footsteps moved slowly away together, echoing hollowly under the curved stone arches of the age-old cloisters.

A shadow moved on the grass beside Amanda and a quiet voice quoted Puck's words: ' "*Lord, what fools these mortals be!*" '

Amanda started up. '*You!*' she said on a gasp. 'What are you doing here?'

'The same as you,' said Steve Howard amiably. 'Eavesdropping.'

Amanda's face flamed. 'I was not eavesdropping!'

'Perhaps not intentionally, but the result was the same. Very instructive, wasn't it?'

'Why are you spying on us all?' demanded Amanda hotly.

'You sound very cross, my sweet. Why shouldn't I come here if I wish? A good many people do. In fact all self-respecting tourists are urged not to miss it. I have been pursuing my Art.'

'I don't believe a word of it!' said Amanda. 'And I'm not cross and I'm not your sweet!'

'I withdraw the adjective. There is, alas, a distinct trace of acidity in your manner this morning; and you are not only cross but getting crosser every minute.'

Amanda opened her mouth and shut it again without speaking. She had remembered an admirable piece of advice frequently given to her by Miss Binns, her Uncle Oswin's elderly and placid housekeeper. She drew a deep breath and counted twenty.

'Why are you here?' she inquired in a more reasonable voice.

'To keep an eye on you.'

133

'On *me?*' said Amanda, startled. 'Why?'

'I find you so attractive that I cannot keep away.'

There was a mocking gleam in Mr Howard's eye and once again Amanda felt her cheeks burn, counted fifteen and said coldly: 'Don't talk nonsense.'

'Don't you believe me?'

'No I don't!' snapped Amanda.

'All right then. I have a brilliant theory that sooner or later someone is going to murder you, and I wish to see who does it. Will that do?'

'Don't you ever speak the truth?' demanded Amanda frostily.

'Not if I can help it,' admitted Steve with disarming candour. 'Truth, Amarantha, as your classical studies will no doubt have informed you, is a naked lady who lives at the bottom of a well. It therefore behoves any gentleman who inadvertently dredges her up in his bucket to look the other way or hurriedly shroud her in a mackintosh.'

Amanda looked at him doubtfully. His brown hair was ruffled into disorder and there was a smudge of blue paint on one side of his chin. He was wearing a blue sports shirt and a pair of grey flannels that had seen better days, and there were paint marks on both.

She said abruptly: 'What have you been painting?'

Mr Howard made an airy gesture of the hand towards the surrounding walls. 'This. From a couple of hundred yards down the road.'

Amanda said: 'I'd like to see it.'

'Suspicious little thing, aren't you? All right — come on.'

They walked back through the Abbey and down the road, and he led the way up a goat track to a point on the opposite hillside some fifty yards to the left of the ilex tree under which Amanda had been sitting.

'Where's your car?' asked Amanda.

'On the upper road; it's not much more than a track.'

134

There was a clutter of painting gear in the shade of some trees, and Steve picked up a canvas that he had left propped against a tree trunk, and held it up for her inspection.

It was a rough sketch in oils, showing the Abbey of Bellapais lifting above a haze of wind-ruffled olives. The thing had apparently been done entirely with a palette knife, for the paint was laid on with a lavish hand; but it in no way resembled the efforts of Mr Lumley Potter. Despite the strength of the technique the unfinished sketch had captured all the dreamlike, ethereal quality of the ruined Abbey that had so forcibly struck Amanda at her first sight of it, and she said again, and unconsciously, almost the same words that she had used on the harbour wall on the previous morning.

'But you *can* paint!'

She lifted her eyes from the picture and looked at Steve Howard, puzzled and uncertain.

'Poor Amarantha,' said Steve softly. 'You don't know whether you're coming or going, do you? Well if it's any consolation to you, I'm not so sure myself. Why did you come to Cyprus?'

The question was abrupt and unexpected, and Amanda looked startled. 'I wanted to come.'

'Why? Any special reason?'

'Yes,' said Amanda slowly, her mouth curving in a reminiscent smile: 'A poem I read at school. Have you ever read something that made you want to see a special place? That – that sort of haunted you?'

Steve's eyes were no longer mocking. 'Flecker,' he said, smiling, and quoted the lines that had captured the schoolgirl Amanda's childish imagination: ' "*I have seen old ships sail like swans asleep beyond the village which men still call Tyre, with leaden age o'ercargoed, dipping deep for Famagusta and the hidden sun that rings black Cyprus with a lake of fire.*" '

'Yes,' said Amanda. She turned to look out across the grey-green mist of olives to the far blue sea beyond them, and spoke

in the soft abstracted voice of one who speaks a thought aloud:
'"*Famagusta and the hidden sun . . .*" The names are so beautiful.
Famagusta — Kyrenia — Hilarion— Paphos.' Her voice changed
to every name, lingering on the syllables. 'Do you know what
the castle on that peak over there is called? Miss Moon told me.
It's called Buffavento. That means "the wind blows". *The wind
blows . . .*' Her voice sank to a whisper.

Steve forbore to correct her translation, and just then a car horn
sounded from the road below.

'That'll be Blaine,' said Steve. 'You'd better get back. See you
at the picnic this afternoon.'

Amanda turned to look at the square of canvas again. She said
a little hesitantly: 'Could I buy it? I'd like to have it for my own.
You do sell them, don't you?'

'I do,' said Steve. 'But not, generally speaking, off the peg.
However, I'd like to give you this one. You can consider it as an
un-birthday present. It's only a rough sketch.'

Amanda smiled at him with a sudden glow in her eyes and
reached out a hand for it. 'It's wonderful!' she said.

'It's wet,' said Steve, removing it. 'I'll keep it for the moment.
You shall have it later.'

Amanda nodded absently, and went slowly back down the
hillside between the olive trees. And all the way back to Kyrenia,
while Persis laughed and chattered as though that brief, emotional
scene in the Abbey cloisters had never taken place, Amanda was
silent and thoughtful.

She was remembering something that Steven Howard had said
in the cabin of the *Orantares*: 'I paint indifferent pictures and have
a passion for meddling in other people's affairs.' She had put her
own interpretation on that and had come to the conclusion that he
was some sort of private inquiry agent, and that it was even possible that Julia had employed him to watch her husband so that she
might have something besides hysterical suspicions with which to
confront Alastair, and acquire thereby an additional hold over him.

But Steve did not seem to fit into that role. And he could paint: there was no doubt at all about that. The conté drawings she had seen on the previous morning had betrayed a considerable talent, but the rough sketch in oils of the Abbey of Bellapais was in an entirely different category and Amanda began to wonder if her imagination had not run away with her.

Had Steve Howard after all come to Fayid and to Cyprus by chance, and with the sole object of painting, and had his subsequent proceedings stemmed, as he himself had suggested, from an amused and analytical interest in the behaviour of his fellow men?

Then there was Persis: Persis and Alastair Blaine, who had apparently met and had a brief affair in London during two short weeks the previous summer, when Alastair had been flown to London on the General's staff to attend some conference. Amanda remembered having heard Julia refer to it once. The conference had been delayed and instead of staying in London for a few days, Alastair had stayed two weeks and — probably as a result of some foolish letter from Julia — reached at last that breaking point to which he had referred. And Persis had fallen in love with him.

Amanda was conscious of a sudden intense pang of pity for Persis Halliday, who had proved to be so vulnerable under that surface shell of glittering, cynical sophistication. It was followed by a surge of admiration. If Persis had indeed received a shattering blow to her heart and her hopes and her pride, there was nothing in her manner to indicate it.

What did she see in Alastair Blaine? wondered Amanda. What had Julia seen? He was tall, blond, sun-tanned and blue-eyed, but not particularly good looking. It was an unremarkable, pleasant and entirely Anglo-Saxon face, and he was in fact, as he himself had said, a 'perfectly ordinary dull sort of chap without an ounce of sex appeal'. Women liked Alastair Blaine, but in much the same way as they liked their brothers. They made use of him and

137

discussed their problems with him in a way that they would never have done had their emotions been involved. It was only Julia's jealousy, Amanda realized, that had built up a picture of Alastair as an irresistible charmer.

Julia was probably the only woman who had ever fallen deeply in love with Alastair Blaine — Julia and Persis. What *did* Persis see in him?

It's because she's an American and she writes, thought Amanda with a sudden flash of understanding.

Persis did not see Alastair as other people saw him. He had looked like her idea of a strong, silent Englishman, and his very indifference to women, as women, had probably lent colour to that view. She had fitted him with a ready-made character and attributes of her own devising, and fallen in love with the result. In love with something that was no more the real Alastair Blaine than a tailor's dummy is flesh and blood.

I wonder what he is really like? thought Amanda. But then what was the real Persis like? — or the real Toby? — or jovial, stupid, easy-going, devoted George Norman? Or, for that matter, Steve Howard?

Amanda frowned unseeingly at the olive groves and the sea; puzzled and disturbed for the first time in her twenty-one years by the realization that despite the dictates of John Donne, each man and woman is, in some way, 'an island unto themselves'.

11

Amanda delivered Euridice's message to Miss Moon, and Miss Moon tut-tutted absently and said: 'I only trust that she will return early enough to cook us some breakfast. At what time are you leaving for this picnic, my dear?'

'Half past two,' said Amanda. 'I'm being collected.'

'I,' said Miss Moon with a regretful sigh, 'shall be leaving a quarter of an hour later. Such a pity that I cannot come with you. St Hilarion always gives me such a feeling of spiritual refreshment and affinity with Time. So much more soothing than Lady Cooper-Foot's bridge afternoons. I shall not enjoy myself at all I fear, and I have a headache coming on — I only trust it does not develop into migraine. But one must not neglect one's duties towards society.'

Amanda said: 'How do I get in if I get back before you, now that Euridice isn't in?'

'Oh, I never lock the house, dear. I have always maintained that any dishonest person who wishes to enter a house will do so despite all the locks and bolts in the world. Locks only serve to incommode the innocent and innocuous. You will find the house open.'

Toby Gates arrived with commendable punctuality on the tick of two-thirty, and Amanda fetched a wide-brimmed hat and a pair of sunglasses and called good-bye to Miss Moon. She received no answer and thought it probable that Miss Moon had already left.

'How are we going, Toby?'

'I've hired a car for the afternoon. Not a bad little bus. The Normans offered to give us both a lift, but as they're already taking Alastair Blaine and all the tea things, I thought it sounded a bit of a squash.'

He ushered her into the front seat of a small grey saloon car and Amanda said: 'What about Persis?'

'Howard is taking her.'

The car drew away from the kerb and gathered speed on the long rising road that leads up from Kyrenia to the pass in the hills, from where it drops again to Nicosia and the plain.

'I can't think why I'm doing this,' said Toby. 'If I were in my right mind I should not be on speaking terms with you.'

Amanda turned to look at him in frank surprise. 'Why, Toby? What have I done now?'

'I like that!' said Toby forcefully. 'Do you realize, you long-haired hussy, that entirely owing to you I am down a matter of fifty quid and in possession of two of the most god-awful eyesores that ever defaced a wall?'

'Oh Toby!' Amanda was suddenly stricken with guilt. 'I'd quite forgotten. You *didn't* buy a genuine Potter?'

'My dear girl, I couldn't possibly avoid it! I sent along a note as per order, and then I quite forgot about the chap and went for a stroll in the town. It was meeting Howard that reminded me of him. And when I got back, there he was, planted in the lounge with a portfolio the size of Cyprus, still waiting. So of course after that I had to do something about it. He stayed for hours! Fortunately it didn't seem to matter if I said anything or not. I let him do the talking, and he thinks I am a connoisseur of the Arts. Well I'm sending you those pictures as a small present, and you can jolly well hang them on your walls. And what is more, you can dine with me tonight. You owe me that at least.'

'Toby darling, I *am* sorry. Yes of course I will. The staff is out for the day, so Miss Moon will probably be only too pleased to have one less to cook supper for.'

140

'Good show. How did your party with the erring wife go? Did she give you the inside low-down on the whole affair?'

'No,' said Amanda repressively. 'We — just talked. Are you sure you know the way, Toby?'

'No,' said Toby. 'But the chap who hired me the car said we can't miss it.'

The road wound up and up through olive groves, firs, cypress, carob, and sunbaked grassy slopes, and just short of the pass Toby turned the car right-handed into a side road signposted to Hilarion. As they turned, a car coming from the direction of Nicosia passed them on its way down to Kyrenia. It was a small green two-seater with a sports hood, driven by a woman, and Amanda thought that she recognized Glenn Barton's secretary, Monica Ford.

Their road skirted the mountain side and presently ran between an outcrop of the hills and past a wide saucer-like depression that Toby said had been a tilting ground — adding that his informant was Persis Halliday, who had been reading up on the subject of Hilarion and had evidently held forth during luncheon.

Rising sheer above it on a pinnacle of rock, over two thousand feet above the sea and silhouetted against the cloudless blue of the sky, stood the ruins of the Crusader castle of St Hilarion — the castle to which, legend says, Richard of the Lion Heart brought his newly-wed bride, Berengaria of Navarre. From this castle he went forth to the Crusades. And from its arched windows Berengaria the Queen must often have looked out on to that same sea to watch for the sails of his ships.

There was another car parked in the shade of some trees below the slope that led up the outer walls of the castle. But it did not belong either to the Normans or to Steven Howard.

'Tourists,' said Toby with contempt.

'Tourist yourself!' retorted Amanda, scrambling out of the car. 'Don't let's wait for the others. Let's go and explore.'

They climbed the stony slope in the hot sunlight and passed into

141

the cool shadow of the Keep. A long flight of worn stone steps led upward to the main bulk of the story-book castle that soared above them, clinging to the naked rock whose sheer sides formed many of its walls. At the foot and to one side of the stairway a man in a vividly patterned sports shirt was seated on a small canvas stool before a large easel. It was Lumley Potter. He turned his head as they approached and his scowl turned to a delighted smile:

'Hullo Gates. Just the man I wanted to see. How does this strike you? Early stages yet, of course, but I feel I have captured something of the tempo and perhaps a *hint* of the aura. At the moment the inner essence eludes me — yes, frankly it eludes me — but I feel that I shall ultimately grasp it.'

'Er – yes – I'm sure you will,' said Toby, staring in horrified disbelief at what appeared to be the portrait of a suet pudding in the making, into which someone had inadvertently stirred a generous dollop of schoolroom ink.

'Well?' said Mr Potter.

'Oh – er – terrific!' said Toby Gates hurriedly. 'I don't think you've met Miss Derington. Amanda, this is Mr Potter.'

Mr Potter expressed himself as pleased to meet Miss Derington and plunged into a discussion of his work that was only terminated by the arrival of the Normans, Major Blaine, Mrs Halliday and Steve Howard.

They left Claire and Major Blaine talking to Lumley — Claire it seemed was entirely familiar with the tempo and aura of art — and continued their exploration of the castle, Persis instructing their ignorance with the aid of a guide book.

Some minutes later, turning a corner, they came unexpectedly upon Anita Barton.

Mrs Barton had spread a travelling rug in a shady corner and lain down at full length with a book and a box of chocolates. The pages of the book were fluttering in a light breeze and a colony of ants were investigating the chocolates. Mrs Barton was asleep. She was wearing an exceedingly becoming dress of corn-coloured linen decorated at the hem and the deep neckline with innumerable small flat flowers cut from white linen and loosely attached by their centres. The effect was charming, but conveyed the impression that Mrs Barton must be exceedingly expensive to dress.

Amanda, gazing down at her, thought that she looked much younger than she had seemed last night — younger, and somehow defenceless — and remembered that Glenn Barton had spoken of his wife as being 'such a child'. Amanda could see now what he had meant. Despite the blue-tinted eyelids, the lavish use of mascara and lipstick and the scarlet lacquer on fingers and toes, there was something oddly childlike about the slumbering figure in the absurd and charming frock.

They turned away noiselessly and left her sleeping.

'This,' said Persis when they were out of earshot, 'is quite a situation. Do we warn her husband that his erring wife is among those present? The guy is due at any moment now. It's almost four. Or do we just ignore the whole thing and let him fall over her and the hell with it?'

'The latter,' advised Mr Howard lazily.

Amanda said anxiously: 'I'd forgotten that Glenn was coming. What time did he say he'd be here?'

'Four, if he could make it.'

Amanda peered over the battlements but could see no car on the white ribbon of road far below. Which was not surprising, for Mr Barton had been delayed ...

Glenn had intended to drive directly from Nicosia to Hilarion, but had found it necessary to go into Kyrenia to deliver some documents to a client who was staying at the Dome. He had been additionally delayed by a puncture just short of the town, and had left his car at a garage on the road and walked down to the hotel, discharged his errand and returned.

He was on his way back to collect his car when he saw Monica Ford's small, shabby two-seater cross an intersection ahead of him and turn down the side road that led past the Villa Oleander.

He was conscious of a slight feeling of surprise. What could Monica be doing in Kyrenia? He had seen her briefly in the Nicosia office that morning, but his work had taken him out to the vineyards and he had not been back to the office. Monica had made no mention of driving over to Kyrenia, and he had never before known her to leave the office unattended in his absence. Had something cropped up that required his immediate attention and had Monica come over in serarch of him?

Glenn glanced at his watch and saw that it was already a quarter to four. He hesitated on the pavement, puzzled and undecided, and then crossed the road and turned down to the Villa Oleander.

Monica's car was not outside the house, but he caught a glimpse of green paint and realized that she had parked it at the mouth of a narrow lane shadowed by mulberry trees on the opposite side of the road. Monica herself had just crossed the road and he saw her push open the gate of the Villa Oleander and disappear from view.

Perhaps there had been some message from Oswin Derington for his niece? But Amanda would be at Hilarion and Miss Moon at Lady Cooper-Foot's, while Euridice and Andreas were attending a fête at Aiyos Epiktitos. Monica would find the house empty.

Glenn turned in at the gate which Miss Ford had neglected to close behind her, and walked up the short flagged path. The front door swung open on oiled hinges and he was in the welcome coolness of the high, dim hall. He heard a movement from the direction of the drawing-room and walked across the hall and through the open doorway.

Monica Ford was standing near the french window and he checked abruptly at the sight of her face.

'Monica! My dear — what's the matter?'

Miss Ford did not answer him. Her face was ashy white and blotched with weeping; so drawn and haggard and aged with grief and emotion that it was almost unrecognizable.

'Monica!'

He went quickly towards her, but she shrank back and he

144

stopped. He saw her lick her dry, trembling lips and she said in a harsh, high whisper: 'What are you doing here? I – I thought you were in Limassol.'

'Monica, what is it? Has anything happened?'

She stared at him for a long moment, her red-rimmed eyes wide and fixed, then turning away she walked stumblingly to the sofa and sank down upon it with her back to him and her head in her hands, and burst into tears.

Oh God! thought Glenn despairingly. Another emotional woman! Anita — and now Monica. For Monica had begun to talk; a flood of hysterical words that fought with her sobs; jumbled, desperate, incoherent, from which a few words stood out, constantly repeated. Her dead brother's name; Anita's; his own — Glenn — Glenn — Glenn.

'... I didn't realize ... I – I loved you, Glenn. I loved you ...'

Glenn shut his eyes and tried to shut out the sound of her gasping voice; aware of a feeling of sick disgust and cold anger. But Monica's voice went on and on. Thick, ugly, choked with tears: '... I didn't realize it until today. I didn't know ... I wouldn't face it. I've always felt that there was something — something I shouldn't ... But I wouldn't admit it. And today you were away and Pavlos came to the office about a damaged case. He said you had gone to Hilarion with – with Claire Norman ... and – and then – then I knew. I loved you ...'

Glenn opened his eyes and looked at the huddled jerking shoulders with rage and despair. A faint scent of jasmine drifted in through the open windows and mingled with the cheap violet scent that Miss Ford affected, borne on a little breeze that billowed the curtains and fluttered the ends of a vivid green *crêpe de Chine* scarf that Miss Moon had left hanging over the back of the sofa. 'Thursday' thought Glenn automatically, noting the colour.

He tried to speak, but could find no words. There was nothing he could say. Nothing that could do any good now. He ought to have sent her away. He ought to have made her go. The ragged, sobbing voice went on and on and he winced at the sound of his wife's name.

'Anita ... Anita must have known. That's why she left you. I should have known too. But I wouldn't let myself know! I wouldn't face it. It's all my fault ... I pretended that everything was all right. But Anita must have known—— '

Anita, thought Glenn with a sudden twinge of almost physical pain. Was it true? Had she known? He had always suspected that she did not really believe the things she had said about himself and Monica Ford — that there was something else behind her sudden defection, and that Monica Ford had been only an excuse. Now Monica herself said that she must have known. And so she had run away. Anita——

The gasping, weeping voice filled the quiet room with ugly sound: 'I don't know what to do! If only it hadn't been for Bobby I could have borne it. But I had to talk to someone — I had to! Glenn! ... Glenn ...'

Monica Ford's voice choked and stopped at long last, like a gramophone record that has run down, and silence flowed back into the dusty, gracious room.

The sun had moved down the sky and now it shone in through the french windows and lay in a bright square of gold on the faded carpet, illuminating Monica Ford's ungainly body and filling the room with a mellow glowing warmth.

Glenn looked down at the slumped, twitching figure with sick distaste. And presently, realizing that there was nothing else he could do, he turned abruptly away from her and walked quickly out of the room.

A clock struck the quarter hour as he crossed the hall, and his hand was on the latch of the front door when he thought he heard a soft sound from somewhere on the bedroom floor.

He turned quickly and looked up. But there was no one on the stairs and nothing moved on the shadowed landing above. Miss Moon was out, and so were Andreas and Euridice, and the up-

146

stairs rooms should have been empty. There could be no one there. Perhaps the sound he had heard had been caused by a pigeon or Euridice's grey cat. He hesitated, frowning and uncertain, his nerves on edge and a cold tremor running down his spine. But there was no repetition of the sound and he did not wish to remain any longer under the same roof as Monica Ford. He turned away and left the house, shutting the door quietly behind him. And it was almost a quarter to five by the time he reached Hilarion ...

He found the picnic party seated about the remains of tea on a grassy space by a ruined buttress, and because he was disturbed and preoccupied he did not notice — or at least did not recognize — Lumley Potter's ramshackle car among the cars parked beside the road.

'So you finally made it,' remarked Persis, making room for him beside her. 'We'd given you up.'

Glenn subsided wearily on to the grass and accepted a lukewarm cup of tea which he drank thirstily.

'I'm sorry I'm late,' he apologized. 'I had to go into Kyrenia first, and I had a puncture just short of the town. And then I met Monica, and that held me up a bit.'

He frowned at the recollection of that interview, and for a moment his mouth twisted in a wry grimace of distaste.

Claire said: 'Monica? What was she doing in Kyrenia?'

'Nothing much. She thought she'd pay a call on Miss Derington, but of course there was no one in the house.'

'On me?' said Amanda, surprised. 'I hope you explained that I was out on a picnic and that the house would be empty until after seven, what with Miss Moon and the servants both out. She won't even get any tea! You ought to have brought her along with you.'

The frown in Glenn Barton's eyes deepened. He said uncomfortably: 'She wasn't really in a picnicking mood. She's feeling pretty upset, what with her brother's death and—— ' He broke off and after a short pause said heavily: 'You'll probably be seeing

147

her later anyway. She may wait if she's nothing else to do,' and changed the subject.

They cleared away the tea things and repacked the picnic baskets, and Amanda seized the opportunity of drawing Mr Barton apart and telling him something of her abortive mission on the previous night.

'I'm sorry it was so useless, Glenn,' she finished, 'but I'll try and see her again when – when she's feeling a bit better. At least you know that you were right and that she's not a bit in love with Lumley Potter.'

'Yes,' said Glenn slowly. 'I suppose that's something; though I was always sure she couldn't be. She's too – too fastidious for such an untidy, messy sloppy sort of chap as Potter.' He smiled at Amanda and added a little awkwardly: 'Anyway it was more than kind of you to go, and I'm very grateful. I am really.'

He took her hand and held it for a brief moment in a hard grip, and Amanda's fingers returned the pressure sympathetically. She smiled warmly at him, and in the next instant became suddenly aware that Steve Howard was watching them with an odd look in his eyes. A hard, bright, speculative look that held more than a hint of anger, and that for no reason at all caused Amanda's heart to give a queer little lurch and brought the bright colour up into her cheeks.

Claire called out: 'Glenn, come and give a hand with these baskets and things,' and Mr Barton dropped Amanda's hand and turned away. Presently he and George Norman carried the baskets and rugs down to the cars, Persis accompanying them.

The sun was low in the sky and the ruined walls threw long purple shadows on the grass and the wild thyme and the sheer rock faces that fell away almost vertically to the olive groves and the quiet blue sea far below.

The sea was as smooth and unwrinkled as polished steel, but high above it the breeze had strengthened with the approach of sundown and blew strongly about the castle, whistling shrilly

148

through the stone arches and along the deserted battlements.

Claire and Toby had walked away together deep in conversation, and Amanda, leaning against a parapet of stone and looking downwards, saw Alastair Blaine standing in an embrasure of the battlements below, talking to Anita Barton. She wondered idly if Alastair too would shortly be the possessor of another Potter masterpiece in Prussian blue, and hoped that Glenn would not meet his wife on his return from the cars. He had looked tired and ill and quite incapable of coping with a situation that involved being faced with a runaway wife and her lover.

Amanda turned her attention to the tilting ground that lay far below, and tried to imagine what it must have looked like when banners and pennants had flown there, and knights in armour had jousted before Richard of England and Queen Berengaria on their wedding day in Cyprus almost eight hundred years ago ...

'What are you thinking of, Amarantha?' inquired Steve Howard coming to lean against the wall beside her. She had not heard him approach because of the croon of the wind, and she turned quickly, considerably startled.

'Penny for them,' offered Steve. 'Or are they worth more?'

'If you really want to know, I was thinking that you and Toby and Glenn and the rest of them ought to be in armour, and Persis and Claire and I should be wearing wimples and "camises of fine white linen" and – and ermine lined pelicons — or do I mean surcotes?'

'Anyone mad enough to wear armour in this climate would be toasted to a crisp inside ten minutes,' observed Mr Howard prosaically. 'And you are wrong about the wimple. You should by rights be leaning out of the nearest window letting your hair down — like Rapunzel. How long have you known this man Barton?'

The question took Amanda by surprise. 'Glenn? I met him at Limassol. You know all about that. Why do you ask?'

'"Glenn",' murmured Steve, and went on to observe with some asperity that considering the shortness of their acquaintance they appeared to be on remarkably intimate terms with each other.

'Hardly that,' said Amanda sweetly, 'though he, like me, is probably worth anyone's while for half an hour in the moonlight.' She saw with satisfaction that she had made him angry, and added with deliberate provocation: 'I must find out.'

'Try it!' said Steve, smiling unpleasantly.

Something clattered on the stone behind them and a mangled tube of Hooker's Green fell at Amanda's feet. Lumley Potter had joined them.

'Damn!' said Mr Potter fretfully.

He deposited a folding easel and a virgin canvas on the ground and stooped to retrieve half a dozen tubes of paint that had fallen from an insecurely fastened box under his arm.

'Thought I'd make a quick study from here,' said Mr Potter. 'Hullo, Howard; you working on anything here?'

Amanda turned to look at Steve in some surprise. She had not realized that he had made Lumley Potter's acquaintance.

'No, alas. I find that it has nothing to say to me,' said Steve with perfect gravity. 'To the eye perhaps; but spiritually, no.'

'Now that's very interesting,' said Mr Potter earnestly. 'I, on the other hand——'

He plunged with enthusiasm into a pond of theory, and Amanda, who considered that Steve had asked for it, wandered away and left them to it.

She had already been up to the topmost part of the castle, but she thought that she would go again, and alone, to sit by the Queen's window where Berengaria must so often have sat, and watch the sun go down. She climbed a long flight of ruined stone steps with a high curtain wall above her and a steep grassy slope falling away below, and passed under an arch of lichened stone and through small, walled enclosures, partially roofless, that had once been guardrooms, granaries, galleries and *garderobes*.

The Queen's chamber was open to the wind and the evening sky, and a large part of the outer walls had fallen away, so that from the edge of the stone-paved floor one looked down on to tree tops and a yawning gulf where the rocky peak on which the castle of St Hilarion was built fell sheer away in a drop of well over two thousand feet.

Only one portion of the outer walls still remained, and from this the Queen's window, a graceful double arch in stone, looked out across the dreamlike landscape spread far below.

The sky and the sea had lost the deep, intense blue of the earlier afternoon and were pale in the evening light, and along the far horizon lay a faint lilac shadow that was the mountains of Turkey.

Amanda turned from the window and wandered away to where the weather-worn stone gave on to nothingness.

The evening wind whistled shrilly past her, whipping back her thin frock and tugging at her hair so that the heavy coils were loosened and fell upon her shoulders, tumbling down her back. Amanda put up a hand to arrest them, and yet another hairpin slid out, bounced upon the stone and fell into the void.

The song of the wind drowned the sound of footsteps behind her. A hand thrust hard against her and she fell forward and plunged downward into that horrible gulf, her scream of terror whipped away on the wind.

It was her hair that saved Amanda. Those long, thick, golden-brown tresses. Her hair and an aged and twisted fir tree that grew outwards from a fissure in the rock-face below the castle wall.

The branches whipped her face and broke under her, but they caught her hair; tangled it and wrenched at it, but held it as Absalom's had once been held. It checked her fall and gave her just time to clutch at a stronger bough.

Amanda hung there, blind and breathless with terror, her hands clinging frantically to the creaking bough, her long hair dragged taut above her and her feet swinging over emptiness.

She heard a shout above her, but she could not turn her head

151

and she dared not move. The muscles in her arms hurt agonizingly, her clutching fingers were numb from her weight, and the wind sang through the pine needles and drowned out all other sounds.

She heard the bough crack, but it did not break, and she knew that she should move her hold and try to swing herself backwards on to the tree trunk; but she could not do so. If she attempted to relax her hold, she would fall.

The tree shuddered as though something heavy had struck it and a voice that she did not recognize shouted to her to hold on. It seemed to come from somewhere close behind her. But no one could climb down that rock-face below the wall — it would be suicide. Someone else was shouting now and a woman was screaming. Amanda felt the tree shake again and the bough to which she clung cracked ominously. And then hard fingers closed about one wrist and a voice said breathlessly:

'Try and get your food on to the branch behind you. Your left foot. Swing it straight back.'

She obeyed automatically, and could not afterwards remember how she had got from the tree trunk to a narrow ledge of rock that had been concealed from above. Once there, with an arm steadying her, it had not been too difficult to reach the level of the ruined battlements.

Someone above her leaned down and caught her hands, and a moment later her feet were on level ground and she had fainted for the first time in her life.

12

Amanda swam slowly up out of blackness into the warm golden glow of the evening sunlight.

Someone was pouring an unpleasant and fiery liquid down her throat and she choked and coughed; swallowed a considerable quantity of the stuff in the process, and choked again.

Steve Howard, very white about the mouth, was looking down at her with a grim anger that startled her. Amanda stared up at him, puzzled and shaken, and momentarily at a loss to know where she was or what she was doing, and why Steve should be in a rage.

She shut her eyes for a brief moment and opened them again. They were all still there, staring at her with pale excited faces. Claire and George Norman, Persis, Toby, Alastair and Glenn.

'What happened?' asked Amanda. 'Did I—— '

And then suddenly she remembered, and stopped on a harsh gasp.

'You fell,' said Steve grimly. 'And I'd like to know what the hell you mean by wandering along parapets that a child of two would realize were unsafe! It's not your fault that you are not unpleasantly dead at this moment.'

It is possible that Mr Howard had a sound knowledge of psychology, for sympathy at this juncture would undoubtedly have reduced Amanda to tears and a return of terror. His curtly callous observation had an entirely opposite effect.

Amanda sat up, her breath coming short, and opened her mouth with the intention of informing him furiously that she had not fallen, but had been pushed.

But she did not say it.

She sat quite still, realizing, with a sudden, appalled clarity, that except for the Cypriot caretaker, Lumley Potter, Anita Barton and herself, there had been no one else at Hilarion that evening but the seven people who faced her.

Then one of nine people — seven of whom stood looking down at her, so close to her that by merely reaching out her hand she could touch any one of them — had meant to murder her. *Her* — Amanda Derington! What was it that Steve had just said? 'It's not your fault that you are not unpleasantly dead at this moment.' It was not someone else's fault either, for one of these people had meant her to be dead. Had tried to kill her——

Amanda shrank back against the sun-warmed stones of the wall, her wide, terrified eyes going from face to face in that circle.

Claire — Alastair — Toby — Glenn — Persis — George — Steve——

No. Not Steve! He was the only one she could be sure of. The only one. Her frightened eyes turned to him and she reached up and clutched at his sleeve.

Steve leant down and jerked her ungently to her feet, and Amanda said breathlessly: 'Please will you all go away. Please! I'm all right. I am really. I'm sorry I gave you all such a fright. I – I think I'd just like to sit here alone for a bit until I feel less peculiar. Please go!'

Her frantic fingers on Steve Howard's arm said *not you! not you!*

Persis said: 'Nonsense! Now see here honey——'

'Persis honey,' remarked Steve pleasantly, 'Scram! I'll see that she doesn't trip over any more walls.'

He glanced at his wrist watch and turned to Toby Gates:

'Would you mind giving Mrs Halliday a lift home, Gates? I'll drive Miss Derington back when she's feeling less scrambled.'

'Of course,' said Toby, looking uncertainly from Persis to Amanda and back again.

'Good idea,' said George Norman, his ruddy features resuming their normal hue. 'Beastly shock for her. Might have been a nasty accident. They really should rail off these dangerous spots. It's a scandal!'

They departed and Amanda was alone with the wind and Mr Howard.

She relaxed her grip on his arm, turned her back on him and said in a muffled voice: 'Would you mind going to the other side of that wall.'

'Why?' inquired Steve. 'Are you going to cry?'

'No,' said Amanda indistinctly. 'I'm going to be sick.' And was.

Mr Howard bore this unalluring spectacle with commendable fortitude, and having provided assistance in the form of a clean handkerchief, remarked that it was a waste of a good brandy and that he hoped for the sake of subsequent visitors that it would rain during the night.

'Feeling better?' he inquired presently.

'Yes thank you. Could we go somewhere where there are four walls and no edge, do you think?'

'Nothing easier.' He drew her hand through his arm and walked her away, keeping her between him and the solid inner wall. They had gone less than half a dozen yards when he checked suddenly and bent down to pick up something that lay wedged between two slabs of stone. It was a small, twisted tube of oil paint from which the top was missing. He turned it over in his hand, looking at it thoughtfully, and then slipped it into his pocket without comment.

They walked back through the roofless rooms, and once again the steep flight of stone steps lay below them.

Amanda stopped and shut her eyes. She had never been in the least affected by heights, but now she knew that she would never be able to look down from any height again without being afraid. She knew that it was ridiculous and absurd; the ruined stairway was wide and safe and the slope that fell away along one side of it was covered with grass and shrubs, trees and fallen boulders. But the fear of falling was on her and she could not move.

155

Steve Howard picked her up without ceremony and carried her down the long, uneven flight to the quiet and shelter of a grass-grown level, where the solid walls of the Outer Bailey towered comfortingly above them and the last of the sun turned the dry grasses to bright gold.

'All right here?'

'Yes,' said Amanda gratefully. 'I'm sorry about that.'

'You'll get over it,' said Steve, striking a match against the stones and lighting himself a cigarette.

Amanda sank down cross-legged on the warm grass and said in a voice that she tried to keep steady: 'I haven't thanked you yet for – for saving my life. That branch wouldn't have held much longer.'

'You don't have to thank me,' said Steve shortly. 'Barton got you out of that.'

'Glenn?'

'Yes — Glenn.'

Steve's mouth twisted a little wryly on the name. 'He's the one you have to thank. He thought he heard someone scream, and ran out and saw you. I was on my way up, and he yelled out to me, and the next thing I knew he had lowered himself down over the edge and found some sort of a foothold and dropped down onto the trunk of that tree. He must have plenty of nerve. I wouldn't have cared to do it myself.'

'And I let him go without saying anything!' said Amanda, distressed. 'I thought it was you——'

'Alas, no,' said Steve satirically. 'I was merely among those present. How did you happen to do it?'

'I was pushed,' said Amanda in a whisper.

'*Say that again!*'

'S – someone pushed me.'

Steve stood very still, looking down at her, his mouth a tight line and his eyes blazing.

Presently he said quite softly: 'Who?'

156

'I – I don't know,' said Amanda, a terrified break in her voice. 'The wind was so loud — I didn't hear any other sound. And then suddenly someone pushed me hard and – and I fell ...' Her voice died out in a whisper and she shuddered uncontrollably.

'You are quite sure it wasn't a sudden gust of wind?'

'Don't be ridiculous!' said Amanda, retreating from the verge of tears. 'It was a *hand*.'

'Man or woman?'

'I tell you I don't *know!* I didn't hear or see anyone.'

'Come on, Amanda — think! Try and remember what it felt like. Was it a small hand or a large one? Hard? Thin? Warm? That dress you're wearing is pretty flimsy, you must have some idea.'

'But I haven't! You see my hair had come down and it was all over my back.'

'*Hell!*' said Steve softly.

He dropped his cigarette on the grass, put his foot on it and sat down beside her with his hands clasped about his knees, and stared fixedly ahead of him at the massive walls of the Outer Bailey. Amanda, watching him, saw that there were harsh lines on his forehead and about his mouth that she did not remember having noticed before, and that his eyes were blank and unseeing.

After a time he said curtly and without turning his head: 'What made you keep quiet up there? — about being pushed?'

'I was just going to say it, and then—— ' Amanda's voice seemed to dry in her throat and she swallowed convulsively.

'And then—— ?' prompted Steve.

'Then I suddenly realized that it might have been one of them. People I know—— ' Amanda's voice wavered and she said desperately: 'Why? I haven't said anything to anyone. Why should someone want to kill me now that it's all over?'

'It isn't all over,' said Steve curtly. 'Not by a long chalk.'

He dropped his chin on his knees and relapsed into silence, brooding with the concentration of a Buddhist considering infinity.

The shadows lengthened and soon the ruined walls of Hilarion would no longer be warmly gold but a cold forbidding grey. The sky above the battlements had already turned to a pale clear green, and the level floor of the tilting ground below the castle began to fill with soft purple shadow.

Steve sighed and moved at last. He stood up, stretching himself, and leaned down to pull Amanda to her feet:

'Come on; it's time we got going. If we don't watch it we shall find ourselves being locked in for the night.'

He put out a hand and lifted a long shining strand of the hair that tumbled in tangled disorder to well below Amanda's waist.

'Beautiful stuff,' observed Steve reflectively. 'I wonder why women will cut it off? Well you can thank your lucky stars you didn't. A crew-cut wouldn't have saved you today, Amarantha. Go on — plait it up or get it out of the way. It gives me ideas — and this is no time for ideas; at least not of that category.'

Amanda's white face flushed with colour and she jerked her head away and plaited her dishevelled hair with quick, unsteady fingers into two heavy schoolgirl plaits.

'You look about six,' commented Steve. 'Can you manage the rest of the way on your own feet?'

'Of course I can,' said Amanda with dignity. 'It was only those stairs.'

He turned on his heel without further comment and walked down ahead of her, whistling abstractedly, his hands deep in his pockets.

There was only one car left beside the roadside at the foot of the slope below Hilarion. The others must have left at least half an hour before.

'Twenty past six,' observed Steve, releasing the clutch and glancing at the dashboard clock. 'You'll just make it.'

'Make what?'

'I gather that you are dining out with young Gates; drinks at seven. He mentioned it during tea.'

158

'Oh!' said Amanda blankly. 'I'd forgotten. Perhaps he could dine with Persis instead.'

'Going to cut your date?'

'Yes. I – I don't think I feel like facing any of them just now. I feel like getting back to my bedroom and looking under the bed and inside and behind all the furniture, and locking every door and window and then getting into bed and pulling all the bedclothes over my head. And that's just what I'm going to do!'

'A very sound programme,' approved Steve. 'You'll feel braver in the morning. Want me to make your excuses to Toby Gates?'

'Would you? Tell him that I — No; don't tell him anything. I'll write a note if you don't mind waiting while I write it. Then you could give it to him. Would you do that?'

'A pleasure, Amarantha.'

Kyrenia and the coast were still bathed in the last warm glow of the sunset when they turned into the quiet side road and stopped before the Villa Oleander. But the shadows were moving swiftly across the garden and up the face of the house, and only the tops of the tallest cypress trees were still touched with gold.

The water trickling from the mouth of the bronze dolphin made a cool, pleasant sound in the silence, and now that the sun had left the garden the scent of roses and jasmine and dust filled the windless air with fragrance. In the embrasures of the old wall behind the house the pigeons cooed and fluttered as they settled down for the night, and the drowsy hum of the town rose murmurously from beyond the trees and the garden wall. But the house itself seemed strangely silent.

Amanda pushed open the heavy front door and stood in the cool, shadowed hall, listening to that silence.

Miss Moon could not be back yet. She was not given to silence except when resting, and the sound of her voice and her jingling jewellery was almost an integral part of the Villa Oleander.

'What is it Amanda?' inquired Steve Howard, watching her face.

159

'Nothing. It – it's very quiet. I thought perhaps that Miss Moon would be back.'

'Scared?'

'Yes!' said Amanda with a shiver. 'Steve——' she turned to him quickly, unaware that she had for the first time used that familiar abbreviation of his name that Persis and Claire used so lightly — 'would you – would you stay until she comes back? I know it's ridiculous of me, but the house feels so empty.'

'Yes of course,' said Steve, in the manner of one who has been asked to pass the salt. His tone was entirely matter-of-fact and oddly steadying. 'Like me to go upstairs and look under the bed for you?' he suggested with a satirical gleam in his eye.

'Do you think I'm being very silly?' demanded Amanda abruptly.

Steve smiled at her. 'No dear. In fact for a girl who has just escaped a particularly messy end by inches, you are behaving like the entire George Cross Island rolled into one, and I'm proud of you, Amarantha. Do you realize that nine hundred and ninety-nine women out of a thousand would have had shrieking hysterics, burst into tears, died of heart-failure and then rushed screaming to the telephone to book an immediate passage to Baffin Bay or North Borneo?'

Amanda laughed a little shakily. 'I've wanted desperately to do all those things,' she confessed. 'In fact with any encouragement at all, I'd have done them!'

'I know,' said Steve with a grin. 'That's why you didn't get any!'

'You've been quite beastly!' said Amanda accusingly.

'The situation,' observed Steve caustically, 'is sufficiently unpleasant as it is, without being further gummed up with tears and hysteria. Is there by any chance a lavatory in this building?'

'Yes of course. Down that passage and first door on your left.'

'Thanks.'

He departed and Amanda, remembering her decision to write

160

a note to Toby Gates, crossed the hall and went into the drawing-room.

The last of the sunlight had only recently faded from the room, but except before the french windows that gave on to the verandah the green wooden shutters were still closed, and the room was hot and airless and very dark. Amanda threw open the shutters to let in the fast vanishing daylight, and sitting down at Miss Moon's cluttered ormolu desk, reached for writing paper and a pen.

She began to write, aware as she did so that the scratching of the pen sounded astonishingly loud in the quiet room. But after completing no more than two lines she paused: listening, as she had listened in the hall, to the silence.

The windless evening was quiet and very still, and there was no sound in the darkening house. But she was not alone in the room. It was not a suspicion but a certainty. There was someone else in the room besides herself. Someone was hidden there ...

Amanda sat rigid while her blood seemed to turn cold and run slowly. She dared not move, and it seemed that she had lost the power to breathe. She knew that she should turn — she would be safer, surely, with her back to the wall? But she could not move. She must call out; scream for Steve Howard——

Steve! Why of course! it was Steve who had returned across the hall without her hearing him.

She whirled round on a gasp of relief. But there was no one there. The dusty beautiful furniture looked back at her, composed and calm and watchful with that curious sense of watchfulness that many old and inanimate objects possess. The open doorway gaped emptily on the dark and silent hall, and there was no sign of Steven Howard.

It was imagination, Amanda told herself — imagination and the silence of an empty house. There was no third person in the Villa Oleander; no one in the room but herself. She forced herself to turn and face the desk; to pick up the pen. But she could not force her hand to write. She could only sit still; and listen——

161

The scent of roses and jasmine and violets filled the airless room with a cloying sweetness: odd that she should not have noticed that there were violets growing in the garden. Amanda laid down her pen very carefully. She seemed to be under some curious compulsion not to make any sound that might break that alert and listening silence. There was — someone else in the room — there was.

She stood up quickly and turned, gripping the carved chairback with cold hands and fighting to control a rising panic. Her wide, frightened eyes searched the darkening room, but except for the solid back of the sofa that stood between her and the french windows the furniture was either too frail or so placed as to afford no opportunities for concealment. The glass-fronted cabinets of buhl and marqueterie stood backed against the corners of the room, their cluttered contents making splashes of pure, gleaming colour in the shadowy room. The fading light glinted on carved jade and ivory, enamelled snuff boxes, bottles cut from rose quartz, chrysoprase and lapis lazuli, and on the tiny, twinkling diamonds that formed the cypher of a murdered Empress on a fabulous Fabergé egg of crystal.

The faded brocade curtains hung straight and motionless and it was not possible that anyone could be standing concealed behind them. An ornately framed looking-glass that hung above the writing table reflected another and similar mirror on the opposite wall, and Amanda could see herself in it; endlessly repeated. A long line of slender, frightened girls standing in a dim, silvery corridor in the disk.

But it reflected something else as well. Something that lay beyond the range of her vision, though not beyond the compass of that glimmering oval. A hand——

There was someone crouching on the floor in front of the french windows, concealed by the sofa.

Amanda froze into stillness; her wide eyes fixed upon the reflection of that hand whose fingers were crooked, claw-like, on the

162

faded carpet; waiting for it to be withdrawn — to slide quietly back into hiding. But it did not move.

A sudden stabbing thought broke the web of terror that held her. It's Miss Moon! She turned and leapt across the narrow space that lay between the writing table and the sofa, reached it and was round it.

But it was not Miss Moon. It was someone who lay sprawled face downwards on the floor. A woman in a tight blue cotton frock patterned with rosebuds, who wore a vivid scarf of emerald green *crêpe de Chine* tied about her neck.

Amanda dropped on her knees and touched that outstretched hand. It was slack and warm, and a wave of incredible relief engulfed her. What a fool she was! This must be some visitor who had waited for Miss Moon, and had fainted. She tugged at the limp, warm bulk and turned it over . . .

There was nothing she could recognize in that swollen, horribly discoloured face with its glazed, protruding eyes and lolling tongue. Nothing except a necklace and ear-rings of garish plastic flowers and the odour of a cheap violet scent that suggested hair oil.

Amanda let the heavy, lifeless body drop back on to the floor and sprang to her feet, backing away from it, her hands at her throat.

There was a sound of leisurely footsteps crossing the hall and then Steve was standing in the doorway——

The next second he had crossed the floor in three strides and his hands were gripping her shoulders so tightly that they hurt.

'What is it!'

Amanda did not speak but her head turned and Steve's eyes followed the direction of her frozen gaze.

His fingers tightened convulsively on her shoulders so that she winced with pain, and then he had thrust her roughly to one side and was on his knees beside that appalling figure.

He touched it once only, noting, as Amanda had done, the warm slackness of that outstretched hand, and after that only his eyes moved, quickly and intently.

He looked up at Amanda and said harshly: 'Did you touch her?'

Amanda wet her dry lips with her tongue. 'I – I turned her over. I thought she had fainted.'

'You know her?' It was less a query than a statement of fact.

'Yes. It's – she's Glenn Barton's secretary. Monica Ford. He – he said that she had called to see me.'

'I remember. That must have been somewhere between four and half-past. Three hours ago,' said Steve thoughtfully.

Amanda said shuddering: 'Then – then she did wait for me. She's warm. She can't have been dead for three hours!'

'Probably less than half an hour, at a guess.' He looked down at the distorted face and said slowly: 'Both you and Barton mentioned at the picnic that this house would be empty. Someone who did not really believe that Miss Ford would wait for you may have seized the opportunity to slip in here and look for something — perhaps that bottle, or the glass — and been surprised by her on their way out.'

Amanda said in a high, breaking voice: 'But I haven't got them! I haven't got them! — I—— '

Steve stood up swiftly and caught her clutching hands in a hard and exceedingly painful grasp.

'Stop that, Amanda. I'm not standing any nonsense from you! Come on, George Cross Island — pull yourself together!'

Amanda gasped, gulped, and clenched her teeth on her trembling lip, and her breathing steadied.

'That's better,' approved Steve. 'Is there a telephone here?'

'Y – yes. At the end of the passage off the hall.'

'Afraid to go there by yourself?'

'No!' Amanda wrenched her hands from his hold and her chin came up with a jerk.

'That's the girl. All right; go and ring a number for me—— ' He gave her a number and made her repeat it. 'Tell whoever answers

164

it that Steven Howard would like to see Mr Jurgan Calder at the Villa Oleander in Kyrenia and that it will be a late party. Got that?'

'Yes.'

'Repeat it ... That's right. Don't say anything else. Only that, and ring off. And when you've done that you'd better get through to the Dome and leave a message for Toby Gates to say that you will not be able to dine with him tonight. Otherwise we shall have him turning up here to fetch you before we know where we are. Cut along.'

He did not watch Amanda go, but turned back immediately to the huddled, hideous figure on the floor. He was on his knees beside it when she returned, but he had switched on two of the lights, and he did not look up or trouble to inquire if she had done as he asked. It was after seven, but Miss Moon had still not returned. They had been back for just over twenty minutes, thought Amanda numbly — how was it possible to live through so much in so short a space of time?

The sun had set and the sky was green with gathering dusk and pricked with the first stars. The house was very still again. And in that stillness Amanda heard the soft, unmistakable pad of shoeless feet in the room above them.

Steve had heard it too, for his head came up with a jerk and his eyes were wide and bright and intensely alert. Presently the sound was repeated and all at once he was on his feet and at the door. He seemed to move with a swiftness and lack of noise that was, in its way, remarkable.

He swung round suddenly and looked at Amanda. His eyes went from her to the open windows and the garden beyond the verandah, and she saw that he was holding something in his left hand. That same small gun that she had seen once before in the cabin of the *Orantares*.

He said curtly: 'You'd better come with me,' and turned away again without looking to see if she followed him or not.

They went up the stairs swiftly and — on Steve's part — silently.

But Amanda's white, flat-heeled sandals clicked on the polished treads and she stumbled and clung to the stair-rail.

It was Miss Moon's bedroom that lay directly above the drawing-room, and Steve glanced over his shoulder at Amanda, and pushing her back against the landing wall with one hand, turned the handle and kicked the door open with his foot.

There was a shrill, feminine shriek and a familiar clash of silver filigree bracelets, and Amanda said on a sob: 'It's Miss Moon!' and brushing past him she ran into the room.

Miss Moon was standing at the foot of her tumbled bed, wrapped in an elderly cotton kimono patterned with a design of storks and chrysanthemums that suggested that its origin was Manchester rather than Matsumoto. She was wearing what at first sight appeared to be a hat, but which, on inspection, turned out to be an ice-bag of antediluvian design tied on to her head bonnet-wise with a black silk stocking. Bedroom slippers of scuffed kid and an assortment of bracelets completed the ensemble.

'Who is this man?' demanded Miss Moon in outraged tones. 'Amanda, send him away at once! I will not have strange men in my bedroom!'

Amanda flung her arms about Miss Moon and burst into over-wrought tears. Miss Moon enfolded her in a protective clutch that smelt of mothballs, menthol and heliotrope, and glared at Mr Howard. Mr Howard looked thoughtfully back at her. The gun was no longer in evidence and he looked entirely relaxed and innocent of guile.

'There, there, dear!' said Miss Moon, patting Amanda's shuddering shoulders. 'Has he been annoying you? Well I shall know how to deal with him. Sir — you should be ashamed of yourself!'

'I must apologize,' said Mr Howard. 'I didn't know that you were in.'

'That,' observed Miss Moon haughtily, 'is quite evident!'

'How long have you been back, Miss Moon?'

'I cannot see that it is any concern of yours, young man. But if it is of any interest to you, I have not been out.'

'*What?*' Amanda lifted a tear-wet face from Miss Moon's bony shoulder. 'But the bridge party ...'

'I was compelled to send my excuses,' said Miss Moon. 'I am subject to sudden and severe attacks of migraine, and it proved quite impossible for me to go.'

Amanda said: 'Then – then you have been here all the time?'

'I have.'

'That's very interesting,' said Steve.

Miss Moon bristled. 'Interesting? Why should it be interesting?'

'Because,' said Steve gently, 'it means that someone is due for the shock of their life, and I would most earnestly advise you, Miss Moon, not to mention to anyone that you did not go out this afternoon.'

'Young man,' said Miss Moon, drawing herself to her full height, 'I do not understand you. Naturally Lady Cooper-Foot and all those who attended her bridge party are fully aware that I remained at home.'

'Then that's torn it!' said Steve.

Miss Moon looked from Amanda to Steve, and her eyes, despite the heaviness that pain and drugs had lent them, were suddenly sharp and shrewd:

'Tell me what has happened,' she demanded crisply. 'Why would it have been advisable to conceal the fact that I have not left the house?'

'Because,' said Steve softly, 'less than an hour ago a woman was murdered in the room directly below this one — by someone who had every reason to believe that there was no one else in the house.'

13

Awaking late on the following morning, Amanda lay for several minutes staring idly at the misty folds of the mosquito net and wondering why the room seemed so airless. She felt drowsy and relaxed and curiously stupid. It can't be more than six, she thought; the room is still dark.

But the air was always cool and fresh in the early morning, not hot like this. Turning her head she saw that the dimness of the room was due to the fact that the shutters, which were always thrown back at night and only used during the heat of the day, were closed and bolted, and she frowned at them; realizing, from the bright chinks of sunlight that showed between the slats, that it was far later than she had supposed, and puzzled by a vague recollection that it was she herself who had insisted on closing those shutters.

A moment later she was sitting bolt upright with all trace of drowsiness gone, for she had remembered why it had seemed so necessary to lock herself into her room last night.

Amanda pushed back the mosquito net and went over to open the shutters, aware as she did so that it was at least midday. And also that someone must have given her a strong sleeping draught, for her head felt unaccountably heavy.

Steve Howard, of course! He had made her drink a cup of coffee. It had been black and sweet and had left a faintly unpleasant taste on her tongue. That must have been late last night, after the police and the doctor had left and an ambulance had taken Monica

Ford's body away to the Nicosia General Hospital, and the endless questions were over at last.

There had been so many questions.

The man she had telephoned for, the man with an odd name, had arrived while they were still explaining the ugly situation to Miss Moon. Steve had gone down to meet him, and Amanda, who had remained with Miss Moon, had not been present at that interview. She had come out onto the upper landing just as he was leaving and had heard him say: 'All right; we'll play it on those lines. It's your deal. I can stack the deck at my end, and—— ' He had heard Amanda's sandals click on the stairs and had stopped.

'This is Miss Derington,' said Steve. He did not complete the introduction and Amanda found herself shaking hands with a slim, quiet man who seemed a little shy and very ordinary. The sort of man, thought Amanda, whom one might meet a dozen times and still not remember. There was nothing in any way remarkable about him except perhaps his eyes, which were as cool and quiet and yet as disconcertingly observant as Steve Howard's own.

A moment later he had gone. It was after that that Steve had telephoned for the police and the doctor, and when they arrived he had gone into the drawing-room with them and shut the door. After what seemed a very long time they had sent for Amanda and Miss Moon and had questioned them. Two of the police officers had been British. C.I.D. men from Nicosia. The third had been a Cypriot who spoke excellent English.

Miss Moon had little to tell them. A migraine had descended upon her with sudden and all too familiar severity, and she had telephoned her excuses to Lady Cooper-Foot and retired to bed in a darkened room with an ice-pack and sedatives. Yes, she had been aware of voices in the drawing-room some time during the afternoon. She could not say when. Three-thirty perhaps? Four? She had been in considerable pain and had paid little attention beyond wishing that whoever was speaking would use a less

169

hysterical tone. Oh yes, it had been a woman, and she had sounded upset. No: Miss Moon had not gone down. She had imagined that it must have been Euridice returned unexpectedly, but soon afterwards the drugs had taken effect and she had slept until past seven o'clock and had barely arisen when Amanda and Mr Howard had burst into her room.

But surely, said a police officer, she must have been aware of some sounds, however slight? The woman had been murdered——

'*"Strangling is a very quiet death,"*' murmured Steve Howard meditatively.

Apparently Miss Moon was familiar with *The Duchess of Malfi,* for she had looked at Mr Howard with a distinct gleam of appreciation in her eye and said: 'Exactly! No, I not only heard no other sounds, but I have no idea — if the woman whose voice I heard was indeed Monica Ford — whom she can have been addressing.'

'Glenn,' said Amanda. And explained that Mr Barton had mentioned meeting his secretary and had added that Miss Ford had wished to see her — Amanda — and that she had seemed upset.

They had questioned her as to her previous meeting with Miss Ford on the day of her arrival in Cyprus, and made her repeat as much of their conversation as she could remember. And then they had asked her to tell them again exactly what Glenn Barton had said on the subject of his secretary at the picnic that afternoon, and having received corroboration from Mr Howard, they had sent for Mr Barton.

Glenn had arrived shortly after half past nine, having driven from Nicosia at a speed considerably in excess of the recognized limits. He had looked grey and drawn and somehow apathetic. Steve had poured him out a stiff portion of Miss Moon's liqueur brandy and he had swallowed it gratefully.

Yes, he had been to the Villa Oleander that afternoon and had spoken with Miss Ford in this room. He explained the circumstances and agreed that his secretary had been upset. She had recently lost her only brother and sole close relative. And there had been other things on her mind—— He checked abruptly and frowned.

What other things?

Glenn's tired face seemed to grow greyer and he had explained in a halting, difficult voice something of what he had told Amanda in that same room on the previous afternoon: of Anita's suggestions concerning the relations between Miss Ford and himself.

'Of course there was nothing in it,' he explained wearily. 'My wife could never believe such a thing. She only spread that story in order to — well, to make trouble I suppose. They had quarrelled and Miss Ford had probably been rude to her.'

'Anita,' put in Miss Moon crisply, 'was well aware that people would be only too willing to believe that Monica had fallen in love with her employer, but that no one in their senses would believe that he was in love with her. So that from Monica's point of view the story would be doubly wounding.'

'Was she in love with you?' asked a police officer.

The colour came up into Glenn's haggard face and his mouth tightened and set hard. He looked at the man who had asked the question and his eyes did not waver.

'No.' The single word was curt and entirely final.

But they had not finished with him. They went back again to the quarrel between his secretary and his wife, and again and again to his conversation with Miss Ford in the Villa Oleander that afternoon. Was he quite sure of the time? Why was he sure? So he had seen the green scarf? Why, having heard a sound from one of the upper rooms, had he still said at Hilarion that the house was empty?

'I didn't know that Miss Moon was in,' said Glenn wearily. 'I thought it must be a pigeon or the cat.'

He turned to look at Miss Moon. 'I'm sorry, Mooney. If I'd known you were ill I'd have come up.'

'I wouldn't have let you in,' said Miss Moon tartly, and departed to cut sandwiches and brew hot coffee.

They turned back to the picnic at Hilarion:

How many people had been present when Mr Barton had spoken of his secretary and mentioned that there was no one at home in the Villa Oleander? At what time had Mr Barton left Hilarion, and where had he gone?

'To Nicosia,' said Glenn tiredly. 'Prove it? Well as a matter of fact I can. The Normans saw me go. We all left at the same time — except Howard and Miss Derington. There were only four cars there. Gates and Mrs Halliday went ahead of my car and turned left for Kyrenia. I turned up right, and the Normans and Major Blaine were behind me and must have seen me turn. They went down to Kyrenia too, of course. I drove straight to the Nicosia office, and as it happens I can prove that too, because I gave a lift to a couple of troops. You can probably check with them. I dropped them off in the centre of the town just after six. Anything more you want to know?'

There appeared to be a great deal more. But they left at last, and it was just as they were leaving that one of the police officers found the little linen flower.

There was a massive carved chest in the hall, black with age and decorated with medallions of beaten silver, and the small white flower had caught on a rough edge of metal at a level where the hem of a woman's skirt might have brushed past it.

The officer reached down and removed it and turned it over between his fingers. There was a thread hanging from the centre of it as though it had been torn from something.

Amanda said incredulously: 'But that's—— ' and saw Glenn Barton's face, and stopped.

Glenn was staring at her with a tense and desperate appeal in his eyes. Amanda looked away quickly and became aware that Steve had been watching them.

The police officer said: 'This is yours, then?'

172

'Yes,' said Amanda without hesitation. She saw Glenn shut his eyes for a brief moment and catch at the edge of the chest as though to steady himself, and she held out her hand for the flower.

The police officer looked at her long and thoughtfully, and then put it into his pocket. 'If you do not mind, I will keep it. It will be returned of course.'

And then they had gone. Glenn first, and the three police officers perhaps five minutes later. The doctor had already left in the ambulance that had taken Monica Ford's body to Nicosia an hour earlier.

Miss Moon departed to the kitchen to make more coffee and Amanda would have followed her except that Steve Howard stood between her and the door that led through to the kitchen, and he did not look as though he intended to move aside for her as he had moved for Miss Moon.

'Amanda,' said Steve softly, 'you are a damned bad liar and several kinds of a fool into the bargain. What possessed you to do such an idiotic thing?'

Amanda did not pretend to misunderstand him. 'I couldn't do anything else,' she said unhappily. 'You didn't see his face——'

'Oh yes I did,' interrupted Steve brusquely. 'But that is no reason why you should have laid claim to the thing.'

'What else could I have done? If I'd said it wasn't mine, they'd have asked Miss Moon; and as it wasn't hers, they would have traced it.'

'They'll trace it all right,' said Steve grimly. 'And when they do you are going to find yourself in an exceedingly unpleasant position.'

'Why?' said Amanda defensively.

'There is such a thing as being an accessory after the fact,' pointed out Steve dryly.

'I can't help it,' said Amanda. 'I – I owed him something.'

'For saving your life?' said Steve with an edge to his voice. 'Perhaps. But he had no right to let you do it.'

173

'You don't understand,' said Amanda. 'He's in love with her.'

'And are you by any chance in love with him?' inquired Steve unpleasantly. 'Is that the real reason for this quixotic gesture?'

Amanda hit him.

She had not meant to do it or known that she would do so. The gesture had been an entirely unexpected and instinctive reaction born of the accumulative terror and shock and emotional strain of the past hours and the last few days. This time he either did not anticipate the action or did not trouble to avoid it.

Amanda stared in stunned dismay at the red mark that her palm had left on Steven Howard's hard cheek; her grey eyes very wide and young.

'I – I'm sorry,' she said in a small, unsteady voice. 'I didn't mean to do that. I——'

'Don't apologize,' interrupted Steve sardonically. 'After all I did offer you a second try, didn't I? — and they say that practice makes perfect.'

'You're very angry, aren't you?' said Amanda in a subdued voice.

'If I am, it's probably with myself,' said Steve curtly.

And then Miss Moon had reappeared with a fresh pot of coffee and they had drunk it sitting round the dining-room table because none of them wanted to go into the drawing-room again, and because Amanda flatly refused to go to bed.

Amanda had not wanted the hot coffee either, and had asked for a cold drink instead. Steve had ignored the request and had poured out a cup of black coffee to which he had added sugar and, undoubtedly, some drug that he had presumably obtained off Miss Moon or the doctor, and had handed it to her without further words. Amanda had looked at his coolly unemotional eyes and uncompromising mouth and had been too tired to argue. She had drunk it, and it had left an unpleasant taste on her tongue.

Steve had embarked on a long conversation with Miss Moon who, it was soon obvious, had entirely revised her first opinion of him and was already addressing him as 'dear boy'. He had not spoken directly to Amanda again, and presently his voice and his face had begun to fade into a misty background in which only a flight of pseudo-Japanese storks and the jingle of Miss Moon's bracelets stood out at all clearly.

Amanda's eyelids had begun to feel strangely heavy and she found that she could no longer prevent them from closing. She slid down a little lower in her chair and a voice that seemed to come from the other end of a long tunnel had said faintly but distinctly: 'I think, dear boy, that she is almost asleep now,' and another voice, equally far away said: 'And about time too!'

Amanda had forced open her eyes in order to see who was asleep, and had looked up into Steven Howard's face and remembered that he had been angry about something; something to do with Glenn Barton. She must explain about that. Steve had not understood. She found that it was an effort to speak, and said drowsily and with difficulty: 'Glenn—— ' and the face above her was suddenly blank and hard and completely expressionless.

Then her eyes closed again and Steve had lifted her and carried her up a long dark flight of stairs, and she had turned her face against his shoulder and clung to him with terrified desperation, because these were the ruined stone steps of Hilarion once more, and she was afraid of falling.

The door opened with a faint creak of hinges and Amanda turned quickly to see Miss Moon peering cautiously around it.

Miss Moon, a vision in lemon yellow, brightened at the sight of her and said approvingly: 'So you are awake at last! I have looked in several times, but did not wish to wake you. How are you feeling, my dear?'

'A bit stupid,' said Amanda with an attempt at a smile. 'Is it very late?'

'Ten minutes to one, dear. Luncheon will be ready in a moment. I expect you are hungry. I do trust that you feel no ill-effects from those sleeping powders? I have always found them remarkably effective, although I confess I have never taken more than one. But Mr Howard thought that in the circumstances two would be advisable. *Such* a dear boy! So thoughtful — and so well read. How *few* people one meets who have read *Il Conte de Carmagnola* in the original and can discuss it intelligently! Dear Papa would have enjoyed conversing with him. I will tell Euridice to run you a bath.'

'Miss Moon,' said Amanda in a halting voice, 'I – didn't dream it by any chance, did I?'

Miss Moon's face changed and her mouth closed for a moment into a tight line.

'No my dear. I am afraid not. We have had the police here the whole morning. I would not permit them to wake you, since you could have told them nothing more than you told them last night. Several people called to inquire after you. That young Captain Gates, and a Mrs Halliday — American I think, and very striking. And Glenn has been here too. There will have to be an inquest, of course, but the police have satisfied themselves as to the reason for poor Monica Ford's dreadful end.'

Amanda sat down rather suddenly on the edge of her bed. 'Who – who do they think did it?'

'A thief of course,' said Miss Moon, and wrung her hands so that the bracelets jingled. 'Oh, Amanda dear, I fear it was *all* my fault!'

'Darling!' said Amanda, jumping up and giving her hostess a sudden impulsive hug. 'Don't be silly! How could it possibly be your fault?'

'Well you see, dear, there are a great many valuable things in this house. My dear Papa was a great collector. And of course I have never kept anything under lock and key, and everyone knows that I never lock the house up — except of course at night. Euridice insists on that. It must have been a temptation. I see that now. Some dishonest person must have come to hear that the house

176

would be empty yesterday afternoon, and have crept in intending to steal what they could. They would not have expected to find anyone in the drawing-room, and may not have noticed Monica until she had time to see and perhaps even recognize the thief. They think that he lost his head and picked up the scarf only intending to stop her from calling out, and did not mean to kill her — I do *hope* he did not!'

Amanda said: 'But nothing was missing.'

'Oh yes there was, dear. Several of the smaller and more valuable items from dear Papa's collection had been removed from the cabinets in the drawing-room. There are so many things there that I did not immediately realize it.'

Amanda was aware of a sudden and overwhelming wave of relief.

She could not have told why she should be so inexpressibly relieved. Surely she could not have believed that one of a small group of people who were personally known to her could have deliberately strangled poor, harmless, unhappy Monica Ford? No of course she had not. All the same she felt as if a black, crushing weight had been lifted off her shoulders.

'It will be a lesson to me,' sighed Miss Moon. 'I shall have to send dear Papa's collection to the bank. So foolish. Beautiful things should be looked at and appreciated; not locked away in vaults. I think I hear Euridice in the hall. Luncheon will be ready and here I am keeping you talking.'

She hurried away and Amanda bathed and dressed quickly, and having brushed out her tangled hair, rolled it up and bundled the shining mass into a coarse white net in the style that had been fashionable in the days when the young Empress Eugenie had netted her beautiful tresses in a similar manner. Amanda would not let herself think of those desperate moments at Hilarion when her hair alone had saved her from a horrible and disfiguring death, but some frightened instinct would not allow her to pin it securely. She had to feel that it was free and unbound.

She turned to look at herself in the long silvery expanse of looking-glass on the wall. The heavy chignon tilted her head back with its weight and made her face appear smaller and more pointed and her slender neck as long as the stem of a flower. White linen dress. White linen sandals. *White linen* — a small flat, white linen flower clinging to a rough edge of metal on the chest in the hall . . .

Amanda caught her lip between her teeth. She had forgotten that sinister little flower. But it couldn't mean anything! Supposing Anita Barton *had* been to the Villa Oleander on her return from St Hilarion? Supposing, even, that she was (as her clothes suggested) extravagant and possibly in debt? That still did not make her a thief, any more than her dislike of Monica Ford made her a murderess. Recalling Anita Barton's relaxed and sleeping face, Amanda was suddenly and comfortingly sure of that.

The police and Miss Moon were right. Some petty thief, snatching the jade and crystal trinkets from the drawing-room cabinets, had been surprised by Monica Ford, and had panicked and killed her.

Amanda applied rose-pink lipstick with a steady hand, made a face at herself in the glass and ran downstairs to join Miss Moon.

The dining-room smelt pleasantly of flowers and fruit and Euridice's special brand of ravioli, and beyond the open windows the garden was brilliant with sunlight and noisy with the coo and flutter of pigeons and the sound of Andreas chopping wood. Euridice was conducting an excitable conversation with a friend in the kitchen and Miss Moon was as talkative as ever.

'No,' said Miss Moon, waving away the barley water: 'I never drink with meals, dear. So bad for the digestion; it dilutes the gastric juices. Only between meals. Though of course one so often forgets to do that, and then so much of it is wasted. It does not really keep in this weather. Try some of this melon, dear——'

Everything was suddenly safe and sane and ordinary again, and the house no longer held its breath to listen but basked comfortably in the hot sunshine. Colour came back to Amanda's cheeks and some of the sparkle to her eyes, and with the resilience and optimism of youth she pushed the recollection of the past few days behind her and felt her spirits rise to meet the challenge of the gay, glittering day. She would forget about all the horrible things that had happened. She would not think of them. She was in Cyprus — in Kyrenia — and the sun was shining. She would go out and bathe with Toby and laugh with Persis, and buy embroidered linen in the shops in the town and photograph the harbour as a hundred thousand carefree tourists had done before her.

Her mood lasted until the end of the meal, and it was Miss Moon who shattered it.

Amanda, admiring a Venetian glass fruit dish, had been suddenly reminded of Miss Moon's stolen treasures. 'And I never even asked you about them,' she said remorsefully. 'How horrid of me. Were they things that you were specially fond of?'

'Oh, but I have not lost them,' said Miss Moon placidly. 'They were all found, you know.'

'*Found?* But where? Then they *have* caught the man!'

'No dear. It was Euridice who found them this morning. Or rather Katina, Euridice's cat. *Not* a very engaging animal. She was playing with something on the path — rolling it about — and Euridice saw it glitter and went to pick it up. It was that crystal egg. The Fabergé egg, you know. And there they all were, in the grass by the path. The thief must suddenly have realized that if he were caught with them it would mean a sentence of death for murder, and dropped them.'

'The — the Fabergé egg?' repeated Amanda in a whisper.

'Yes dear. Such a pretty thing. He made a great many of them. For the poor Czarina, you know. This was a specially beautiful

179

one, and of course the diamonds probably add to its value. There is a jewelled bird in it, that sings. I am not very fond of it. Such a tragic story. It makes one wonder, does it not, if Russians are ever to be trusted?'

But Amanda was not listening. She was seeing again the shadowed drawing-room as she had seen it on the previous evening when, rigid with the terrified conviction that the silent room contained someone besides herself, she had looked about it with panic-stricken eyes. The diamonds on the Fabergé egg had sparkled in the last of the daylight.

The egg had been in the buhl cabinet less than a minute before she had discovered the dead body of Monica Ford. It had not been stolen. Someone had removed it later in the evening, together with a handful of similar small objects, in order to convey the impression that Monica Ford had been murdered by a thief. And quite suddenly Amanda knew who had done it and when.

Steve Howard had sent her out of the room to make a telephone call that he could have made with more speed himself. But it had served a double purpose. He had got her out of the way for at least ten minutes, and it must have been then that he had opened the corner cabinet.

Amanda could see him doing it — moving with that noiseless swiftness that had surprised her. Lifting each small, gleaming object in his handkerchief so as to leave no finger-prints, as he had lifted the small bottle with the red poison label in the cabin of the *Orantares*.

'All right — we'll play it on those lines; it's your deal,' the slim, ordinary-looking man with the odd name had said; and the half a dozen or so trinkets from Miss Moon's cabinet had almost certainly been in his possession as he said it. He had shaken hands with Amanda and gone out into the darkness and had dropped that misleading evidence in the overgrown grass by the edge of the flagged path, to lend colour to the theory that Monica Ford's murder had been a chance occurrence instead of part of a hidden,

180

ugly pattern that had begun to form in Fayid, and that involved that small group of people who had sailed for Cyprus on the S.S. *Orantares* — one of whom must have planned the death of Julia Blaine.

14

Amanda did not do any of the things that she had meant to do that afternoon. She ran up to her room instead, and having looked under the bed and inside the cupboards and behind every piece of furniture, she locked the door and wrote three letters. One to her Uncle Oswin, one to her aunt in Fayid, and the third to the shipping company. After which she threw herself on her bed and wept stormily, and had not the least idea why she should do so.

Whatever the reason, she felt considerably better for it; and more than a little ashamed of herself. Presently she heard the clock in the hall strike four and realized that the afternoon had almost gone, and Euridice would be laying tea in the verandah outside the drawing-room.

Amanda sat up and pushed her tumbled hair out of her eyes. She went over to the dressing-table and stopped with a sudden shock of dismay at the sight of her own reflection in the oval looking-glass.

She stood there for a long time, staring at herself. Her hair had escaped from its confining net and had tumbled about her shoulders and half-way down her back in tangled disorder. Her white face was blotched with tears and her dress crumpled and creased.

Looking at herself, she had a sudden and disturbing vision of Julia Blaine, tear blotched and unsightly, giving way to hysteria in the cabin of the *Orantares*. If she wasn't careful, she, Amanda Derington, would soon be behaving as Julia Blaine had behaved.

There was already something about her tear-stained face that was unpleasantly reminiscent of Julia's.

A familiar, mocking voice seemed for a moment to speak in Amanda's ear: '*Come on, George Cross Island — pull yourself together!*'

Amanda straightened her bowed shoulders with a jerk and set her small jaw, and there was a sudden defiant sparkle in her eyes.

The three letters that she had written lay on the writing table by the window. She picked them up, tore them into small pieces and dropped them into the waste-paper basket, and ten minutes later went down to tea with her head high and her red mouth set in lines of determination.

There were voices on the drawing-room verandah and Amanda suffered a momentary qualm. Could it be the police again?

But it was only George Norman.

Mr Norman, who was holding a tea-cup in one hand and a small plate in the other, stood up hurriedly at the sight of Amanda and instantly dropped a piece of toast butter side down on the matting.

'Mooney's been telling me about this terrible business of Glenn's secretary,' explained George Norman, stooping to retrieve the toast and spilling his tea in the process. 'Ghastly show! I can't tell you how shocked we all were. Told Mooney a thousand times if I've told her once that having all that stuff lying round loose was simply asking for it! Ought to be in a bank. Terrible business! Claire's very upset about it. Couldn't sleep a wink last night.'

'Last *night?*' Amanda's voice was startled and incredulous. Did Claire always get bad news ahead of other people? How could she possibly have known last night about Monica Ford?

'Glenn told her,' said George Norman, spreading bloater paste on his toast. 'He telephoned at about half past ten last night. Extraordinary chap. Actually wanted us to go at once and see Anita about something. Seems he didn't dare go himself. Some silly idea that the police might see where he went. He said he couldn't ask you because the police were in your house, and that only left us. Well of course we've been friends of Glenn's for years, but there are limits! He knows perfectly well that Claire and Anita never hit it off. And since then Anita has been spreading all that scandal about him and Claire. However urgent the matter was I do not feel that he should have traded on our personal friendship for him to that extent. Anita Barton is a thoroughly bad lot and he is lucky to be rid of her.'

Miss Moon said: 'I confess I do not understand Anita. I would never have thought her capable of such crudely vulgar behaviour. It does not seem to be at all in keeping with her character. She has changed sadly of late.'

'Drink,' said George Norman succinctly.

'My *dear* boy!' said Miss Moon in horrified protest, 'I am quite sure you are mistaken. Although of course I have heard rumours——'

'I bet you have! It's true, I'm afraid. Drinks like a fish. And that's the girl who never used to touch anything stronger than tomato juice.'

'Perhaps there is a reason for it,' said Miss Moon with a small sigh. 'I cannot help feeling that despite her brazen behaviour Anita is very unhappy. Perhaps she hoped that drink would give her forgetfulness — or courage. "Dutch courage", my dear papa used to call it.'

'She deserves to be unhappy,' said George Norman. 'Impossible woman!' He drained his tea-cup and helped himself to a slice of cake.

Amanda said abruptly: 'What did you all do yesterday? After you left Hilarion?'

'Eh? Oh yesterday. Nothing much. Came down to the Club, you know. I wanted to see a chap who I thought would be there, but he wasn't. Hardly anyone there. Lumley dropped in for a minute or two. He's not a member as a matter of fact. Came up to show a chap some pictures. Claire went off to do a bit of shoppin' and

184

Alastair went for a stroll, and we all forgathered at the Dome for a drink about eight. Alastair was dining there with Mrs Halliday, and she suggested we all stay, so we did. Didn't get home until half past ten, and then the telephone went and there was Glenn going on about this appalling business. Couldn't believe it when Claire told me. Thought the poor chap had finally gone off his rocker.'

Amanda said carefully: 'What happened to Toby — Captain Gates?'

'Oh, he fetched up too. I think he dropped Mrs Halliday at the hotel and drove the car back to the chap he hired it off. He joined us for dinner.'

Amanda relapsed into silence. So they had all separated. All or any of them could have come to the Villa Oleander and gone away again without anyone else knowing about it. They had all been within five minutes' walk of it, and there were three separate entrances to the garden: the front gate, the gate at the far end of the garden that led to the garage, and the small, sun-blistered door in the old Turkish wall that ran the length of the back garden, and which gave onto a narrow secluded lane.

I won't think about it, thought Amanda. I won't ... It was somebody who broke in to steal ... It must have been ... Ordinary, nice people — people that you know — don't do these things. And yet — there was Hilarion. I won't think of it, Amanda told herself again and with desperation.

Miss Moon was saying: 'Yes, a great many people have called. To offer sympathy of course. And two of Amanda's friends came to inquire after her. Lady Cooper-Foot and Mrs Teenley telephoned. Everyone realizes what a shock it must have been to me. But I could not see them all this morning. The police were here you know. And after luncheon dear Amanda went up to her room to rest, so I told Euridice to say that we were "not at home" and to take the receiver off the telephone. So kind of people; but in the circumstances—— '

'Nosey Parkers!' snorted George Norman indignantly. 'All the old gossips dying to get the details.'

'Oh surely not, dear boy,' protested Miss Moon, shocked. 'After all, *you* are here, and although of course we did discuss the whole affair, I am sure that you did not come only for that.'

George Norman's already ruddy countenance turned a rich shade of puce and he said hurriedly: 'No, of course not. I mean Claire told me to — I mean—— '

He floundered into incoherence and Miss Moon, taking pity on him, offered him another cup of tea and urged him to move his chair a little farther into the shade afforded by the climbing roses.

'I always like to take tea out here,' said Miss Moon. 'The view is so beautiful. Quite uninterrupted. I often sit here to watch the sunset, though facing west, it has its drawbacks. Almost too much sun; it has sadly faded my drawing-room carpet. But then I myself am a sun-worshipper. I do not think — except during the real heat of the day of course — that one *can* have too much of it. Do you not agree?'

George Norman sighed, and for a moment his face had a wistful look. 'Yes. I suppose so.'

'You sound rather doubtful,' said Amanda, only too anxious to keep the conversation firmly on the weather. 'Don't tell me that you prefer grey skies and drizzle to this heavenly climate?'

'But of course I do,' said George Norman, surprised. 'England is my own country. This foreign stuff is all very well for a time, but one gets tired of it. The heat and the smell and jabbering foreign voices, and this damnable sun, sun, sun. No; give me Suffolk on a grey day with the wind blowing over ploughed fields, and chaffinches and yellow-hammers in the hedges, and—— ' He broke off with a sharp sigh. 'Oh well; no good talking about it. It doesn't suit Claire. If it wasn't for Claire—— ' His voice trailed off into silence and he sat staring at the slowly cooling tea in his cup as though he had temporarily forgotten Amanda and Miss Moon, his square, ruddy face suddenly bleak and bitter.

Miss Moon, said: 'Try a piece of the gingerbread, dear boy. I made it myself. A recipe of my dear grandmother's.'

George Norman awoke from his meditations with a visible start and said hurriedly: 'No thank you. I must be getting back.' He gulped down the contents of his cup and added that he had not meant to inflict himself on her for tea: 'I really only came to——'

'I know. To collect the details,' finished Miss Moon wickedly. 'Well I hope you have them all. Tell Claire that I am sorry to hear that she is feeling so upset, and that I advise a strong dose of Gregory's powder. My dear Papa used to say that it was a sure cure for all imaginary ills. Good-bye, dear boy. So kind of you to call.'

Miss Moon watched him depart and clicked her tongue impatiently.

'It is frequently a matter of surprise to me,' she remarked tartly, 'what some men will put up with. And the nicest men put up with the most. Look at Glenn! As for George, he puts me out of all patience.'

'Why, Miss Moon?' Amanda was interested in the Normans. She was interested, with a shrinking, frightened, fascinated curiosity, in every one of that small group of people who had known Julia Blaine and who had picnicked at Hilarion.

'Because,' said Miss Moon, 'he has got into the habit — Claire has seen to that! — of putting his own wishes and desires and convenience second to those of his wife. There is nothing wrong with Claire's health and George knows it! But he has to keep up the fiction of believing in it for the sake of his own self-respect. It is, of course, a case of "he who pays the piper calls the tune". The money is Claire's, and that has put her in a position to dictate. All the same, George is able bodied and reasonably intelligent. There is no reason why he should not be able to obtain some remunerative employment in his own country if he insisted on returning there. With or without his wife!'

Amanda said: 'But he's so devoted to her.'

'Is he? I suppose so. But I have frequently wondered of late if

187

perhaps he might not be almost relieved were she to emulate Anita Barton. Poor Anita: I fear she made a bad enemy when she came up against George's wife. So foolish of her! But she was always high-spirited and reckless. Anita will always "rush her fences", as my dear Papa would have said. And that so frequently leads to disaster. Claire is far more subtle. Yes, I am afraid that Claire is a bad enemy.'

Miss Moon sighed and Amanda said: 'You like Mrs Barton, don't you?'

'Well ... yes, dear. One could not help being fond of her. She was such a child.'

'Glenn said that too,' said Amanda slowly.

'He was right. Some adults seem to retain the more endearing qualities of childhood longer than others. Though many, of course, retain the worst ones for ever. Anita Barton was one of the former. A little spoilt perhaps, but very trusting and honest, and not very clever. A woman like Claire Norman, for instance, could make rings round her. It seemed that Anita and Glenn would be perfectly happy. Of course she was gay; she always liked parties and people and pretty clothes. And Glenn, poor boy, was very overworked and perhaps did not take her about as much as he should, so that——'

Miss Moon stopped suddenly and was silent for a moment or two, frowning.

'What is it?' asked Amanda curiously.

'Well dear, it suddenly struck me that if one hears a thing repeated sufficiently often, one begins to believe that it is true, even if it is not. We have all heard so often of late that Glenn neglected Anita. But now I come to think of it, they appeared to go about together a great deal. One certainly never heard that he was remiss where the social side of life was concerned. Of course she may just have found him dull. One does not know.'

'I don't see that she can have it both ways,' pointed out Amanda. 'If — as she says — he was behaving like a Don Juan and making love to about six different women at once, he can't have been exactly dull. He must have had *something* — plenty of spare time, for a start!'

Miss Moon sighed again. 'One would think so. Although of course women do like Glenn. I am very fond of him myself. And so was Claire. She was not at all pleased when he married Anita. All the same, it was exceedingly foolish of Anita to be rude to her, and I have always had a suspicion — uncharitable of me, I fear — that Claire was in some way responsible for the break-up of that marriage. What is it, Euridice?'

Euridice was standing in the french windows behind them, wearing the patient expression of one who has been waiting for at least five minutes. She made a brief and unintelligible remark and went to collect the tea-cups, and Miss Moon turned to Amanda and said: 'Someone asking to see you, dear. If it is that nice Mr Howard, ask him to stay and dine with us.'

Amanda stood up quickly and put her hand to her hair in a gesture that was purely instinctive and feminine.

Miss Moon smiled at her with warm understanding and said: 'You look exceedingly nice, dear. In fact, if I may say so, quite charming.'

Amanda blushed, laughed and went quickly through the french windows and across the drawing-room into the hall: to check abruptly at the sight of her visitor, aware of a sudden and ridiculous sense of disappointment.

It was not Steven Howard who stood waiting for her in the hall of the Villa Oleander. It was, surprisingly enough, Anita Barton. And Anita Barton was frightened. That fact was immediately and startlingly apparent, and it sent an odd cold shiver of apprehension through Amanda.

In the dimness of the high, dark hall Mrs Barton's face had the appearance of a white paper mask on which a child has scrawled features in crudely coloured chalks. The patches of rouge on her cheeks, the vividly lipsticked mouth, the blue-tinted

eyelids and heavily mascara'd lashes, stood out in harsh and painful artificiality in a face that was drawn and drained of all natural
colour, and eyes that were as wide and glittering as a terrified
cat's.

There was no longer any trace of prettiness in that face, but
strangely enough its look of haggard fear was not ageing, and with
the loss of her hard defiant assurance, Anita Barton seemed to
have become all at once younger, and as though she were indeed
only the foolish, frightened child to which both her husband and
Miss Moon had likened her.

Amanda was aware of a sudden pang of pity and an instinct of
protectiveness, and she went forward quickly with her hand outstretched. 'What is it? Did you want to see me?'

'Yes—— ' Anita Barton's frightened-cat eyes darted quick
glances about the hall and the long staircase that stretched up into
the shadows of the upper landing, and her fingers tugged
nervously at a small lace-edged handkerchief so that the delicate
fabric tore with a small ripping sound. She dropped it, startled,
and said breathlessly: 'But not here. Can't we go somewhere else.
Will you walk down the road with me?'

Amanda looked at her, puzzled and disturbed. 'All right. Just
wait a moment while I tell Miss Moon.'

She returned to the verandah and informed Miss Moon that she
would be going out for a short walk. Miss Moon looked interested.
'Anita, you say? I was not aware that you knew her. *Hardly* a
suitable companion for you just now dear. People talk so. Do you
not think that perhaps it would be wiser to decline the invitation
— tactfully, of course?'

'I can't,' said Amanda, distressed. 'I think she's in trouble. I
don't suppose I shall be long.'

Once outside the gates of the Villa Oleander Anita Barton
turned to the right and away from the main road, and as soon as
they were out of sight of the house she clutched Amanda's arm and
spoke in a harsh, breathless voice:

190

'Is it true that something of mine was found in Miss Moon's house last night? — a flower off that dress I was wearing?'

'Yes,' said Amanda briefly.

She heard Anita Barton catch her breath in a hard gasp and the fingers that held her arm tightened convulsively so that the pointed scarlet nails dug painfully into her flesh.

Mrs Barton stumbled and recovered herself and stopped near a group of dusty tamarisk trees by a high, white-washed wall in what appeared to be a deserted cul-de-sac:

'Then it is true! I didn't believe it. I thought that it was only – only a spiteful story. But Lumley said—— ' she stopped, and her wide, hunted eyes searched Amanda's face with a desperate intensity. 'Tell me about it, please. I must know.'

Amanda told her. There was not much to tell, but the bare facts were ugly enough and Anita Barton's white face seemed to grow whiter and more pinched as she listened.

She said at last in a harsh whisper: 'Didn't they ask whose it was?'

Amanda hesitated and once more the lacquered fingernails dug into her arm. 'Didn't they?'

'Yes,' said Amanda unhappily. 'I – I said it was mine.'

'You *what?*' Mrs Barton's voice was suddenly strident. 'Why did you do that? Why should you do a thing like that for me?'

'I didn't,' confessed Amanda. 'I did it because of your husband. You see—— '

'*Glenn?*' Anita Barton relaxed her grip and took a quick step backwards, staring. A stare that changed suddenly to a look of scornful comprehension:

'Glenn,' repeated Mrs Barton, her mouth no longer slack-lipped with fear but twisted and derisive. 'So you've fallen for him too, you silly little fool!'

Amanda's chin came up with a jerk. Her grey eyes were suddenly cold and angry and her voice as scornful as Mrs Barton's own:

'I think it is you who are the fool, if you really imagine that I have any interest at all in your husband. Perhaps no one else has ever had any interest in him either, and you are just another Julia Blaine. Someone who imagines that no other woman can speak to her husband without falling in love with him. You do love him, don't you? You're only behaving like this because someone has made you jealous. Julia was like that.'

For a long minute Anita Barton did not speak, but the scorn and bitterness left her face and it was once more frightened and quivering. She put her hand up to her throat and said in a voice that was barely above a whisper: 'Yes, Julia was like that. And Julia died. But I don't want to die!'

She swallowed convulsively and her eyes came back to Amanda:

'If Glenn doesn't mean anything to you, and I don't, why did you tell the police that the flower was yours?'

'Because I owed your husband something. My life,' said Amanda bluntly.

'Your *life?* What do you mean?'

Amanda told her, omitting only the fact that her fall had not been accidental. 'So you see,' she concluded, 'I thought that I owed him something in return.'

'So that's why you said that flower was yours!' Suddenly and without warning Anita Barton threw back her head and laughed. A loud peal of hysterical mirth that was somehow incredibly shocking. It stopped as abruptly as it had begun and she reached out and clutched at Amanda's arm once more:

'Listen, I never went near Miss Moon's house yesterday. Do you hear? I never went near it?'

Her teeth chattered suddenly as though she were cold, and Amanda said quickly: 'If you didn't, you'll be able to prove it, and then——'

'But I can't prove it!' interrupted Anita Barton desperately. 'Someone telephoned the café on the quay and asked them to give a message to Lumley. Some visitor who wanted to know if he

192

would take a few of his pictures up to the Club. But the man never turned up, and Lumley waited and didn't get back until late. I was alone in the flat; but I can't prove it. I might have gone out. The floors below are empty. They're used for storage. And there are two ways out of that house.'

'Perhaps you wore that dress to Miss Moon's house some other time?' suggested Amanda. 'That flower thing could have been there for ages, you know. Euridice doesn't seem to be very good at dusting and I don't suppose that anyone would have noticed it.'

'I haven't been at the Villa Oleander since the winter,' said Anita Barton, 'and that flower couldn't have come off my dress there because I've never worn it to the house. Someone put it there; and I know who it was. I know how they could have got it and why they did it. And then you said it was yours, which might have spoilt it all. But it won't — you'll see! The police and everyone will know soon enough.'

Her voice died out in a frightened, hopeless whisper and Amanda's fingers closed over the hand on her arm in a comforting grasp.

'No they won't. Don't look like that, Mrs Barton. The police think that it's mine; and they won't worry about it any more because Miss Moon says that they think it was a thief who killed Miss Ford.'

Anita Barton drew a long shuddering breath and her eyes seemed to look through and beyond Amanda as though they did not see her. She said in a barely audible whisper: 'I shall have to be careful. I shall have to be very careful ...'

The sky beyond the dusty tamarisk trees was tinged with gold and the deserted lane was in shadow, and high above the tree tops Amanda could see the distant, rocky outline of St Hilarion, bright with the sunset. It would not be long now before the swift tropical twilight would be upon them, to merge once more into another night of moonlight and stars. She heard a cart creak past the end of the lane, and from somewhere behind the high, white-washed

193

wall a woman began to sing a plaintive Turkish ballad that was old when the Empire of Byzantium was young.

Anita Barton's eyes seemed to focus Amanda again and she drew a short, hard breath and said: 'Thank you for trying to help. It was kind of you. I don't think you'd better be seen with me, so I'll go back a different way.'

Amanda said, impulsively: 'If there is anything I can do — to help I mean — I'd like to do it. I really would.'

Mrs Barton smiled crookedly. 'That's nice of you. I'll remember.'

She turned on her heel and walked quickly away, and Amanda, following more slowly, saw her take the turning that led into the narrow lane behind the wall where the pigeons of the Villa Oleander cooed and paraded in the ruined embrasures of the time-worn stone.

15

Amanda walked slowly back to the house, but at the gate she suddenly changed her mind, and instead of going in, went on and turned down towards the centre of the town.

She would go and see Steve Howard and tell him about that odd, disturbing interview with Anita Barton. Steve would know what to do.

There was a man loitering at the corner of the road, and as she passed him Amanda had the odd impression that he had taken note of her; not as a pretty girl, but as one who observes and files away a piece of information.

She looked quickly back over her shoulder, but the man was leaning against the wall, apparently intent upon removing a stone from the sole of his shoe, and she wondered if her imagination had tricked her, or if the police were not so satisfied as Miss Moon supposed with the theory that Monica Ford had been killed by a thief, and were watching the Villa Oleander?

It was an uncomfortable thought, and yet she had to admit that she would sleep easier that night if she could be assured that the police were keeping an eye on the house.

She saw Claire Norman and Toby Gates in the town, but they did not see her. They were talking earnestly outside Karafillides' shop, and as she approached they turned and walked away together.

Amanda saw no one else that she knew, with the exception of several children who grinned cheerfully at her and were presumably among those admirers of Steve Howard's whose acquaintance she had made on her first morning in Kyrenia. And struck by a sudden thought, she did not go directly to the Dome, but turned instead towards the harbour, where the low rays of the setting sun had turned the massive walls of Kyrenia Castle to molten gold, and dyed the long range of the hills with rose and cyclamen and lavender streaked with soft blue shadows.

The quiet water of the sleepy little harbour lay like a vast opal in the shelter of the sea wall, mirroring all the clear colours of the evening and the orange-brown mainsail of a small blue sailing boat whose owner was manoeuvring her to her moorings at the far side of the harbour. It was a picture to delight the eye of the least appreciative: a back-drop for a ballet or the setting for an opera by Puccini. But there was no one painting on the wall that evening and Amanda could see no sign of Steve Howard.

She turned to look at the row of tall, flat-roofed houses that ringed the far side of the harbour, one of which contained Lumley Potter's studio flat. The french windows of the Potter studio gave on to a small iron-railed balcony, and Amanda saw a man step out on to the balcony and peer down on to the quay beneath. The distance was too great for her to be able to make out his features, but against the dark square of the open window behind him the man's blond head stood out in sharp relief, and Amanda wondered if Alastair Blaine — if it was Alastair — was being inveigled into purchasing a companion piece to 'Sea Green Cypriots'?

The man turned and went in again and Amanda's gaze wandered along the quays and over the crowded tables of the little café, but Steve Howard was definitely not among those present, and after a time she turned away and walked slowly back towards the Dome Hotel.

The girl at the desk glanced at an array of keys and said that she was afraid Mr Howard must be out. He had left his key at the desk and had not reclaimed it. Perhaps Amanda would care to wait?

Amanda lingered, uncertain whether to stay or to leave a

196

message asking Steve to call at the Villa Oleander. But as she hesitated, there was a click of high heels on the floor behind her, a waft of *'Bois des Iles'* and Persis Halliday said: 'Hullo there! Just the girl I wanted to see! Amanda honey, I was round at that old Palazzo of yours this morning trying to see you, and I rang up twice this afternoon. But your phone must be out of order. I hear you've been right spang in the middle of a front page story? Come and have a shot of something and tell me all about it at once. Am I thrilled!'

She took Amanda's arm in an affectionate and possessive clasp and swept her off to a corner of a wide lounge where the lights had already been lit and the windows that looked out onto the placid ocean were filled with the last daffodil glow of the sunset.

Persis, thought Amanda, was showing signs of strain. There were lines about her eyes and mouth that Amanda did not remember having seen before, and she looked less glossy and well dressed than usual. There was a large flake of crimson lacquer missing from one fingernail, and for the first time since Amanda had known her, her gleaming hair was less than immaculately sleek.

She questioned Amanda about the events of the previous evening in a low, eager voice that was entirely unlike her usual gay, high-pitched and incisive tones.

Amanda gave her an outline of the story, but avoided details, and eventually Persis abandoned the catechism and relaxed in her chair.

She had apparently called at the Villa Oleander that morning, after hearing the news of the murder from a hotel acquaintance, and had met Miss Moon.

'She wouldn't let me see you,' explained Persis. 'Seems you were asleep. The place appeared to be crawling with cops and your hostess was dealing with them with considerable firmness. She's quite a character. Glenn was there too. And Toby dropped around to ask after you. We all went upstairs and sat in the boudoir and had a quiet smoke, while the cops milled around in the drawing-room. It was quite a party.'

'Why was Glenn there? Were they——?'

'They'd been doing a bit of reconstructing the crime I gather,' said Persis, hailing a passing waiter and throwing him into temporary confusion by demanding rye-on-the-rocks:

'It seems that Glenn was their Public Enemy Number One, until someone tripped over a handful of valuables on the garden path. Will you have sherry or gin? Okay waiter, make it tomato juice.'

Amanda said: 'You mean they thought that *Glenn* had killed her?'

'Sure. Why not? After all, on his own say-so he was the last person to see her alive, and it seems that his wife's been tooting it all over town that he had an affair with the dame. They had it all doped out. Even the local cops have read that one about the secretary who is seduced by the boss!'

'Did you ever see Monica Ford?' demanded Amanda heatedly.

'Nope. But I've heard plenty from those who had that privilege. I gather that she would not exactly have reached the finals of the Beauty Contest at Mud Flats, Pennsylvania. Am I right?'

'You are. She was plain and efficient and thick and thirty-five-ish, and——'

'I get you, honey. But I guess the cops must have been reading *Candid Confessions*, for they were quite a little taken with their theory. Seems they thought the guy had gotten tired of amorous games around the office and had tried to toss the gal aside like a soiled glove, and she wouldn't toss. So he upped and strangled her, left the corpse in Miss Moon's drawing-room, came on up to Hilarion and callously ate a hearty tea to celebrate. That was their theory and they were crazy about it.'

'They must be mad!' said Amanda. 'She hadn't been dead for any time at all. She was *warm*!'

'Yeah, I know. But they probably thought he just pretended to turn off to Nicosia and really turned back and followed the

Normans to Kyrenia, whipped into Miss Moon's, strangled his secretary, sprang for his steed — I mean his Studebaker — and hey, for that mad ride for the border! Could be.'

Amanda said scornfully: 'How was he supposed to know that she would still be there? It sounds a lot of poppycock to me.'

'Well it blew a fuse early on. Seems the guy gave a lift to a couple of enlisted men just back of that turn, and they've turned 'em up and checked the times, and he couldn't have made it. Not unless he's mastered the art of being in two places at once. And then there was all that jade and junk lying around the garden path, and they figured that though he might indulge in a little murder, he'd probably draw the line at theft.'

'How did you hear all this?' demanded Amanda. 'Did Miss Moon tell you?'

'Good grief no! She was too busy telling the police what she thought of them. Glenn told me. I brought him back here with me and we had a few drinks and discussed this and that. I like that guy. It's a pity he's still carrying a torch for that wife of his. She sounds a bit screwy to me. Anyone who could leave a nice guy like Glenn, to elope with a set of ginger whiskers and a smell of turpentine, must be rocking on the rails with their signals mixed.'

Persis sipped her drink in silence for a moment or two and presently said thoughtfully: 'Steve was there too.'

'Where?' asked Amanda sharply.

'At your Miss Moon's this morning. That guy's a smooth operator. He's wasted on art. He ought to be giving Dulles and Eden a few lessons in diplomacy.'

'What do you mean?'

'When I gate-crashed your villa this morning,' said Persis with a reminiscent grin, 'the situation was a little complicated. Glenn was not taking too kindly to the suggestion that this Monica had been his mistress, and your Miss Moon was addressing the senior cop in a manner which many a high-school teacher would have envied. Then that housemaid of hers — or cook or what-have-you

— was having hysterics in the kitchen, and the bootboy was offering to fight a cop who seems to have suggested that he might have tipped off a pal that the villa would be empty yesterday afternoon, so why not slide in and swipe a few trinkets? It was quite a situation and I doubt if UNO could have done much better. Then in strolls Steve like a flock of doves bearing olive branches, and in no time at all everyone is sitting around drinking vino and relaxing, and Miss Moon is calling the Head Cop her dear boy. Yes, it was certainly quite a performance.'

Persis lit a cigarette from a small diamond and platinum lighter and looked thoughtfully at Amanda through the smoke:

'You're in love with him, aren't you?'

'Who? Steve Howard? Don't be absurd! I hardly know him.'

'You sound almost convincing, honey — but not quite. And it isn't necessary to know someone to fall in love with them. In fact the less you know about 'em the easier it is.' There was a trace of bitterness in Persis' voice. 'Has he kissed you?'

She saw the vivid colour flood up into Amanda's face and said dryly: 'I see he has. Ah well, some girls have all the luck.'

'Persis,' said Amanda severely, 'don't you ever think of anything but love?'

'Not if I can help it,' said Persis candidly. 'I'm nuts about love! Romance is my business — and a very paying proposition I have found it.'

'Are you going to use everything that has happened here for one of your books?'

A shadow seemed to pass over Persis Halliday's face, and then she laughed. It was a short and rather bitter laugh.

'No. Not quite everything.'

Amanda looked at her curiously and said suddenly: 'Persis — are we real to you? Or are we — are we all just people acting out parts that give you ideas for stories?'

Persis leant back in her chair and blew a smoke ring at the ceiling. She said in a soft, abstracted voice: 'You know, it's queer that you should ask that. Sometimes I do feel that way. As if I was on the other side of a sheet of plate glass, watching a puppet show and thinking "that's interesting". Sometimes the people I write about seem more real to me than a lot of people I meet, because I know them and I own them. It's — I suppose it's a little like being God. I can make my characters do just what I want. Fall in love, get married, hate each other, jump through hoops. I can kill 'em off or make 'em achieve fame and fortune in a coupla' lines of print. But – but real people won't always do what one wants ...'

Her voice sank to a half-whisper on the last words and she relapsed into silence, leaning back in her chair with her abstracted gaze on the darkening sky and the first stars that lay beyond the open windows, while the cigarette burned out between her fingers.

A soft, fluting voice made itself heard from the direction of the door and Persis dropped the stub of her cigarette into her glass and looked over Amanda's shoulder.

'Here comes Teeny-weeny-me,' she observed. 'Why, hullo Claire. Brought the baseball team with you I see.'

Claire Norman, accompanied by her husband, Alastair Blaine, Toby Gates and Lumley Potter, crossed the room and sinking into a chair, announced that she was exhausted. She appeared surprised at seeing Amanda and murmured a few soft words of sympathy on the subject of the *terrible* ordeal that Amanda must have been subjected to.

'We've just been to see Miss Moon,' she said. 'We thought you'd be there too of course, but Mooney said you'd gone out. She was rather secretive about it. She wouldn't say who with. I thought it must be Steve. I didn't think of Persis. Lumley, you're not going, are you?'

'Afraid I must,' said Mr Potter reluctantly. 'I said I'd be back around six, and it's well after seven, and——'

'*Poor* Lumley!' interrupted Claire in her soft, clear voice. She reached up a small hand and laid it on his arm in a brief gesture indicative of sympathy and understanding, and Mr Potter flushed pinkly.

Persis, who had watched this bit of byplay with considerable interest, caught Amanda's eye and winked, and Amanda bit back a laugh and turned hurriedly to Toby Gates who had seated himself on the arm of her chair was inquiring solicitously as to her health.

Mr Potter removed himself, Alastair Blaine ordered a round of drinks, and George Norman asked Amanda to supper at their house:

'Would have asked you before,' he said, 'but didn't think you'd feel up to it. Be delighted if you'd come. Only pot luck of course. Claire, I've just asked Miss Derington to join the party for supper tonight.'

Claire Norman raised her delicate brows and smiled charmingly at Amanda, but Amanda received the sudden and distinct impression that she was not pleased, and said quickly: 'I'm so sorry, I'm afraid I can't come. I couldn't walk out on Miss Moon at such short notice. She had a horrid time yesterday, and today hasn't been exactly peaceful for her.'

'Of course,' sympathized Claire. 'We quite understand. Some other time perhaps.'

Toby said in a low voice: 'Why didn't you give me a ring last night and tell me what had happened? It must have been hellish for you. You know I'd have come up.'

'Thank you Toby,' said Amanda with real gratitude. 'But there wasn't anything you could do.'

'I gather Howard was there,' said Toby with a trace of resentment in his voice.

'He brought me back from Hilarion, that was why. Toby, did you really all call in on Miss Moon again this evening?' She indicated Claire and her entourage with a brief gesture of the hand.

'We just thought we'd look in and see how you were. We all happened to meet rather by accident up at the top of the town, and as it was only about two minutes' walk we went along. It's an astonishing house, isn't it? The old girl took us all over it. Simply crammed with stuff that would make an antique dealer drip at the mouth. Do you know that there's a Constable sketch in one of those bedrooms? Must be worth a packet. No wonder some enterprising burglar had a crack at it. The only thing I can't understand is why the whole shooting match wasn't pinched years ago. I don't believe the old girl would have noticed it if it had been!'

Claire was saying, '——Toby will tell us. Toby dear, is it true that your Regiment is coming here in the autumn? Alastair is being very cagey and Security-Minded about it. As if it mattered!'

Major Blaine laughed. 'I'm not being in the least cagey. I don't know. And I bet Toby doesn't know either. It is commonly supposed that the policy of the Broadmoor graduate responsible for the placing of units is to decide all changes at the last possible moment with the aid of a pin, in the hope — only too frequently realized — of causing the maximum confusion not so much to the enemy but to the units involved. Amanda, now that you've dealt with that tomato mush, how about trying the effects of a gin and lime?'

Amanda smiled and shook her head. 'No thank you, Alastair. I'm afraid it's time I was going. I don't like to keep Miss Moon waiting.'

'Nonsense. You've masses of time for another drink.'

'This is my round,' said Toby quickly. He rose and went to the bell and Alastair Blaine crossed over, and having removed Amanda's empty glass took Toby's place on the arm of her chair and began to make desultory conversation to which Amanda paid little attention.

She was watching the clock and wondering if Steven Howard had returned, and if he too was dining with the Normans? If so it would be too late to tell him about Anita Barton tonight, and she would have to let it keep until tomorrow.

She became aware that Alastair Blaine had lowered his voice to an undertone and had asked her some question. Amanda jerked her gaze from the clock and looked at him.

'I – I'm sorry, Alastair. What did you say?'

Alastair glanced quickly at the four other members of the party, but George was explaining the intricacies of cricket to Persis, and Claire and Toby were discussing a mutual friend in Alexandria. His gaze came back to Amanda and he asked a low-voiced question that was an echo of one that Amanda had already heard once that evening:

'Is it true,' asked Alastair Blaine, 'that something off Anita Barton's dress was found by the police last night?'

'Who told you that?' asked Amanda, startled. 'Did Miss Moon?'

Alastair shook his head. 'No. Claire told me.'

'*Claire?* How did she know?'

'Seems that Barton told her. He rang up in a bit of a stew last night and wanted her to go down and see his wife or Lumley and warn 'em to burn the dress or bury it or get rid of it somehow. Didn't dare go himself for fear the police were tailing him. But I think he must have been a bit worked up to suggest it, as Claire isn't exactly sympathetic to Mrs Barton. However, she and George have always been pretty good friends of his so I suppose he felt that in the special circumstances she might rally round for his sake, if not for Anita's.'

'And did she?'

'No,' said Alastair Blaine slowly, and frowned.

'She seems to have made it her business to tell a good many other people,' said Amanda tartly. 'Is that why you were down at Lumley Potter's?'

Alastair Blaine looked startled.

'I thought I saw you on the balcony,' explained Amanda.

'I did drop in for a minute,' admitted Major Blaine uncomfortably. 'I thought someone should tip her off. But she wasn't in, and Lumley said he'd already told her. Don't know how he got hold

204

of it. Then we met the Normans and Toby in the town and went up to see you. I thing Claire wanted to find out from Miss Moon if it were true. But your peculiar old hostess wasn't giving anything away. *Is* it true?'

Amanda hesitated, but before she could reply Claire looked up and called out in her sweet, fluting voice:

'Steve! What have you been doing with yourself? You're looking very well dressed. Is this in honour of dining with us?'

Amanda turned quickly, aware of an odd breathlessness.

Mr Howard had not, apparently, been occupying himself with art. His hair was unusually smooth, and in place of his normally somewhat casual attire he wore a thin checked suit. He had, it is true, removed the coat, which he carried slung over one shoulder, but his silk shirt was impeccable and he wore the tie of a famous public school.

'No,' said Steve smiling lazily down at Claire. 'Nothing short of a white tie and tails could do justice to that, but as I omitted to pack 'em, this is the best I can do. And damned hot it is too.'

Persis said: 'Where have you been, Steve?'

'Troodos,' said Steve, and offered no further comment.

'*Troodos?*' exclaimed Claire surprised. 'Do you mean you've been the whole way there and back this afternoon? Whatever for?'

'Oh, just to see a man about a dog,' said Steve amicably.

He pulled up a chair and sat down, stretching his long legs before him and driving his hands deep into his pockets.

Claire smiled archly at him and said: 'I don't believe a word of it! Who is she, Steve? I am quite sure that you would never have dressed up in a suit for any mere male — unless you've been to see the Governor, of course!'

She laughed, as though such an idea was preposterous, and Steve grinned at her and turned to George Norman with some query as to whether there was any fishing obtainable in the Island? George rose to the bait with the alacrity of a trout in May and Claire's question remained unanswered.

205

Persis stood up and said: 'Well I'm for a bath. Toby, collect me in about half an hour and we'll walk up to Claire's.'

Amanda looked at the clock again and rose hurriedly to her feet. 'I'm afraid I must be going too,' she said, addressing the company in general. 'I hadn't realized it was so late.'

George said: 'Change your mind and come on to supper.'

Amanda smiled and shook her head, and Steve, who had risen, said: 'I'll see you home,' thus checkmating Toby Gates who had been about to make a similar suggestion.

Amanda, catching Persis Halliday's amused and mocking eye, said a little stiffly: 'Please don't bother. It's no distance, I can easily go by myself.'

'I'm quite sure you can,' said Steve equably, 'but as I have sundry messages to deliver to Miss Moon, I might as well go up now as later.'

'What messages?' asked Amanda. 'Can't I take them?'

'One or two things about the inquest. It's for eleven tomorrow in Nicosia, and we shall all have to put in an appearance.' He grinned at Amanda with a good deal of comprehension in his gaze and said: 'Of course if you are averse to my company, I can always give you three minutes' start.'

'Don't be ridiculous,' said Amanda with dignity, and walked towards the door.

'Dinner at 8.15, Steve,' Claire called after him. 'Don't be late.'

'I won't.'

Persis said: 'Goodnight honey. Enjoy yourself!' And then they were crossing the hall and a moment later were out in the warm moonlight under a sky that was thick with stars.

Amanda started off at a brisk pace, but as Steve refused to be hurried she was compelled to slow down as the only alternative to having him wandering up the road a yard or so behind her — a proceeding that must appear more than a little ridiculous.

'That's better,' approved Steve, linking his arm casually through hers. 'I have had a tiring day, and just at the moment a marathon race is not in my line. What did you want to see me about?'

Amanda checked and stumbled. 'How did you know I——?'

'No, I am not omniscient, worse luck,' said Steve regretfully. 'The girl at the desk told me that a young lady had been inquiring for me. She added a description that was flattering but reasonably accurate, and a natural modesty forbade me to suppose that all you required was the pleasure of my company. What is it?'

Amanda hesitated, frowning and uncertain.

'Changed your mind?' inquired Steve.

'No,' said Amanda doubtfully. 'Perhaps there isn't anything in it, but Mrs Barton came to see me this evening——'

Steve Howard's leisurely pace did not alter but Amanda had a fleeting impression that the muscles of the arm that was linked through hers had tightened for an infinitesimal moment.

'Did she indeed? What about?'

Amanda told him, repeating that short conversation word for word as accurately as she could remember it. Steve made no comment, except to ask her if she had mentioned the finding of the small linen flower to anyone.

'No,' said Amanda. 'It was Glenn.'

This time there was no mistaking the sudden rigidity of that arm, and perhaps Steve was aware of it, for he released Amanda's arm and thrust his hands into his pockets.

'Ah, the hero boy,' he remarked satirically. 'So he blew the gaff, did he? Now I wonder why?'

Amanda explained the circumstances, her voice quick and indignant, and Steve said caustically: 'Dear Glenn would appear to make quite a habit of getting his girl-friends to pull his chestnuts out of the fire for him.'

'Why must you always sneer at him?' demanded Amanda with some heat. 'I know you all think he's a fool not to say "good-riddance" to Anita, but he can't help it if he's still fond of her. You

207

can't stop loving people just because you want to. It's nothing to do with sense or logic or——'

She stopped suddenly and Steve gave her an odd sideways look and said: 'You do rush to his defence, don't you? No; love has nothing to do with sense and even less with logic. In fact, taking it all round, it is an infernal nuisance and a booby trap laid by Mother Nature with a view to spreading alarm and confusion, defeating the ends of justice and leading inevitably to over-population and the atom-bomb.'

Amanda laughed and Steve said sadly: 'It is no laughing matter I assure you. Just as it becomes vitally necessary to keep one's eye on the ball, along comes a naked and nauseous infant with a brain suitable to its tender years, whom someone has inadvisedly armed with a lethal weapon in the form of a bow and arrow. And *whang!* — there is a spanner in the works.'

'Are you speaking from personal experience?' inquired Amanda with interest.

Mr Howard sighed. 'Yes, alas!' he looked down at her and grinned. 'In fact you can take it that my recent crispness on the subject of dear Glenn is caused by the demon of jealous gnawing at my vitals. No one ever rushes to my defence or sobs sympathetically over my woes. And neither do I win rounds of applause by risking my neck rescuing damsels from certain death. I find it very discouraging.'

Amanda looked at him doubtfully. There was a derisive gleam in his eye and she was quite sure that he did not mean a word of what he had said. Or was there, perhaps, a grain of truth in it?

They had reached the turn down to the Villa Oleander and Amanda noted that once again there was a man standing in the shadow of the wall, lighting a cigarette. It was not the same one who had been there when she had passed earlier that evening, but there was about him the same indefinable suggestion of deliberate and observant loitering that the other man had had.

The quiet, tree-lined road was white with moonlight, but the

208

pavement was a dark patchwork of shadows and Amanda was suddenly intensely grateful to Steven Howard for insisting on accompanying her. It would not have been pleasant to walk through those black shadows alone.

Steve stopped at the gate, glanced at the luminous dial of his watch and said: 'See you tomorrow at the inquest. Don't let them faze you and don't get led off into side issues. Just answer the questions in as few words as possible and lay off unnecessary detail. Keep it short and you'll be okay. Goodnight.'

Amanda said: 'But I thought you wanted to see Miss Moon.'

'She'll have been told all about it by now. You were being a bit haughty about accepting my offer to escort you, so I had to bring pressure to bear. Be seeing you.'

He turned away and Amanda said: 'Steve——'

Steve Howard stopped and turned rather slowly. 'Yes?'

Amanda said: 'It *was* you who took those things from the cabinet, wasn't it? The——'

Steve took a swift stride towards her and the palm of his hand was hard and warm over her mouth. She saw him throw a quick look left and right into the shadows and draw a short breath of relief. He dropped his hand and said low and tersely: 'What makes you think that?'

'The Fabergé egg,' said Amanda in a whisper. 'I noticed it in the cabinet just before I – before I found Monica Ford. The diamonds glittered——'

'*Damn!*' said Mr Howard softly.

He looked down at Amanda and the moonlight showed a deep crease between his brows.

'Have you mentioned that to anyone?' he demanded curtly.

Amanda shook her head.

'Then don't! Not to anyone at all — do you understand?' His voice held a hard edge of command.

'Yes,' said Amanda in a whisper.

Once again he turned his head to look into the shadows and then he shrugged his shoulders in a faintly fatalistic gesture and turned and walked quickly away, his footsteps audible in the silence long after his tall figure had been swallowed up by the shadows.

16

'Is that you dear?' called Miss Moon, peering over the banisters of the upper hall. 'I shall be down in a moment. Tell Euridice we will dine at once.'

Amanda delivered the message to the kitchen and went upstairs to brush her hair. She came down to find Miss Moon awaiting her in the dining-room, arrayed in a regal robe of yellow velvet and wearing a magnificent parure of topazes that would have been greatly improved by cleaning.

Amanda looked down a little guiltily at her own short cotton frock and apologized for not changing.

'Nonsense dear. You look exceedingly nice as you are, and had you delayed to change, the soup would have been cold. I only change from habit. Dear papa would have considered it most odd had I not, but I often think how foolish I am to continue doing so. What did Anita wish to see you about? Such a pity she should have called just then, for Claire and several of your friends dropped in not so very long afterwards. I had a most social evening. They inquired so kindly after you: although I fear that on Claire's part it was less a visit of condolence than of curiosity. But perhaps I am being unkind. That Major Blaine is a very quiet, pleasant-mannered man. His wife committed suicide I hear — so tragic for him. It seems that she—— But of course dear, you know all about it. You were on the same boat. Quite dreadful.'

'Yes,' said Amanda in a colourless voice. She did not in the least wish to discuss the death of Julia Blaine, and hoped that Miss Moon would not pursue the subject. Miss Moon did not. She was

211

far more interested in the fact that Lumley Potter had had the effrontery to accompany Claire and her friends to the Villa Oleander.

'*Such* impertinence, dear! I have always considered him a most tiresome man. Spiritual aromas indeed! Anyone who can depict our enchanting harbour in a *welter* of dirty browns and blacks — and that particularly unpleasant shade of Prussian blue — I cannot but feel to be lacking in *honesty*. And when he knows quite well how fond I have always been of Glenn — not to mention Anita — his action in calling at this house becomes quite inexplicable. Naturally I could not turn him from the door; particularly as Claire had brought him. But I let him see *quite* plainly that I considered his visit an unwarrantable intrusion. He did not look at *all* comfortable,' added Miss Moon with satisfaction.

Amanda was suddenly reminded of something that Anita Barton had said about Lumley Potter and Claire, and she turned to Miss Moon and said abruptly: 'Do you think he wants to marry Mrs Barton?'

'Marry Anita?' said Miss Moon as though such a thing had never occurred to her. 'I am quite sure he does not.'

'Then why do you suppose he ran off with her?'

'I do not think he did — though of course I may be wrong. I think Anita ran off with him. Just to make a scandal. So that Glenn would divorce her. She is obviously quite determined, for reasons of her own, to obtain her freedom; though I am convinced that her object cannot be marriage with Lumley Potter. But Anita — as I think I told you — has a strangely childish streak. When she wants something, she wants it badly and at once and without counting the cost. And you would be surprised, dear, what silly and quite childish things many people will do when their tempers and emotions get the upper hand of them. Things that they would never *dream* of doing if only they would give themselves time for reflection.'

'No I wouldn't,' said Amanda sadly. 'I'm just as bad. I lost my temper and slapped someone across the face the other day. I didn't think that anyone ever really did things like that.'

'Mr Howard,' said Miss Moon placidly. 'It left quite a mark did it not? I own I was interested. Such a dear boy! What had he done to provoke you?'

Amanda laughed, and followed the laugh with a frown. 'He asked me if I'd fallen in love with Glenn Barton.'

'What a foolish question!' said Miss Moon. 'But then gentlemen are often *so* unobservant, dear. Even the most intelligent of them. And when they are jealous they can behave with quite surprising stupidity. Look at Lumley Potter, who has always been devoted to Claire. Not that I consider *him* intelligent: quite the reverse! I imagine that Mr Howard thought that you had laid claim to that flower of Anita's to please Glenn.'

Amanda said: 'Do you notice everything, Miss Moon?'

'Oh I wouldn't say that, dear — but I hope that I am not *too* unobservant.'

'How did you know that it belonged to Mrs Barton?' inquired Amanda curiously. 'Had you seen her in that dress?'

'No,' said Miss Moon. 'Not to my knowledge. But I was aware that both you and Glenn had recognized it, and when I saw him look at you like that of course I knew at once that it must be something of Anita's. I supposed that you had seen her wear it.'

Miss Moon selected a peach and peeled it while Amanda wondered how many other things Miss Moon had noticed and had kept to herself?

'Claire had heard about it too,' said Miss Moon presently. 'She was trying to pump me. I soon put a stop to that! I imagine Glenn, poor boy, must have asked her to warn Anita. He should have known Claire better. But then, as I have said, gentlemen are lamentably unobservant in such matters, and I do not think that Glenn is a particularly good judge of character, or he would have seen through Claire years ago. Let us take coffee in the drawing-room.'

She rose with a clash of bracelets and jewellery, and over the coffee informed Amanda that a police officer had called earlier to notify her that both of them would be expected to attend the inquest on Monica Ford the following morning.

'Only a formality, my dear,' said Miss Moon. 'Nothing to worry about. I understand that all those who were at Hilarion that afternoon have also been asked to attend. I cannot think why. Corroborative evidence on the times of arrival and departure I suppose. Even Lumley and Anita have been requested to be present. Quite unnecessary I should have thought. So hard on poor Glenn.'

Miss Moon turned the conversation on to general topics and shortly after nine o'clock expressed her intention of retiring to bed:

'I feel that we could both do with an early night, dear.'

Amanda was feeling far from sleepy, but she had no intention of remaining alone in the shadowy drawing-room with those shimmering circles of looking-glass that had reflected Monica Ford's lifeless hand.

Euridice had already retired to bed — Andreas slept out — and Miss Moon turned out the lights, closed and bolted the french windows and went into the dining-room to fetch a jug of barley water off the sideboard, the train of her yellow velvet dress trailing regally behind her and collecting a small wash of dust.

'I usually take a jug of this up with me to my bedroom during the hot weather,' said Miss Moon. 'Can I offer you a glass of anything, dear? No? Then let us turn out the lights.'

Amanda relieved her of the jug and carried it upstairs to her room, and Miss Moon said: 'Thank you, dear. Just put it on the bedside table.'

Amanda did so and turned to look about her. She had not been inside Miss Moon's bedroom before, except for those few frantic minutes on the previous evening, when she had had no attention to spare for her surroundings. Miss Moon's bedroom was worth a second look, comprising as it did a magnificent mixture of

French baroque and Victorian mahogany. The massive dressing table and wardrobes belonged to the later period, while the carved and gilded vastness of the canopied bed would have done credit to the Pompadour in her hey-day.

On either side of the bed two marble-topped console tables supported a clutter of books, bottles and other oddments, and on one of them stood a massive silver candelabrum that had been converted into a bedside lamp. Amanda switched it on, and the warm glow illuminated the jumbled contents of the table and glinted on gilded garlands and the worn brocaded hangings of the bed.

Something moved on the pillow and she gasped and took a quick step backwards. But it was only Euridice's grey cat, who had been lying curled up in a warm nest formed by an elderly lace-edged bed jacket.

'What is it, dear?' inquired Miss Moon, looking round. 'Oh it is that dreadful cat! Chase it off, dear. I do wish that Euridice would get rid of it. I suppose that there will now be hairs all over the pillow. How very vexing.'

Amanda scooped up the cat, deposited it in the passage, and returning, shook out the bed jacket and picking up the pillow beat off the few short grey hairs that clung to it.

She bent to replace it and stood suddenly very still, her eyes wide with shock and an icy prickle of panic running down her spine.

Something had been lying under that pillow. An insignificant object that was yet horribly familiar.

A small bottle containing a few white tablets and bearing a red poison label.

But it could not be the same one! It could not possibly be! She had not brought it away with her. Steven Howard had taken it. He had wrapped it carefully in his handkerchief and had put it into the pocket of his dressing-gown. Yet it was the same bottle — or its twin.

215

Amanda found that she was shivering, and she caught her lip hard between her teeth to stop it trembling.

Miss Moon had seated herself before her dressing table and was engaged in removing various necklaces, bracelets and rings and replacing them in an old-fashioned and much worn morocco jewel case the size of a small hatbox. She was still talking, but the flow of her words slid over Amanda without making any impression on her. She could only stare and shiver.

Discovering that she was still holding the pillow, she laid it down carefully on the bed and reached out a shrinking hand for the bottle. But just before she touched it she remembered what Steve had said about finger-prints, and stopped.

There was a small, crumpled lace-edged handkerchief on the table beside Miss Moon's bed, and Amanda picked it up and lifted the bottle with it, holding it with extreme care.

She looked at Miss Moon's unconscious back and suddenly her brain seemed to clear, and she knew——

She knew that there would be no finger-prints on that bottle and just exactly why it had been placed there.

There was to have been a repetition of a scene that had been planned to take place in a cabin of the S.S. *Orantares*. But this time it would be Miss Moon and not Julia Blaine who would die. Miss Moon who should have been at Lady Cooper-Foot's bridge party, but had stayed at home instead, and who might therefore have heard or seen something or someone at the hour that Monica Ford had died. Miss Moon who knew and noticed so much and who might be waiting her chance to say a word that might lead to the hanging of Monica Ford's murderer ...

She would have laid her head on that single down pillow and have felt the small hard lump of the bottle, and would have removed it, looked at it in some surprise and put it aside until the morning — as Julia would have done.

Amanda could almost hear the coroner's verdict. Elderly and eccentric lady, shocked by Miss Ford's murder and distressed by the consideration that her own refusal to keep her house locked was responsible for it, felt herself unable to face a public inquiry and allowed the tragedy to prey on her mind, and the recent suicide of Mrs Blaine to suggest a way out. Yes, it would have been something like that. And but for Euridice's cat and the fact that Amanda had carried up the jug of barley water for her, Miss Moon would have been found dead in the morning.

The barley water!

Amanda whirled round and stared at it. Someone who knew that Julia drank lemon juice and water had made use of that knowledge to disguise the acidity of a poison. Because Miss Moon drank barley water, had that someone laid the same trap for her? There was no innocent iced drink on Miss Moon's bedside table, but there was an empty glass — and the jug that Amanda herself had placed there.

Amanda forced herself to speak, waiting until Miss Moon ceased talking, and not having heard one word that she had said.

'May I have some of your barley water please?' Her voice sounded high-pitched and like a gramophone record, as though it did not belong to her.

Miss Moon turned. 'Why, of course dear. Help yourself.'

Amanda said: 'There's a glass in my room. I'll take some if I may and bring the jug back.'

'Do, dear.'

Amanda thrust the small bottle in its crumpled handkerchief into her pocket and picked up the jug. Once in her own room she filled her own glass from it, her hands shaking so badly that the liquid splashed on to the table. She poured the remainder out of the window, and ran down the passage to the bathroom where she turned on both taps and rinsed the jug again and again. Having dried it on a towel she half-filled it with cold water, and returned to Miss Moon; her face chalk white and her hands still shaking uncontrollably.

'I'm most awfully sorry,' explained Amanda breathlessly, 'but

I'm afraid I've spilt your barley water. I've brought you some water instead.'

Miss Moon tutted indulgently and said that Amanda was not to bother about it.

'I – I have to telephone someone,' said Amanda, finding it difficult to keep her voice under control. 'Something I have to ask about. Do you mind?'

'No dear, of course not. You know where the telephone is, do you not? Now don't stay up too late. You are not looking at all well.'

Amanda said goodnight and left the room hurriedly, shutting the door behind her and standing for a moment with her back to it, fighting off an absurd feeling of faintness and aware that her heart was beating unpleasantly fast.

The stairs stretched down into the blackness below, and she was suddenly afraid to go down into the darkness of the deserted hall and past the open doorway of the drawing-room where Monica Ford had died. Supposing that there was someone hiding there, waiting to make sure that Miss Moon died too? Waiting to make sure that they were safe for ever from Miss Moon's observant eyes and chattering tongue?

But of course that was absurd! Whoever had laid that deadly trap for Miss Moon would make certain of being as far away as possible from the Villa Oleander that night. There was nothing to be afraid of. Nothing except the darkness and the silence . . .

Amanda set her teeth and forced herself to walk down that long dark stairway, remembering as she did so that other stairway and the footsteps that had crept down behind her. She groped her way to the electric light switch, and a moment later the hall was flooded with soft light from the few candle bulbs in the dusty crystal chandelier that hung from the high ceiling.

The passage off the hall yawned shadowy and silent, and facing it the door stood open on to the dark drawing-room. Amanda shivered and walked resolutely down to the end of the passage, and after a few moments of ineffectual groping, found the switch of the small lamp that hung above the telephone.

It took an absurdly long time to find the number she required. The pages of the telephone book fluttered in her unsteady hands and her fingers refused to obey her, but she found it at last.

It was George who answered the phone:

'Who? . . . Oh, Howard. Yes, he's here. Do you want to speak to him?'

'Yes please,' said Amanda, trying to keep the fear and urgency from her voice; trying to speak quite calmly.

'Who is it?' George's voice was maddeningly loud and slow. 'Who? I can't hear you. Amanda? — Oh, Miss Derington! Sorry; didn't recognize your voice. Like me to give him a message? Or would you rather——'

The receiver was abruptly removed from his grasp and Steve's voice said crisply: 'What is it, Amanda?'

'*Steve!*' Amanda's voice wavered suddenly and she clutched at the edge of the table to steady herself. 'Steve, I must see you! Could you — could you come here? At once. I know it's late but — Steve *please!*'

Mr Howard's voice said cheerfully and surprisingly: 'Oh she does, does she? I can't have made myself clear. Perhaps I'd better come round and have a word with her. No, tell her it's no trouble at all. I'll be right along.'

There was a click and he had rung off.

Amanda stared stupidly at the receiver in her hand and was just about to ring the number again and tell him that he had not understood her, when it dawned on her that Steve was once again manufacturing an alibi for the benefit of those who might be unduly interested.

She replaced the receiver slowly, but she could not return to the hall. There were too many doors leading off the hall into too many dark and silent rooms. Too many old, beautiful, silvery mirrors that reflected her and watched her . . . as they had watched Monica Ford.

The passage was narrow and bare and smelt strongly of dust and boot-polish and faintly of garlic, and the house was uncannily silent: it did not creak or stir as many houses do after dark. And outside it the windless moonlight night was as silent and as still as the house.

Amanda was seized with a sudden fear of that silence. Surely she should be able to hear Miss Moon moving about in her room? Or had there been another glass somewhere in that room? A glass that she had overlooked? Was Miss Moon even now lying sprawled face downwards on the floor like Julia Blaine? Like Monica Ford——?

Amanda ran down the short passage and raced up the stairs, taking them three at a time, and burst into Miss Moon's room, white with panic.

Miss Moon, clad in a nightgown reminiscent of the one in which the Princess Victoria was popularly supposed to have received the news of her accession, was seated before her dressing-table rolling her hair up in curl-papers. She said: 'What is it, dear?' without looking round.

Amanda clung to the door handle and strove to regain her breath.

'N-nothing. I – thought I heard you call.'

'Probably someone in the road, dear. Did you put your call through?'

'Yes,' said Amanda, her eyes searching the room and seeing no sign of any other glass. 'Steve — Mr Howard — asked if he could come round for a minute or two. About – about the inquest I think. I hope you don't mind.'

'Of course not, dear. I did not realize that it was Mr Howard you were telephoning. Such a delightful man. You will find biscuits and brandy in the sideboard. Gentlemen usually like brandy; although I have often wondered why. *So* unpleasant — except in hard sauce. Do not let him keep you up too late.'

'I won't,' promised Amanda.

She went slowly downstairs again, feeling a little foolish and wondering if she had not, after all, dragged Steve Howard out on a fool's errand? Supposing there was nothing in the barley water, and that the bottle contained some drug that Miss Moon took for her migraines? She should have questioned Miss Moon about it instead of leaping to wildly melodramatic conclusions. Her nerves must be badly on edge and Steve would undoubtedly laugh at her. She had better go up at once and ask Miss Moon.

She turned back, but as she did so someone came rapidly up the flagged path and took the six stone steps in two. The fall of the knocker echoed through the quiet hall and Amanda went slowly to the door, thinking that if it was Steve Howard he must have run most of the way.

If he had, he gave no sign of it. He looked very tall and slender silhouetted against the bright moonlight, and he did not appear to be in the least out of breath. He studied Amanda's face for a long moment and the tension went out of his own.

He said amicably: 'Are you coming out or am I coming in?'

Amanda flushed and drew back, and he strolled into the hall and closed the door behind him. He looked about him, glanced up at the landing above the staircase, and evidently deciding that the hall was an unsuitable spot for conversation, moved towards the drawing-room.

'No!' said Amanda sharply. 'Not in there.' She went past him into the dining-room and switched on the lights.

The dining-room was friendly and lacked the shadowy corners and the ugly memories of the drawing-room. Steve followed her in and shut the door.

'Well, Amarantha? What is it now? Judging from your voice on the telephone I rather expected to find another body on the door-step.'

221

'I'm sorry,' said Amanda uncertainly. 'I found something and I got into a panic. And now I think that perhaps it doesn't mean anything after all, and that I've made a fool of myself.'

'Let's see it,' suggested Steve, and held out his hand.

Amanda drew the small bundle of lace and cambric from her pocket and handed it over. He accepted it without much apparent interest, unfolded it, and then stood very still.

A minute ticked away into the silence and there was no longer any trace of casualness in Steve Howard's face or his tall figure, and his eyes were wide and bright and intent. Presently Amanda heard him let his breath out between his teeth and he lifted his head and looked at her.

'Where did you find this?'

Amanda told him, and he listened without interruption, his eyes on her face, and when she had finished told her curtly to fetch the glass of barley water. Amanda left the room and came back a few moments later, breathing a little unevenly, with the glass in her hand.

Steve was standing where she had left him. He had unscrewed the top of the bottle, and two small white tablets were lying in the full glare of the lamplight on the polished surface of the dining-room table. He took the glass from her hand, smelt it, and then wetted the tip of one finger in the contents and touched it to his tongue.

He made a quick grimace and jerking a handkerchief out of his breast pocket, rubbed it over his tongue. Amanda said breathlessly: 'Then it is poison?'

'H'mm?' said Steve in a preoccupied voice.

Amanda repeated the question and he looked at her as though he had momentarily forgotten her existence, and said impatiently: 'Of course it is.'

He pushed the glass away and sat down on the nearest chair with his elbows on the table and frowned at the two white tablets. Something about the handkerchief caught his attention and he

222

reached out a hand for it and spread it flat. It was, or it had been, an expensive trifle. A monogram consisting of three entwined initials was embroidered in one corner, and the lace had been badly torn along one edge.

'A.B.H.,' said Steve pensively. 'Where did you get this, Amanda? It isn't yours.'

'It was on Miss Moon's table, by her bed,' said Amanda, leaning over to look at it. 'And it isn't A.B.H. The centre initial overlaps the other two. Its A.F.B.'

'Anita F. Barton in fact,' said Steve thoughtfully.

'Why, of course!' said Amanda suddenly. 'I remember seeing her drop it. She had it here, in the hall. I suppose Miss Moon picked it up and took it upstairs, meaning to ask whose it was.'

'Mrs Barton seems to be a bit careless with her possessions,' observed Steve grimly. 'Her husband's secretary is found murdered, and a bit of nonsense off Mrs Barton's skirt is discovered in this hall. And if Miss Moon had been found dead tomorrow morning, that handkerchief wouldn't have looked so good; however innocently it came to be there. 'Unless . . . I wonder——'

He twisted it absently about his hand, frowning the while, and after a moment inquired abruptly if Miss Moon always took a jug of barley water up to her bedroom at night.

'She told me that she usually did in the hot weather,' said Amanda. 'She doesn't seem to drink anything else. Euridice makes it fresh every day.'

'Have you ever drunk it?'

'No. Only Miss Moon. But no one else would know that.'

'Oh yes they would. I have a tolerably retentive memory, and someone, either you or Glenn Barton — I think both — mentioned the fact at that lunch party at the Dome. Which means that quite a few people knew of Miss Moon's addiction to barley water, and someone put the knowledge to good use.'

'Like – like Julia,' said Amanda, shivering.

'Julia?'

223

'The lemon juice.'

Steve's face was suddenly blank and unreadable. He looked at Amanda for a moment or two and seemed about to say something, but changed his mind.

Amanda said in a voice that was little more than a whisper: 'You thought that something like this might happen, didn't you?'

'Yes. It had occurred rather forcibly to me that whoever put paid to Monica Ford was going to be scared into next week by the news that Miss Moon had been in the house the entire time. We took certain precautions.'

'Then the house *is* being watched! I thought it was.'

'You could hardly miss it,' said Steve dryly. 'In fact, you were not meant to. The knowledge that the place was bristling with cops would, it was hoped, tend to discourage any rough stuff. And then,' he added bitterly, 'someone walks in right under our noses and plants this neat little booby trap. Mind if I touch you?'

He reached out and laid the tips of his fingers briefly against Amanda's arm.

'What's that for?' inquired Amanda, puzzled.

'For Luck. If it hadn't been for you and that cat of the cook's, Miss Moon would have gone the same way as Julia Blaine. In addition to which you appear to bear a charmed life. You ought by rights to be sliced into small sections and distributed in the form of amulets.'

Amanda said in a small, frightened voice: 'But if there are police watching the house they must know who came in——'

'My dear child,' said Steve impatiently, 'of course they know who came in! And that's the hell of it. I can give you a list myself. Barton was here for most of the morning, and during that time Mrs Halliday and young Gates called round to ask after you and stayed a considerable time. George Norman dropped in to tea and then Anita Barton came in to see you, casually shed her handkerchief on the premises and took you out for a walk. While you were out, a squad of sympathizers that included Claire Norman, Major

224

Blaine and Lumley Potter called round and were actually taken on a conducted tour of the house. That makes quite a nice little list of people, all or any of whom could have easily dropped a slug of poison into the barley water and slipped that bottle under Miss Moon's pillow. The thing was a gift, and I ought to be shot for not thinking of it. I considered a good many other possibilities, but not a repeat performance of a previous flop.'

Amanda said: 'Mrs Barton couldn't have done it. There wasn't time. And she didn't go upstairs.'

Steve lifted his eyes from a contemplation of the exhibits before him and looked thoughtfully at Amanda.

He said: 'Let's hear about that visit of hers again. Details please Exactly when did she arrive and how long was she alone in the hall and where was she standing when you first saw her? Everything.'

Amanda told him all that she could remember; hesitantly but in detail.

Steve leant back in his chair, drove his hands into his pockets and frowned at the ceiling: '*H'mm*. I wonder. She would probably have had plenty of time to doctor the barley water, and as she knew Miss Moon fairly well the odds are that she not only knew about the stuff, but where it was kept. Thirty seconds would have been enough for that job. But from what you say, it sounds impossible for her to have made a quick trip to Miss Moon's bedroom and back in the time. Anyway, the risk would have been too great, for if you'd seen her coming down the stairs you would have been curious, to say the least of it.'

He brooded for a while, rocking his chair gently to and fro until it creaked protestingly, and presently he said in a softly meditative voice: 'I think a few words with the cook-general would be in order. I'll get on to that in the morning. However it begins to look as though Mrs Barton is in the clear, and that means ...'

He did not finish the sentence, and presently began to whistle '*Sur le pont d'Avignon*' very softly through his teeth.

Amanda waited for a minute or two and then, as he did not

speak, asked anxiously: 'What does it mean?'

Mr Howard transferred his gaze from the ceiling to Amanda's white face and said thoughtfully: 'It means that one should not go to Birmingham by way of Beachy Head. In other words, if one wishes to get from A to B with the minimum loss of time and temper, one should stick to the main road and not allow oneself to be lured down intriguing but unprofitable bypaths. An error to which I must regretfully plead guilty.'

'I don't understand,' said Amanda with a catch in her voice.

Steve returned the front legs of his chair to the floor with a crash and stood up:

'God forbid that you should! But I should have known better. I had the whole thing cold, but owing to the entirely fortuitous fact that a varied assortment of emotional crises got mixed into the works, I began to look at this thing from another angle. In fact from several other angles. A mistake, Amarantha. There was only one angle. Just as there was only one person who could possibly have been able to push you over the battlements at Hilarion.'

Amanda said in a small, frightened voice: 'Does that mean that you — you know who it is?'

'I think so,' said Steve soberly. 'But the difficulty is going to be to prove it. The obvious procedure of course is to tie up a kid with the object of luring the tiger. That would probably work all right. But I'm not sure that I'm a good enough shot.'

'You mean – you mean deliberately let a murderer have another try at killing her just so that you could see who it is? Steve, you can't! You can't risk it!'

Steve Howard looked down at her and his face and voice were suddenly and inexplicably raw with anger and bitterness:

'No!' he said savagely. 'I can't risk it. That's the damnable part of it. I should, but I daren't — because I've lost my nerve!'

He stared down at Amanda for a long moment as though he

226

hated her, and then swung round violently and jerking open the door walked out of the room.

A minute or two later Amanda heard him strike a match, and followed him into the hall, bewildered and shaken by his sudden rage.

He was standing with his back to her under the dusty chandelier, the light turning his brown hair to bronze, and he must have heard her but he did not turn.

Amanda waited in silence, studying the back of his head and thinking that she could draw it with her eyes shut, and wondering why this should be so when she had only known him for so short a time? The smoke from his cigarette spiralled up into the still air and the scent of it mingled pleasantly with the smell of beeswax and dust and the tall orange lilies that filled a vast copper jar by the carved chest.

Presently he reached out a hand behind him and drew Amanda absently into the curve of his arm, still without turning his head.

He continued to stand quite still, holding her against him; staring ahead of him and drawing thoughtfully at his cigarette as though his mind were several hundred miles away — as indeed it was.

After a time he looked down, blew a smoke ring at the top of Amanda's head, released her and dropped his cigarette end into the jar of lilies:

'Time you were in bed, Amarantha. And quite time I got back to the Normans'. I am supposedly instructing Miss Moon in the procedure at an inquest, and there is no point in overdoing it. Do you think you can find me an empty bottle that'll take the remains of that barley water?'

'I can try,' said Amanda. She disappeared in the direction of the kitchen and presently returned with a bottle that had once contained cooking sherry.

Steve had gone back into the dining-room and was engaged in

replacing the tablets and wrapping the small bottle in a sheet of paper.

'Is it the same stuff that killed Julia?' asked Amanda in a half-whisper.

'No. That would have been inviting odious comparisons.'

'But there would have been anyway. Because of that bottle——'

'You've forgotten something. You kept quiet about that first bottle. Which is why it was tried again — for the simple reason that having once kept your mouth shut you would have to continue to do so, or else land yourself in an exceedingly nasty spot indeed. An angle which I admit should have occurred to me, but didn't.'

Steve decanted the barley water into the sherry bottle with infinite care and pushed the empty glass over to Amanda.

'Run that under the tap half a dozen times, will you? Oh, and you'd better take this——' He tossed over Anita Barton's torn handkerchief. 'Ask Miss Moon about it in the morning and let me know what she says.'

Amanda nodded and put it in her pocket. She removed the glass and carrying it out into the pantry, rinsed it and left it on the draining board and returned to find Steve waiting for her in the hall.

He glanced at the clock and said: 'See you in court,' and pulled open the front door.

Amanda said with a catch in her voice: 'But aren't you going to call in the police?'

'What for?'

'To tell them about the poison, of course!'

Steve shook his head. 'No. I don't think we'll tell anyone for the moment. Not even Miss Moon.'

'But — but surely whoever did it will try again?'

'Oh, sure to. But not that way. It was a good idea, but it's back-fired twice. Someone is due for an unpleasant headache tomorrow trying to work out what went wrong this time; and because they won't know they will lay off that tack and try another. And I think we can block anything else.'

He saw Amanda throw a quick look over her shoulder at the empty hall behind her and said: 'There's nothing to be frightened of tonight, dear, I promise you. The person who planted that stuff is going to make quite sure of being well in the public eye and surrounded by alibis up to a late hour tonight. Nor are they going to come near the place or ask any questions tomorrow. And in any case, the chaps who are watching this house won't let so much as a bluebottle past them between now and tomorrow morning.'

'They let you in,' said Amanda unsteadily.

'That,' said Mr Howard, 'is different. Word has gone round that I am really Marilyn Monroe in disguise, and they are all hoping to get my autograph.'

He removed himself into the night and Amanda bolted the door behind him and went upstairs to bed; but not to sleep.

17

The inquest on Monica Ford was unexpectedly brief. The jury system did not prevail in Cyprus, and an apparently bored judge listened without much interest to the pathologist's report and an account of the police findings. But Amanda received the unpleasant impression that the perfunctory questions did not add up to lack of interest or any conviction that the comfortable theory that a casual thief had been responsible for the murder was necessarily correct. It seemed more as though the officials involved were acting under orders, and she wondered uneasily if someone was being lulled into a false sense of security.

The proceedings had been too smooth — too suave. The voices too silkily polite and the eyes too hard and watchful.

They were all there. Claire and George, Persis and Toby, Alastair and Glenn, Lumley and Anita, Steve, Miss Moon and herself.

Amanda had found that she too was watching them with furtive, frightened eyes, afraid that one face might betray surprise or fear at the sight of Miss Moon. But she had surprised no such expression and did not know whether to be relieved or sorry.

She and Steve Howard had described the finding of Miss Ford's body, and Glenn had told of his meeting with his secretary earlier that afternoon and explained about her brother's death and her recent agitation of mind. He had not looked at his wife, and no further questions had been put to him beyond asking him for the time of his departure from Hilarion and his arrival at Nicosia. The latter had been corroborated, according to the police, by the two young National Service men to whom he had given a lift, and the various members of the picnic party had confirmed the times of his arrival and departure from Hilarion.

Miss Moon had stated that owing to an attack of migraine she had, in fact, been in the bedroom in the Villa Oleander throughout the afternoon, but had heard nothing beyond the sound of a woman's voice raised in apparent agitation some time during the earlier part of the afternoon.

They had accepted the statement without comment and had returned unexpectedly to Amanda. They had asked her four questions, and this time the suave voices had been considerably less suave.

Was it true that she had seen a great deal of Major Blaine in Fayid?

Was it true that Mrs Blaine had died in her cabin on the way to Cyprus?

Was it true that she had been alone in the drawing-room of the Villa Oleander for several minutes — perhaps five or even ten? — before Mr Howard had found her standing beside the body of Miss Ford?

What dress had she worn that day, and would she describe it?

The room had been stiflingly hot and airless and it was pleasant to get into the open again and feel a faint breath of breeze and smell the scent of sunbaked dust and flowering trees.

Miss Moon declined an invitation from the Normans to return to their house for a glass of sherry, and announced her intention of returning home immediately. Andreas was driving her in her own elderly car, and Toby had offered Amanda a lift. Miss Moon went over to talk to Persis Halliday, and someone touched Amanda's arm and she turned to see Glenn Barton.

'I haven't had a chance to talk to you before,' said Glenn in a low voice. 'I wanted to thank you. For saying what you did. I – can't tell you how grateful I am. I know I shouldn't have let you do it, but — well I think you're a brick!'

231

Amanda said quickly: 'Don't Glenn. Anyone would have done the same; but not many people would have risked their necks for me at Hilarion. And I never even thanked you for that.'

Glenn Barton smiled at her and held out his hand. 'Shall we call it quits?'

Amanda put her hand into his, and an exceedingly dry voice behind them said: 'I'm sorry to interrupt you, but I'd like a word with Miss Derington.'

Amanda snatched her hand away and turning quickly looked up into Steven Howard's face and experienced a sudden shock of dismay.

Steve was looking at her as though she were some complete and not particularly attractive stranger whom necessity compelled him to address, and his voice was cold and remote and entirely devoid of expression.

He said: 'I understand that you have a guardian who is at present somewhere in the Middle East. I suggest that you write to him as soon as possible and ask him to come over.'

Amanda stared at him, bewildered. 'But – but why?'

'Because it looks as though you are going to need some responsible person to advise you. You made a statement to the police two nights ago that was entirely untrue and which looks like leading to a lot of trouble.'

He threw a glance of cold dislike at Glenn Barton, and continued curtly:

'In these circumstances I think that you would be well advised to let your uncle know what is going on, and let him decide if he thinks it is worth coming over or not. You won't find that it is in the least amusing being mixed up in a murder case in this part of the world.'

'But he's in Tripoli!' said Amanda.

'I know. Miss Moon told me. That's why I wanted to speak to you. I have a friend in the R.A.F. here who happens to be flying to Tripoli tomorrow, so if you can let me have a letter before midday tomorrow I'll see that your uncle gets it the same evening. He can probably pull enough strings to get here by Monday or Tuesday at the latest. Think it over.'

Steve turned on his heel and walked away and Amanda stared after him; helplessly aware that there were tears in her eyes, and restraining herself with a strong effort from running after him to catch at his arm and demand to know why he had looked at her and spoken to her like that? He could not be jealous of Glenn Barton! — he could not be. Couldn't he *see*——?

Glenn said soberly: 'He's right you know. You ought to let Mr Derington know about this. Would you like me to cable him instead?'

Amanda winked the tears from her eyes and said: 'I – I'll think about it.'

She did not believe for one moment that she was in any danger of arrest. The idea was too ludicrous to be entertained even for a second. She had not, as Glenn Barton and several others had, taken in the significance of those three final questions, and she did not think of them now. She could only think of Steve's face and voice and feel hurt and bewildered and angry.

A police officer came up and spoke to Glenn Barton and Glenn excused himself and they walked away together and re-entered the building.

There was a jingle of bracelets and Miss Moon patted Amanda's arm with a be-ringed hand and said affectionately: 'There, there dear. You must not mind. He is not in the least annoyed with you. Only with himself. And with Glenn of course. Gentlemen are *so* foolish!'

Amanda laughed a little shakily and said: 'You don't miss much, do you Miss Moon?'

'No dear. It is only the young who seem unable to see what is under their noses. Of course he knows quite well that you cannot really have the slightest interest in poor Glenn, but I think that he has a great deal on his mind and that it annoys him to realize that he cannot prevent his attention being distracted by – by extraneous emotions, shall we say?'

'Not extraneous emotions,' corrected Amanda with a somewhat watery chuckle. ' "Unprofitable by-paths".'

'Is that what he said, dear? Well there you are! What did I tell you. And now, as I understand that Captain Gates wishes to drive you back to Kyrenia, I think I will return home. I shall be seeing you for luncheon.'

She turned away as Persis and Toby, who had been buttonholed by Lumley Potter, detached themselves at last and came towards Amanda. A few yards away George Norman, Alastair Blaine and Claire were standing on the kerb in a patch of shadow talking to Steve Howard who was sitting at the wheel of his car. Amanda noted resentfully that he appeared to be in excellent spirits and that the group beside his car, despite the fact — or possibly in reaction to it — that they had just been attending an inquiry into murder, were laughing at something that he had just said.

Anita Barton was standing by herself, a little apart. She was looking forlorn and unhappy and there were dark shadows under her eyes. Her usual air of defiant disregard for public opinion was entirely lacking and she looked noticeably ill at ease.

Amanda, studying her, saw that she was not quite steady on her feet and suspected that she had been drinking — perhaps to give herself courage to face the curious gaze of those who knew how much she had disliked her husband's secretary.

Persis, looking as usual like an advertisement for Saks, Fifth Avenue, caught Amanda's arm in an affectionate clasp and said in plangent tones: 'Well honey, how does it feel to be Suspect Number One?'

'Shut up, Persis!' said Toby crossly. 'Your humour is misplaced. Come on Amanda darling, we're all going along to the Normans' to get drunk. Only possible course, after a session like that.'

'Who's "all"?' inquired Amanda.

'The gang, honey,' supplied Persis. 'The Associated Society of

Suspects. Little did I think when I decided on visiting the birth-place of Venus that all I should get handed in lieu of Love would be a coupla' corpses. It's time the boys at the Tourist Bureau rewrote that "Come to Sunny Cyprus!" stuff, and urged the prospective visitor to pack a gat and bring a lawyer with them.'

'The trouble with you, Persis,' said Toby sourly, 'is that you can't really believe anything you don't see with your own eyes. None of this is any more real to you than one of your own stories, merely because you never saw the bodies of either Julia Blaine or this secretary woman.'

'And did you, Toby dear?' inquired Persis softly.

'No. But Amanda did.'

Persis turned swiftly to Amanda and said contritely: 'He's right. I keep forgetting what heck and hades it must have been for you honey. What would like me to do? Prostrate myself on the pave-ment as a penance, or dedicate my next book "To Amanda, who stole all my beaux"?'

'Meaning Toby?' inquired Amanda with a smile. 'Was he your beau?'

'He certainly was. But humiliating as it is to own it, I am compelled to classify him as one of the ones that got away.'

'What you really mean is one of the ones you couldn't even bother to gaff,' said Toby, lifting one of her hands and kissing it.

'Toby! What a Continental gesture!' exclaimed Persis in mock admiration. 'I had no idea that——' She broke off and said rather sharply: 'Say, what's bitten Glenn?'

Amanda, turning to follow the direction of her gaze, saw Glenn Barton come quickly out into the sunlight, and realized what had prompted that startled exclamation.

Glenn's mouth was compressed into a tight line and he looked frightened and desperate. He stood for a moment looking about him with his eyes narrowed against the glare, and then seeing his wife walked swiftly over to her and put a hand on her arm.

'Anita——'

Anita Barton whirled about, her face white under its heavy make-up, and almost in the same movement she wrenched his hand from her arm and turned as though to walk away.

Glenn's hand shot out and he caught her arm again and swung her round to face him. 'Anita, please! I've got to talk to you. Just for a few minutes. It's for your own sake. Darling *please*.'

His voice was hoarse and desperate and he appeared to be entirely oblivious of the fact that his words were perfectly audible to everyone within a dozen yards and that at least as many inquisitive, interested or appalled pairs of eyes were openly watching him.

An ugly wave of colour flooded up into Anita Barton's livid face and she wrenched herself from his grasp and struck him across the face with the full force of her arm. She stood there for a moment staring at him, her breath coming fast, and then turned on her heel and walked rapidly away, leaving her husband standing in the bright sunlight with the red marks of her fingers showing clearly against his haggard face.

Persis was the first to recover herself and to rush in where angels might justifiably have feared to tread. She went swiftly across to him and said: 'Why, Glenn Barton — I thought you'd gone!' and slipping her hand through his arm almost forcibly turned him round: 'Have you got a car here? Because if you have, you've gotten yourself a passenger. Will you take me some place to get a drink before I drop dead from sunstroke?'

Glenn looked at her with a dazed expression, and then seemed suddenly to focus her, for he smiled a stiff-lipped puzzled smile and said: 'Why – why of course, Mrs——?'

'Persis,' supplied Persis briskly. 'Is that your car over there? Good. Let's go.'

She led him firmly away, talking animatedly and at random, and the entertainment was over.

Steve Howard's car, followed by the Normans', slid away down the road. Lumley Potter hurried off in the wake of Anita Barton, and Amanda, suddenly deciding that she could not bear the prospect of a social gathering at the Normans', asked Toby to drive her instead to the Villa Oleander.

She was feeling mentally and physically exhausted, and by two-thirty was much inclined to follow Miss Moon's example and retire to her bedroom for a siesta. She was still considering the advisability of this course when she heard someone run quickly up the front steps and walk into the hall without knocking. It was Glenn.

'Amanda——!' He gave a quick gasp of relief at the sight of her. 'Amanda, can I talk to you please? Somewhere where we can't be overheard?'

His voice was jerky and uncontrolled and he appeared driven to the verge of collapse. Amanda looked at him for a long moment and then turned without a word and led the way into the drawing-room.

He came in after her, and shutting the door, leant against it.

'What is it, Glenn?'

'Anita,' said Glenn desperately. 'She won't see me. She doesn't understand! Amanda, I know she didn't kill Monica. I *know* she didn't. She may do rash, silly things, but she *could* not kill. I tell you I *know*. Good God! — who should know, if I don't? I don't pretend to know what she was doing in this house that day; she must have been here I suppose, because of that hellish flower. But whatever the reason, it can have had nothing to do with Monica Ford's death. She probably came in to see you, or Miss Moon, and found Monica dead, and panicked. No one could blame her for that!'

Amanda said urgently: 'Glenn, don't stand there. Come and sit down here and tell me what has happened. There's no sense in tearing yourself to pieces like this.'

Glenn laughed. It was a short, curiously wavering laugh that had no amusement in it. He walked unsteadily to the sofa and sank down on it as though his knees had suddenly given way under him.

Amanda looked at him with an anxious frown and left the room

237

abruptly; returning a moment later with a glass containing a stiff proportion of Miss Moon's brandy. Glenn took it from her hand and gulped it down gratefully.

'You're a brick, Amanda. I seem to have said that a good many times of late, don't I?'

He looked up at her with a crooked attempt at a smile and Amanda said: 'What is it, Glenn? What has happened?'

'The police,' said Glenn wretchedly. 'It's that damnable flower. I think they've found out who it belongs to. They asked me if I'd recognized it. And — they asked a hell of a lot of other questions too. About her quarrel with Monica, and wasn't it true that she had told me that either I sacked Monica or she'd leave me, and – and that when I wouldn't, she had left me. They went over and over it. And then they – they wanted to know if I knew that she was friendly with Major Blaine——'

'With *Alastair!*'

'Yes. Oh, I know they asked you the same thing, but that was just routine. This was far more serious.'

Glenn stood up abruptly, and walking over to the french windows stood staring blindly out across the garden, his back to Amanda.

He said in a harsh, jerky voice: 'They suggested that she knew him rather well and that – that his wife's death had made him a rich man. They pointed out that she — Anita——' His voice failed suddenly and Amanda saw his shoulders jerk in a small shudder. Presently he said in a more normal voice:

'They wanted to know if she could have got her hands on any poisons, and asked if it were true that her father had been a doctor. They – they seemed to know so many things. I got scared then, and I tried to talk to her, but she wouldn't speak to me——'

His voice held a sudden hurt, bewildered note. He turned and walked back to Amanda and stood looking down at her, his hands clenching and unclenching at his sides, and said in a flat, exhausted voice: 'I know I shouldn't ask you — I know it's an unforgivable thing to do, but I can't think of any other way out. Will you help me?'

'Yes,' said Amanda, lightly and quite steadily.

Glenn stooped quickly and lifting her hand, kissed it. 'Bless you!' There was a sudden break in his voice.

'What do you want me to do?'

'Persuade her to go away. Lumley's a useless fool. He'll be no help to her. She must get away for a while; to give them time to find out who really did kill Monica.'

'But Glenn, how can I! Persuade her to go where?'

'Lebanon. We have friends there who I know would take her in. And I've got a good many friends among the local fishermen here. I could arrange all that; if only she could be persuaded to go.'

Amanda looked at him with a crease between her brows. She said slowly: 'Glenn you know that won't work. You must know that if they are suspicious of her, and she disappears, it would only confirm their suspicions, because then they'd be sure that she had done it.'

'Yes,' said Glenn heavily. 'I know.'

'Then – then there must be some other reason why you want to get her away. What is it?'

Even as she spoke she was aware of a sudden suspicion that Glenn, whatever he might say to the contrary, was secretly and terribly afraid that his wife might just possibly be more deeply involved than he would admit.

Glenn lifted his tired, red-rimmed eyes to hers and looked at her for a long moment. And when he spoke it was in a voice that was so low that it was barely audible:

'Yes. There is another reason. There is something about all this that I don't understand, and it frightens me. You see I think – I think there is going to be another murder. An attempt at one anyway. If I'm right, there's got to be.'

He heard Amanda catch her breath and did not know that she

was remembering that Steve had said almost those same words that night on the harbour wall.

Glenn said: 'Perhaps I'm wrong. I hope I am. But I'm beginning to think that there's — oh, I don't know — something behind all this. A plan. Something that may even have been worked out a long time ago. But now it hasn't gone right, and someone who still means to go through with it is getting frightened and needs a scapegoat. That's why I want to get Anita away. Because I think that she is playing straight into — someone's hands. Once she is safe with friends in the Lebanon, whoever is trying to hide behind her will have to think of something else. And then, if there is another attempt, we can tell the police at once where she is and why she went there. She'll be safe then. But I can't guard against something that I can only sense and guess at, but not see ...'

His voice died out in a whisper and Amanda said quickly: 'You think you know who it is, don't you?'

He did not answer, and she repeated the question. Glenn's eyes came back to her again.

'Yes.'

'Who?' There was an odd tremor in Amanda's voice.

Glenn shook his head. 'I wouldn't tell you, even if I were sure — and I'm not. It might be dangerous. And I can't be sure; not yet. I think that there is a way to find out, but I daren't use it as long as Anita is here to – to pin things on. Once it cannot possibly be her, then it must be someone else. You do see that, don't you? That would prove it.'

Amanda was conscious of a sudden stab of fear and a vivid recollection of Steve Howard's words about tying up a kid to lure the tiger. So Glenn intended to use himself to lure a tiger into another killing. And provided Anita was safely out of the Island, even if he failed to avoid death himself, it would at least be proof that she was in no way responsible. But he must not do that! — it was too foolhardy a risk. Steve had said 'a killer knows quite well that even if he kills a dozen people, or twenty, he himself can only hang once'. Someone who had killed twice would not hesitate to kill again.

She said breathlessly: 'You can't do it, Glenn. If it's dangerous for Anita it's just as dangerous for you.'

'Me? Oh I can look after myself. But Anita's got no one but that ass Lumley. I've *got* to get her out of it. If I can only do that, without anyone knowing or even guessing that she's gone, there is a chance.'

'But Glenn! even if you do, don't you see that if someone is really trying to pin this on Anita, and – and nothing else happens, and she has disappeared, their object is achieved?'

'Anita's suicide would achieve it in a far more final and satisfactory manner,' said Glenn grimly.

'*Suicide!*'

'Yes. An artistically staged suicide. It wouldn't be so very difficult to arrange. Anita found dead: verdict, suicide rather than face trial and conviction for murder.'

'*No!*' said Amanda in a whisper. 'Oh no, it couldn't be——'

But she knew that it could. Once again she saw, in an ugly flash of memory, Julia Blaine lifting an innocuous, frosted glass, drinking from it, and dying. Felt again the little hard lump of a bottle under her pillow, and stared down with wide, frozen eyes at a similar bottle that had lain under Miss Moon's pillow only last night.

Glenn was quite right. Someone needed a scapegoat, and Anita Barton's death — supposedly by her own hand — would tie up a good many loose ends in a very neat and final manner.

Glenn said: 'She may refuse to go. If she does — well I shall just have to think of something else. But if you can persuade her——'

'I'll try,' said Amanda unsteadily.

Glenn turned quickly away and began to pace up and down the room, his hands in his pockets and frowning concentration on his face. Presently he came to a stop in front of her again

241

and said abruptly: 'It must be tonight. Tomorrow may be too late. If she agrees, would you help her to go? To see that she is safe.'

'Yes.'

'Can you drive a car?'

Amanda nodded.

'Then this is what we'll do. I'll leave a car on the road tonight — against the kerb by that open bit of ground on the main road about fifty yards below the turn out of this road, opposite that house with the blue shutters. If you can get Anita to agree, tell her to take only what she can carry, and to give out that she's got a bit of a headache and intends to go to bed early. There's a little cove just beyond the five-mile beach on the road to Larnaca. Anita will know it. I'll get Yiannopoulos to be there with a boat not later than ten. It will mean leaving here around nine-thirty, which will give her an alibi from then on, as you would be with her. And as it's in the opposite direction from Nicosia, if anything should happen tonight they can't think——' He checked abruptly and then said: 'As soon as she's away, drive back here and leave the car in the same place. I'll pick it up later. There's only one other thing . . .'

Glenn pushed his hand wearily through his hair and his mouth twisted bitterly:

'You'll have to pretend that it's your own idea, or Miss Moon's. If she thinks that I've had anything to do with it, she won't touch it. Just at the moment I really believe that she'd rather be arrested for murder than be beholden to me. You see she doesn't understand. She thinks that she can do what she likes and get away with it. She doesn't realize that murder is a deadly thing.'

Once again the words brought an echo of Steven Howard. Steve standing in the bright moonlight on the harbour wall with his arms about Amanda and saying: 'Murder is a diabolical thing.'

Amanda said: 'I'll do my best.'

'I know you will. Make her see that it's serious. Don't let her brush it aside and take the line that nothing can really happen to her.'

Amanda nodded wordlessly.

Glenn said: 'I can't thank you enough, dear. I shouldn't risk getting you involved in anything; I know that. But I'm in a corner. If I could think of any other way out I'd take it; but I can't.'

He was silent for a moment or two, and then his mouth twisted in a wry smile and he said: 'I did try one other way. But it didn't work and I only made rather an ass of myself.' The smile faded and he said: 'The car will be there at nine o' clock. If Anita won't go, well——'

He shrugged his shoulders and turned away, and a moment later Amanda heard the hall door close behind him.

18

Amanda came out on to the quay and walked slowly in the direction of the café at the corner of the harbour.

She felt curiously exhausted, but her exhaustion was mixed with a feeling of elation. Anita Barton had been difficult and suspicious and more than a little tipsy. But she had been frightened too, and it was her fear that had tipped the scales. She had agreed to go.

Amanda had succeeded in convincing her that she and Miss Moon were responsible for the scheme, and perhaps it was Miss Moon's name that had brought about Anita Barton's sudden capitulation. That, and the fact that Amanda had reported the gist of the questions the police had asked Glenn Barton about his wife, hinting mendaciously that they had been put to Miss Moon. She had also allowed it to be supposed that Miss Moon had arranged with the owner of a fishing boat to convey Anita away from the Island; it being unlikely that she herself would have been able to arrange such a thing.

She was to pick up Mrs Barton at a turn of the road near the Post Office at half past nine. Less than half an hour's driving would bring them to the beach where the boat was to wait, and that would give them an ample margin in which to get from the road to the shore — a matter of less than a hundred yards of rough ground and rocks.

The sun was setting in a blaze of gold and rose and apricot and the tall, picturesque houses that ringed the harbour threw long lilac shadows across the quays and the quiet water. A church bell was ringing and from the minaret of a mosque a muezzin intoned the call to prayer.

Amanda turned down the sea wall of the harbour and sat down tiredly on the warm stone. She wished desperately that she could discuss the coming night's work with someone. Glenn had not bound her to secrecy in the matter; but then he would not have considered such a course necessary. It was so obvious that if danger threatened Anita Barton, her departure must not be known or talked about.

Amanda thought longingly and resentfully of Steven Howard. Steve at least would be safe. She could have gone to him and asked for his advice and help. But she could not forget the caustic words that he had spoken only last night on the subject of Glenn Barton: 'Dear Glenn would appear to make a habit of getting his girlfriends to pull his chestnuts out of the fire for him.'

Mr Howard, apprised of the present situation, would undoubtedly consider that dear Glenn had no right to ask Amanda to involve herself in anything that might conceivably be dangerous, and be correspondingly scathing on the subject. He would, in addition, refuse to allow her to have anything whatever to do with the scheme, and might even take steps to prevent Anita Barton leaving the Island. However, even if she had wished to tell him, she could not, for she had passed him on her way to the harbour. He had been driving up the main road that led out of Kyrenia towards Nicosia, and though he had undoubtedly seen her, he had given no sign of having done so.

Amanda sighed and rested her chin on her hand.

A shadow fell across her and a cheerful voice said: 'What's eating you honey? Is it love — or indigestion?'

Amanda turned quickly. 'Persis you beast! You've nearly made me bite my tongue in half? No it isn't love — *or* indigestion. And nothing's eating me.'

'No? Then you're lucky!'

Persis subsided gracefully on the sea wall beside Amanda and said abruptly: 'Honey, I'm worried.'

Amanda turned sideways to look at her and saw that Persis was staring out to sea, her white forehead wrinkled in a frown.

'What's worrying you?'

'It's Glenn,' confessed Persis. 'You know, I like that guy. I like him quite a lot. He makes me feel all maternal; and that's something I've certainly never felt about anyone before. Maybe it's a sign of old age!'

Amanda said cautiously: 'What has he been doing now?'

'Acting like a fool!' said Persis with unexpected violence. 'Do you know what that crazy guy did this morning? He walked right back to see the police and confessed to murdering his secretary!'

'He *what*? He must be mad!'

'That's right. Plain cuckoo! I tried to drag him out. Told the boys he'd had a brain storm. But he had it all doped out and he was perfectly sober about it. Talked away as cool as a mint julep in July. Said he had not gone straight back to Nicosia from Hilarion after all. He'd lied about it. He'd waited out of sight until George's car had turned down to Kyrenia, and then followed it, gone into Miss Moon's, strangled this dame and streaked for home. So they asked him what about the two hitch-hikers he'd given a lift to? And he had that taped too. Said he'd put back the hands of the dashboard clock to fake an alibi, and the boys had taken their time from that. He said it had been preying on his mind, and asked to be arrested.'

'What happened then?' demanded Amanda breathlessly. 'Why didn't they arrest him?'

'Because they aren't that dumb,' said Persis with a sigh. 'They'd thought of that one too. They turned up the statements of the two guys, and the thing came unstuck at once. Seems the boys hadn't taken their time from any dashboard clock — it's busted anyway. They both had wrist-watches and they swear to the time they got back. Glenn tried to argue it, but the cops threw him out with the

246

greatest charm. I thought he was going to cry, and I don't mind telling you honey that it was all I could do not to put my arms round him and kiss him right there in the roadway and say: "There, there, son! Tell Momma all about it and she'll see that you're arrested for murder if that's the way you want it!" And what I want to know,' said Persis with feeling, 'is am I nuts, or is he?'

'So *that's* what he meant!' said Amanda, enlightened.

'How's that?'

'Nothing much. Just something he said about trying something, but that it hadn't been any use and he'd only made rather a fool of himself.'

'When did he say that?' demanded Persis quickly. 'Have you seen him this afternoon?'

'Yes,' said Amanda hesitantly.

She looked at Persis Halliday, frowning and uncertain. Persis could never have seen or heard of Anita Barton until that afternoon on the S.S. *Orantares* at Port Said, and could not previously have been aware of her existence, or that of Monica Ford. She had never been to Cyprus before, and she could have no possible reason for wanting to pin a murder — two murders! — on Glenn Barton's wife.

Quite suddenly Amanda made up her mind. The terror and strain and emotional tension of the last few days had been too much for her, and she had to confide in someone. It should have been Steve, but Steve had been curt and unkind, and he had apparently gone to Nicosia.

Amanda said: 'Persis, if I tell you something, will you promise me that you won't tell anyone else? — anyone at all?'

Persis looked at her for a long moment with narrowed speculative eyes, and then held out her hand. It was a strong hand, with long, intelligent, square-tipped fingers, and its clasp was comfortably firm and reassuring.

'Shoot!' said Persis laconically.

She listened to Amanda's account of the afternoon's interview with enthralled interest, and when it was finished said: 'Well if this doesn't beat Erle Stanley Gardner! When do we start?'

'We?' echoed Amanda.

'Sure. I'm going with you. You don't really think I'm going to let you stick your neck out like this without standing by with a blackjack just in case anyone tries any rough stuff? Why I wouldn't miss it for a million dollars! I'm in on this, honey, and you can't get me out.'

Amanda laughed, conscious of a sudden and overwhelming flood of relief. She would not have admitted to anyone how little the thought of that coming night's adventure had appealed to her, or how frightening she had found the prospect of that long, lonely drive back to Kyrenia. But now that Persis would be with her the affair lost its terrors, and became instead merely an exciting escapade.

Amanda threw an arm about Persis and gave her a sudden and impulsive hug.

'Persis, you're an angel!'

'So I have frequently been informed,' said Persis dryly. 'And now let's take a stroll up to that villa of yours and break it to Miss Moon that you will be dining with me at the Dome. Then there will no hitch over getting to that car on time. What do you say?'

They scrambled to their feet and carried out this programme, and Amanda, not without some qualms, left Miss Moon to dine alone. She reassured herself, however, with the reflection that Steve Howard would have taken every possible precaution to safeguard Miss Moon from further danger, and was relieved to see that the usual loiterer was industriously engaged in doing nothing at the corner of the road.

They met Alastair Blaine coming out of the Dome. He appeared to be in a hurry and said that he had a date to dine at Antonakis' Restaurant in Nicosia.

'I'm told that the speciality is octopus,' said Alastair. 'I've always wanted not to eat octopus, but life catches up on one. I'll probably be seeing you sometime tomorrow — if I survive!'

Persis said: 'Who's your date with, Alastair?' But Alastair was already striding rapidly away into the dusk, and it is doubtful whether he heard the question.

Claire came out of Zari's lace shop opposite the hotel, and seeing them, waved, but did not come over to speak to them and also appeared to be in a hurry.

They saw no one else they knew, beyond a few hotel acquaintances of Persis Halliday's, and Lumley Potter, who was eating a lonely meal in a far corner of the dining-room, and who left early. Anita had evidently thought it best to send him out for the evening. There was no sign of either Toby Gates or Steven Howard, both of whom were obviously dining elsewhere that night.

The lingered over their meal as long as they could, but the hands of the clock seemed to crawl and stop and crawl again. Even Persis began to be affected by tension, for she lit one cigarette from the next in endless succession, jerking the ash on to the floor with nervous fingers and fidgeting restlessly in her chair.

At last it was nine o'clock and Persis glanced at the tiny diamond-ringed dial of her wrist-watch, checked it with a hotel clock, and rose:

'Let's go.'

They went first to her room where Persis fetched a thin tussore silk coat from the cupboard and peered intently at her face in the looking-glass. She tied a chiffon scarf over her smoothly waved hair, applied some lipstick with careful concentration, and declared herself ready.

They walked up through the town, and were pausing at the junction of two roads when George Norman passed them, driving his car. As he slowed down for the cross traffic, the headlights of an approaching car fell full on him, and they saw that his pleasant, rubicund face was looking as sulky as that of a small boy whose play has been interrupted by a request to help with the washing up. He did not see Persis and Amanda, but drove on up the main road out of Kyrenia.

'A dime'll get you a dollar that Teeny Weeny Claire has sent him out to run errands,' commented Persis with a grin. 'What that guy needs is a nice bellhop's outfit with a dandy set of buttons down the front. Then he'd be right in character.'

They found a car parked in a patch of shadow near the edge of the vacant lot. But it was not Glenn's car.

'Sure this is it?' inquired Persis, speaking entirely unintentionally in a whisper.

'It must be. It's empty and the key's in it. He wouldn't have left his own, because his wife would have recognized it.'

'You're dead right. Okay, get in. I'd better sit in the back and put up a silent prayer that this contraption does not belong to some honest but absent-minded citizen who has chosen an unfortunate spot to park his jalopy. I do not fancy the prospect of spending the rest of my stay in Aphrodite's Island in the can!'

Amanda settled herself behind the wheel and turned on the dashboard lights. The ignition key was already in place, and she switched on the engine and pressed the self-starter. A moment later the car moved softly off down the road.

Anita Barton was waiting in the shadow of a jacaranda tree. She wore a dark linen coat and a scarf over her head, and was carrying a small suitcase.

Amanda threw open the car door and the next moment Mrs Barton was beside her, breathing quickly and shivering with fear or tension. She slammed the door behind her, and as the car drew away from the kerb, caught sight of Persis Halliday's reflection in the windscreen and whipped round with a choking cry that was almost a scream.

'*Who's that!*'

'It's all right,' said Amanda quickly. 'It's only Mrs Halliday. She's a friend of mine. She came along to – keep me company on the way back.'

'I don't think we've met,' said Persis sociably. 'I'm pleased to know you. I hope you won't think I'm butting in, but I thought maybe Amanda could do with a bit of support. It's going to be a long ride home.'

'You're an American, aren't you?' said Anita Barton in a hard voice.

'Dyed in the wool,' said Persis.

Mrs Barton fell silent, but it was not a relaxed silence. She sat tense and quivering, and every now and again she threw a quick, hunted look over her shoulder as if she feared to see the headlights of a pursuing car. Twice a car overtook them and passed in a cloud of dust, and she cowered down in her seat; bending her head so that her features were hidden by the dashboard.

The winding road and the olive groves, and the steep stony sides of the Kyrenia range, were milky with moonlight. The sea was a placid sheet of polished silver, and the night was warm and white and wonderful. The road dipped and turned and climbed through the streets of little white-walled villages and fell away into minia-ture valleys where small stone culverts spanned the stony beds of streams; and the miles unwound behind them ...

'We're nearly there,' said Anita Barton, speaking for the first time in almost twenty minutes. 'Stop here. By those trees. We can see from here if the road is clear and if it's safe to go on.'

Amanda pulled the car to a stop where a ragged clump of scrub and casurina trees made a pool of freckled shadow.

'Turn off the lights,' commanded Anita Barton in a harsh whisper.

Amanda switched them off obediently, but left the engine running softly as Mrs Barton opened the car door and stepped out into the moonlit road and Persis and Amanda followed her.

The shore lay some fifty yards or so to the left of the road and was separated from them by a stretch of rock-strewn ground covered with coarse grasses, stunted shrubs and mulberry trees.

Anita Barton spoke in a whisper: 'I'm going to walk to the turn

251

of the road to see if all's clear. Sometimes there are picnic parties here on moonlight nights. Miss Derington had better stay by the car. You' — she turned to Persis — 'will you go to the cliff edge and see if you can see a boat out there? It should be off the rocks about half a mile ahead. You can see straight across from this point. We won't go on if it isn't there.'

'Okay,' said Persis with a sigh. 'I guess it will ruin my nylons to say nothing of my nerves, but it's all in a good cause.'

She turned away and vanished into the shadows of the casurina scrub, her high-heeled slippers making no sound in the soft, sandy soil beyond the road's edge.

Anita Barton waited for a moment or two and then walked round to the front of the car. She stopped suddenly and bent down, and Amanda heard her catch her breath.

'What is it?' asked Amanda sharply.

'*Look!*' said Anita Barton in a frightened whisper.

Amanda ran round to her and bent down, staring at the white, dusty road where Anita Barton's trembling finger pointed.

'What is it?' she said. 'I don't see——'

And then she saw the shadow on the moonlit road.

Anita Barton's shadow. A shadow that held something in its hand and swung its arm silently upward and swiftly down again.

Amanda tried to turn, but it was too late. Something crashed with a cruel force on to the back of her bent head and she fell forward into blackness and lay sprawling on the moonlit road.

Anita Barton laughed. A soft, unsteady, hysterical sound in that silver silence.

She looked behind her with wide, panic-stricken eyes, but there was no sound or sign of Persis Halliday, and she turned back to Amanda and stooping down, gripped her by the shoulders and half dragged, half lifted her into the car. She closed the door on her, ran round and climbed into the driver's seat and released the brake.

The car slid away with barely a sound down the moonlit road, its lights still switched off — a grey shadow in the black and white and silver of the night. At the bottom of a long slope the road swung round a curve and began to climb again, and the car, having gathered speed, took the gradient at fifty and roared on down the coast road with the needle of the speedometer touching seventy-five.

The rush of the night air revived Amanda and she stirred and moaned with pain and opened her eyes.

For a minute or two she could not remember where she was, or think of anything but the agonizing pain of her head. It seemed to her that she was looking into a red haze shot with stabbing scarlet lights. Then the haze lifted slowly and the night air was cool and pleasant against her throbbing forehead, and she remembered Anita Barton's shadow on the moonlit road ...

Anita had hit her with something; something hard and heavy and made of metal. But the thick coils of her hair had cushioned her from the full force of the savage blow.

Anita——

Amanda lifted her head slowly and painfully and saw Anita Barton's face in the faint glow of the dashboard light. A white mask of a face, the red lips drawn back over the teeth in a purely animal grimace. There was a touch of froth at the corners of that mouth and the wide eyes were fixed and glaring and bright with fear.

She felt Amanda stir, and turned her head. The next moment she had taken her foot from the accelerator and jammed on the brakes.

The car screeched to a standstill and the shock of its sudden stop flung Amanda's numbed body forward against the dashboard.

Anita Barton drew something out of her pocket, and the moonlight glinted along the barrel of a heavy service revolver.

'Don't do anything silly,' she warned, her voice harsh and high and uncontrolled.

She put up her left hand and tore at the silk scarf that was tied

253

about her head, jerked it free and said: 'Turn round with your back to me and put your hands behind you. Quickly!'

Amanda, with that cold ring of metal thrust against her, obeyed numbly. She felt Anita Barton's hot unsteady fingers winding the silk about her wrists and wrenching the knots painfully tight, and realized that she must temporarily have laid aside the gun.

'That's right,' Mrs Barton's voice was panting and breathless. 'Now your ankles.' She dragged Amanda over roughly and tied her ankles with a length of cord that she must have brought with her and then savagely and unexpectedly thrust a handkerchief into Amanda's gasping mouth and wound another length of material across it, pulling down her hair with a ruthless hand so that it would not impede the tightness of the gag. It was quite obvious that she had made her preparations with some care.

'There!' said Anita Barton with breathless satisfaction.

She stared down into Amanda's wide, terror-filled eyes and laughed long and loudly; a high, hysterical laugh.

'So you're another of Glenn's girls, are you. You planned this with him, didn't you? Darling Glenn! What a fool you must have thought me! So he's going to wait for me with a boat, is he? He's going to get a surprise. The very last surprise of his life. He arranged it all so beautifully, didn't he? But he's the one who is going to disappear. Not me. I've kept this gun for him. I thought of using it on myself once, but I shall use it on him instead. It *was* Glenn who put you up to this, wasn't it? — *wasn't it!* Of course it was. Well it's the last thing he'll do. You thought you'd fooled me, didn't you? All that stuff about doing this for my sake; for my safety; when all the time you were doing it for the sake of dear Glenn. Why you little——!'

She used an unprintable word. Her eyes were not sane and her face was ash-white in the moonlight and contorted with rage and fear — the rage and fear of a hunted animal turning at bay. She glared at Amanda, her breast heaving with her panting breath, and suddenly and unexpectedly she laughed again and turned to release the brake.

She drove more slowly now; and presently, at the top of a rise, switched off the engine and let the car coast down a long, gentle sloping stretch of road, and braked it softly near the edge of a patch of shadow thrown by some tall, windworn rocks.

She sat quite still, listening intently, and after a moment or two opened the car door and slipped out.

She turned and looked back at Amanda and said in a whisper that was barely a breath of sound: 'When you hear a shot you'll know that you've helped dear Glenn to a death that will probably be painful. I've never used a gun before, so I shall make quite sure I don't miss him. You can stay here and listen for it. I'll deal with you later.'

She turned away and moved silently out into the moonlight to vanish down a narrow, sandy track between tumbled rocks that led to a low headland, some fifty yards distant, below which the unseen sea purred softly against a shelving beach.

Amanda turned and twisted frantically, wrenching helplessly at her bound wrists. Glenn would not be there, but since his wife did not believe that, it would be some harmless, friendly fisherman who would die. He would be waiting for her, and she would shoot him down without mercy and without warning — killing him as she must have killed poor, helpless Monica Ford. And because she had never used a gun before she would play for safety and fire at the man's chest or stomach, and he would die horribly, coughing blood.

Anita Barton was not sane. Fear for her own safety had driven her over the narrow line that lies between sanity and madness. Had Glenn really suspected all the time that she might be a murderess? Was that why he had tried to get her away — and used any and every excuse to that end?

Amanda writhed and wrenched and tugged at her bonds in helpless, frantic fear. She must not let Anita kill again. She could

255

not lie there and wait for the sound of a shot, and know that she herself would be the next to die. She tried to get her chin on to the car horn, thinking that if she could sound it, it might cause Anita Barton to take fright; but she slipped and fell to the floor, and hit her head on the steering wheel trying to get upright again.

Then all at once hands were gripping her and dragging her up, and there was an urgent, hissing whisper in her ear:

'For Pete's sake stay still! How in heck can I get you outa this while you're hopping like a jumping bean?'

Persis! Amanda's slim body was suddenly limp with relief. Fingers fumbled at the knot behind her head and Persis' voice whispered: 'Damn and blast this hair of yours! Why the heck you want to——'

And then the bandage was whipped away and Amanda spat out the sodden handkerchief and was breathing in deep gulps of air.

'Persis! — how did you get here?'

'*Ssh!* Keep quiet! Do you want that dame back on us?' Persis started on the knotted scarf that bound Amanda's wrists and explained in a whisper:

'I didn't like the look of the set-up. There was a gleam in that gal's eye that I've seen in the eye of a horse in my day. And I don't buy nor ride those horses! I walked round the back of those trees and counted ten and came right back again, and found you out like a light and the girlfriend making a getaway. So I jumped a ride on the luggage grid, and here I am. A very dusty and unpleasant journey, and I nearly broke my neck when she slammed on the brakes a mile or so back. There you are——'

Amanda's wrists were free. She bent and tugged at the knots about her ankles, and a minute later she was out of the car and standing in the bright moonlight.

'Hey, come back!' hissed Persis. 'This is where we beat it!'

'I can't,' said Amanda desperately. 'She thinks it's Glenn down there on the beach, and she'll take a shot at him. Can't you see, I've got to stop her!'

'Okay,' said Persis, resigned. 'I guess I'll come with you. Let's go.'

She jumped out into the road and gave a brief and muffled yelp of pain.

'Holy cat!' gasped Persis, hopping on one foot.

'What is it?'

'Lost a shoe back there, and I've trodden on a rock.'

'Well you can't come on one foot,' said Amanda in a feverish whisper. 'Stay here and find a spanner or something, and if she comes back, see if you can lay her out!'

She turned and ran in the direction that Anita Barton had taken a few minutes before.

The path came out on the top of a low cliff below which lay a tangle of sea grass and huge tumbled rocks. Amanda could see no sign of Anita Barton and imagined that she must be lying in wait in the shadows of one of the big boulders. She crept forward, grateful that the wash of the sea on the shelving beach blurred the sound of her movements, and reached the level of the shore.

The sand was warm and dry and deep and she edged her way between the high, wind-worn rocks and found herself looking out on a small curving beach bounded on one side by the low headland that she had just descended, and on the other by a long natural breakwater of tumbled rocks.

A boat was drifting in from the shining sea; a boat that had evidently been waiting off the point of the rocks. She could hear the soft splash of oars above the hush of a slow tide that broke gently on the beach with a sound like the rustle of dry leaves in a light autumn breeze. Then a keel grated on wet sand.

There was only one man in the small boat, and Amanda saw him ship the oars and jump out into the creaming surf to draw the prow a little farther up the beach.

He turned and walked towards her, and the moonlight fell full on his face.

It was Glenn Barton.

257

For a moment the shock of that knowledge deprived Amanda of the power to call out. Then she opened her mouth to scream a warning and stopped — checked by the terrified knowledge that Anita must be somewhere ahead of her, and that if she cried out Glenn would stop and Anita, realizing that she was discovered, would fire.

She edged her way forward, keeping to the shadow of the rocks and nearing the point where Anita must be standing.

Someone moved out of the shadows barely half a dozen yards ahead of her and Glenn stopped and said quietly: 'Anita.'

The single, softly spoken word sounded astonishingly loud in that white silence where the only other sound was the lazy, murmurous whisper of the tide.

Anita Barton moved out into the moonlight, one hand in the pocket of her loose linen coat. She drew the hand out slowly, and Amanda raced forward and flung herself on Mrs Barton's arm, dragging it down so that the shot went harmlessly into the sand.

The small bay seemed full of the echoes of that sound, and Amanda's hands were on cold metal, wrenching it, twisting it free and flinging it away.

Glenn stooped slowly and picked it up, and Anita Barton turned on Amanda screaming; clawing at her like a frenzied cat:

'*You fool!* Oh you fool! Can't you see he'll kill us. *No* Glenn! – no – no! I don't want to die!'

She crumpled at Amanda's feet in a sobbing, shuddering heap.

Glenn Barton looked down at the weapon in his hand and then at his frantic wife. He raised the revolver quite steadily and said in a pleasant, soft voice:

'Yes. I shall kill you. You were really becoming too dangerous altogether. Both of you. No, don't move, Amanda! I am an excellent shot and I happen to have my own gun as well as the one my dear wife — my very dear wife — has so thoughtfully provided me with. I am sorry that you will have to disappear too. You will, of course, have accompanied Anita to the Lebanon and a telegram to that effect will be handed in there in a day or two. Anita, naturally, has left a letter which will explain everything to Miss Moon and to anyone who may be interested: I can really copy her handwriting very well. When, eventually, you fail to reappear, it will of course be obvious that my wife has committed another murder.'

Amanda said breathlessly: 'Glenn! — Glenn, what are you talking about? I don't understand——' Her voice did not seem to belong to her, but to some stranger.

'I think you do,' said Glenn softly. 'You came here to spy on me, didn't you Amanda? To report on me to your uncle. I'm sorry that I shall have to shoot you. It's noisy and bloody, and I dislike noise and blood. But there appears to be no alternative. You seem to be immune to poison. Some friend of yours drank the stuff that was meant for you on the ship, and you wouldn't even touch the drink I offered you at the Inn. I'd got either contingency worked out to look like suicide, and it would have saved a great deal of trouble. Then I had what looked like the chance of a lifetime at Hilarion, but a fluke saved you, and when I tried to get back I found Howard was on his way up behind me. As there was no other way down and no one else up there, the only possible way out of a very sticky situation was to risk my neck and save you. The irony of that should appeal to you.'

'*No!*' said Amanda in a sobbing whisper. 'No Glenn. You're mad. You don't know what you're saying!'

'Oh yes I do. I thought I could get you both once before. You practically handed it to me on a plate. I meant to throw you down Anita's stairs, and then go up and send her after you. They'd have said she must have been drunk and pushed you, and then fallen herself. Those banisters are like matchwood. But that interfering idiot Howard wrecked that too.'

Amanda said chokingly: 'I don't believe it! It isn't true.'

'Anita believes it. Don't you Anita dear? Stand up Anita — stand up my darling. You won't like it if I put a bullet through you

259

while you're on the ground. It might hit you where it would hurt. You won't know anything about it if you stand up. The fish will leave nothing that can be identified if you should ever come up on a trawl. But I don't think you will. I'll weight you well. Stand up Anita——'

Anita Barton grovelled in the sand, sobbing and choking and pleading. She crawled forward on her knees, her face a mask of tears and sand, crazy with terror.

Glenn Barton looked down at her with cold disgust and fired with complete indifference.

Anita screamed at the sound of the shot and leapt to her feet, but Glenn did not fire again.

He stood staring, wide-eyed, at the gun in his hand; then he dropped it on to the sand and whipped a second one from the pocket of his coat.

A shadow moved out of the shadows of the piled rocks: and another, and another, until the moonlit curve of the narrow beach was ringed with silent men, and a familiar voice remarked pleasantly:

'You won't find that one any good either, I'm afraid.'

19

Glenn Barton whipped round on the speaker, gun in hand, and Amanda flung herself frantically between them.

'Steve——!'

There was an orange flash of flame and for the third time that night the quiet cove echoed to the sound of a shot.

Steve Howard removed Amanda's clinging fingers and said: 'It's only blank,' and Glenn Barton flung the useless weapon savagely at his head.

Steve ducked, thrust Amanda to one side, and leapt at him.

Amanda heard the blow go home on Glenn Barton's body and saw him bend double and throw his head up, gasping for air. There was the crack of a second blow to the jaw; a crisp, sharp sound that seemed almost as loud as the report of the useless revolver. Glenn Barton's body appeared to leave the ground, and came to rest a yard or so away, spreadeagled and unconscious on the sand.

'I have been aching to do that for days!' observed Steve, breathing a little unevenly.

He turned to a man who was standing beside him, and Amanda saw with a numbed lack of surprise that it was the man with the odd name whom she had seen once before in the hall of the Villa Oleander on the evening that Monica Ford had died.

'Well there he is,' said Steve. 'He's all yours.'

He turned to Anita Barton: 'If you're feeling all right, Mrs Barton, we'll get back to the car. Amanda, you can't cry here! Save it for the journey back and I'll lend you my shoulder.'

He took hold of Anita Barton's arm with one hand and

Amanda's with the other and urged them up the narrow path towards the car. Someone was limping towards them down the path and Steve checked suddenly.

'It's Persis,' said Amanda.

'Good grief!' said Mr Howard, exasperated. 'What the hell is she doing mixed up in this?'

'She came with me,' explained Amanda.

Persis materialized out of the moonlight.

''Lo Steve. Sugar Ray Robinson in person, I presume? I'm sorry I missed the first two acts and the intermission, but I had a grandstand seat for the finale. It certainly packed a punch.'

She turned and accompanied them back to the car, limping a trifle, and subsided abruptly on to the running board.

Steve produced a flask from his coat pocket, removed the cap, filled it and handed it over.

'Thanks a lot,' said Persis, gulping the contents. 'Boy! did I need that. Sling some into Anita; her need is greater than mine.'

Anita Barton drank with chattering teeth and looked at Steve Howard. Her face was still white and tear-streaked, but her voice was no longer hysterical.

'I can't thank you enough. When did you — how did you know about Glenn?'

'You knew, didn't you?' said Steve gently.'

'Of course. That was why I left him. I tried to warn that fool Monica, but she wouldn't listen. She was crazy about him.'

'How did you find out?'

'Oh — little things. A lot of little things that all added up. Then I began to watch him, and – and in the end I found out. I was frightened then. I knew that if he once realized that I knew, he – he'd kill me. He was always a killer. Quiet and decent and – and *deadly*. He'd been making love to Monica, and I used that as an excuse. I had to get away from him. I *had* to!'

Persis said sharply: 'I'll believe almost anything after what I've seen tonight, but I will not believe that guy ever made a pass at a middle-aged dame with buck teeth and a forty-two inch waist!'

'But he did,' said Anita Barton drearily. 'You see she'd been sent out to see what was going on. Mr Derington sent her. He always believed that women had an instinct over shady business. I think he must have heard a few rumours, so he sent out a competent secretary who was to find out what went on, and report.'

Anita Barton subsided wearily onto the running board beside Persis, and leaned her head back against the car door. She said: 'Glenn made love to her. He could always make women fall for him. He has that "little-boy-lost" look about him that makes fools of the best of them — it made a fool of me too! Monica went overboard about him. He was probably the only man who had ever looked twice at her, and he reduced her to a pulp. After that he could do anything with her and make her swallow any lie. I'd stood for his affairs with half a dozen other women including Claire — Claire used to send and carry messages for him that he couldn't risk sending himself. I don't think she realized what he was doing. He probably told her some convincing lie; and anyway she can look after herself. But the Monica business sickened me. When I tried to warn her she was rude and hysterical, and I got Lumley to let me move in on him. He only did it to score off Glenn and Claire, and because he has an inferiority complex as a result of being a Conscientious Objector during the War, so he feels he must pose as a flouter of public opinion.'

Amanda said helplessly: 'I don't understand! What was Glenn doing?'

'Gun running,' said Steve Howard briefly.

'What?' Persis straightened up abruptly and nearly fell on her face on the roadside. 'Why — say Steve, where do you come in on all this?'

'Oh, I'd been told off to find out who was back of the racket,' said Steve. He looked over his shoulder and said impatiently: 'How much longer do you suppose those sleuths are going to be?'

'Never mind them,' said Persis firmly. 'Spill it, honey — you have our undivided attention. I for one am not shifting from this spot until I've got all the dirt, and you can't drive off with a gal on the running board!'

Steve laughed a little grimly. He accepted one of Persis' cigarettes, lit it from her lighter, and said:

'We knew that someone was shipping guns into Africa and we knew that they were coming from a satellite country, via Cyprus. We did not know how it was done, but we narrowed it down a bit and became interested in, among others, Glennister Barton. It seemed just possible that he was using the wine business as a cover for something more profitable. He was. And things were going tolerably smoothly for him until Amanda suddenly put a cat among his pigeons.'

'*I* did?' said Amanda incredulously. 'How?'

'You decided to go to Cyprus, and your Uncle Oswin sent an exceedingly official letter demanding that you be put up and taken round and offered all facilities, and all the rest of it. It was a misleading document, and bearing in mind your uncle's preference for females in the role of snoopers, Glenn Barton imagined that you were being sent here expressly to spy on him — as Monica had been. He might have tried to carry it off, if it hadn't been for his matrimonial mess-up.'

Amanda said: 'But why should that matter?'

'Your uncle,' said Steve Howard, 'is a notorious prude in such matters. A hint from you that his nominee for the post of Barton's secretary was rumoured in love with the Boss — not to mention the rest of the set-up! — and Barton would probably have had the sack by wire. Or — more likely — your Uncle Oswin would have arrived on the next plane in order to clean the matter up.'

'Yes,' said Amanda slowly. 'He might have done. He's a bit rabid about that sort of thing.'

'Exactly. Barton couldn't risk it either way. He had a hell of a

264

big deal coming off, and all he needed was just three more weeks and he'd have been in a position to clear off to some salubrious spot like South America, and keep himself in champagne and caviare until he died. It was as close as that. He daren't say that he couldn't have you, so he tried to stop you getting here. The stuff that Julia Blaine drank was meant for you.'

Persis said sharply: 'Julia! You mean that was *murder*?'

'But — but it was in her lemon juice,' said Amanda helplessly.

'It wasn't lemon. It was sweetlime. And there was plenty of sugar in it as well. The carpet was sticky with it. You merely jumped to the conclusion that it was lemon juice and meant for Julia because you hadn't ordered it, and, by a fluke, had happened to change cabins with Mrs Blaine much earlier in the day. Julia would never have ordered or touched such a thing. But a nice icy lime squash left in a cabin on a hot night was a pretty tempting bait. And when you told me that Mrs Blaine had gone to bed around ten o'clock, it began to look even more as though that glass had not been in the wrong cabin after all.'

'But why, Steve?'

'Ice. You didn't go down until nearly eleven, but there was still ice in that glass. There were chips of it on the carpet when I got there. If that drink had been in your cabin before ten the ice in it would have melted. Yet if it had been meant as a trap for Mrs Blaine it would never have been put there almost three-quarters of an hour after she had left the deck and gone to her cabin with a certain amount of attendant publicity. You, however, were dancing.'

Amanda said on a gasp: 'But – but Glenn! ... Glenn couldn't have done it. He wasn't even there!'

'No. But one of his thugs was. You don't really suppose that anyone could run a racket of that description single-handed, do you? There were a gang of 'em up to their necks in it! This was a man called Kostos who was masquerading as a deck-hand. The husband, incidentally, of a woman who keeps an inn on the road to Limassol where you appear to have almost lost one of your nine lives.'

'It can't have been! Glenn told me that her husband was an old wreck of a man who——' She stopped suddenly and said in a shaken voice: 'I see now. He had to say something to make me turn round and look away from the table, so he said the first thing that came into his head. And then she — the woman — said that her husband had been on the ship. Why didn't I notice that? And Glenn dropped his cigarette into my glass. To make sure that no one else would drink it I suppose.'

'He also,' said Steve grimly, 'arranged for the disposal of the deck-hand. He was taking no chances. The chap was supposedly killed in a bar-room brawl: which was, oddly, enough, the reason why Miss Moon's staff, who were related to the widow, did not return on the day that Monica Ford was murdered and you were so neatly shoved over the battlements at Hilarion.'

Amanda shivered violently. 'But *why* Steve? Surely if – if I'd died here it would have been just as bad for him? Uncle Oswin would have come over then.'

'Would he? From all I've heard of him he doesn't sound like a man who would allow his niece, who was also his ward, to be buried in a place like this. It would have been the Derington Family Vault or nothing! Barton would only have had to cable your uncle that he was arranging to fly your corpse home in a coffin, pronto, and would he please meet? And it's my bet that your grief-stricken relative would have scrubbed the rest of his business schedule and taken the next plane to England, so that he could collect the dear-departed at London Airport, and lay on a suitable funeral. And if he *had* come here, he would have been in no state to start bothering about his wine business. That's for certain!

'If he'd come, it would only have been to collect the coffin from scratch, so that he could escort it home in person. Either way, he wouldn't have had the time or the inclination to start investigating the affairs of Mr Glennister Barton until he'd got your mortal remains parked in the family vault. And by that time, Barton would have been living it up in Buenos Aires or Montevideo, or wherever.'

'Yes, I see,' said Amanda with a shiver. 'You're right about the family vault; and about Uncle Oswin too. He'd never have left me here . . .'

'Exactly. I expect Barton was banking on that. But once you'd arrived in Cyprus — presumably to spy out the land — Barton could not risk letting you leave here alive. It was the time factor. He had to have those extra weeks, and the money involved was worth taking risks for. Any risks! He would have killed you and half a dozen others cheerfully for it.'

Amanda said: 'But why on earth should I have committed suicide? What possible reason could I——'

'Judging from statistics,' interrupted Steve impatiently, 'the average adolescent can decide to "End It All" for any number of footling reasons. Unrequited love coming high on the list — the "I can't live without him" syndrome. That would always have been a safe card to play, since it would have been difficult to disprove, once you were dead. After all, it even occurred fleetingly to me — and a lot less fleetingly to the police! — that you might have bumped off Julia Blaine in the hope of snaffling her husband. It was considered a possibility. And if you'd died of the same poison in that pub; it could have been written off as remorse!'

'Yes, you told me about the "possibility",' snapped Amanda, torn between indignation at remembered outrage, and annoyance at being classed as an 'average adolescent': 'But what about Monica? It wasn't possible for Glenn to have killed her. Not by any stretch of even *your* fertile imagination!'

'Oh yes it was. He saw her going into Miss Moon's that afternoon, and followed her in. She had come to see you.'

'But why? What did she want to see me for?'

'Because both she and Barton, as a result of your uncle's letter, had it firmly fixed in their heads that you were really here as a sort of private agent for him. And she had found out what Barton was up to.'

'But surely, she must have known before?'

'She'd probably always known or suspected that there was something pretty peculiar going on, but I think she deliberately shut her eyes to it and tried to pretend that it was merely a matter of smuggling a few cigarettes. Something on those lines. But that afternoon a case, supposedly containing wine, got broken, and as Barton was out, she opened it herself and realized what he was doing. A week earlier and she might still have looked the other way, for she was about as completely under Barton's thumb as a frustrated spinster can be. But her brother had just been murdered by Mau Mau terrorists — armed by Glenn Barton! It broke her up, and she rushed into Kyrenia to see you and spill the beans. And Barton strangled her.'

Amanda said: 'He can't have done, Steve! He can't possibly have done it. The police proved that he went straight from Hilarion to Nicosia.'

'He did. But he killed Monica Ford before he ever arrived at Hilarion.'

'But she was *warm*!'

'I know. That was what put us all out of step for a bit. He'd left her in front of the french windows, where the sun had been full on her from the time he killed her until just before it set. It had barely gone from the room when we got back; remember? Of course she was warm! It's never as easy as detective fiction would have you believe to fix the exact time of death. It depends on a good many things, and temperature has a lot to do with it. Glenn Barton had his wits about him, and made very good use of the fact that the sun would be on that bit of the room from roughly four fifteen onwards. He came on to Hilarion, mentioned having seen the woman, and provided himself with a nice alibi all round. And when he was telephoned for by the police — as he knew he would

268

be — he arrived complete with that neat bit of evidence against his wife, and planted it as he came through the hall.'

'I knew it was Glenn who had done that,' said Anita Barton with a shudder. 'It couldn't have been anyone else. There were several of those flowers in the house. They were always coming off, and I'd left a lot of my stuff behind. He must have gone through my dressing-table drawers, and found one.'

'I imagine so,' said Steve. 'He then provided an affecting scene by registering sufficient horror at the sight of it to attract everyone's suspicious attention. And Amanda nearly spoilt the whole show by rushing into the breach like Florence Nightingale or Flora Macdonald, and claiming it as hers. However, just in case the police proved bat-witted enough to believe her, he took the precaution of ringing up Mrs Norman and spilling the beans under cover of a distracted plea that she should go and see you, Mrs Barton, and tell you to destroy the dress. He knew dam' well that she'd see you dead first, and also that she could be trusted to spread the story around the whole of Cyprus.'

Anita Barton said: 'He meant to get me hanged for murder!'

Steve shook his head. 'I don't think so. The last thing he wanted was a court case of that sort. He was working up to an artistic disappearing act, so that people would jump to the conclusion that you had lost your nerve and bolted. He worked round to that angle very nicely, and I added the last touch by ordering Amanda to write at once to her uncle. That tore it. If she had done so, and her uncle had arrived by return of post, the whole thing would have blown up in his face. I thought that threat would fetch him, and it did.'

Amanda stared at him, speechless, and Anita Barton said wearily: 'And I thought she was in it with him. That she'd fallen for him too, like Monica and all the other fools. I hit her over the head with that gun, and I thought I'd killed her. I'm sorry, Amanda. I knew he was trying to kill me, and I thought you were helping him.'

Amanda was not listening to her. She was clinging to the door handle of the car and looking at Steve:

'You mean you *knew* that he'd do something like this?' demanded Amanda breathlessly. 'You told me to write that letter just to make him — to make him . . .' Words appeared to fail her.

'I had to darling,' said Steve. 'We had to panic him into showing his hand. But if it's any consolation to you, it was quite the most unpleasant thing I've ever had to do. We'd have got him on the gun-running without it. But we might well have failed to pin him with murder. And we did at least go to a great deal of trouble to remove the bullets from any guns he possessed and replace them with blanks. Which wasn't as easy as it may sound. However, I will admit that I had left out of my calculations the possibility that Mrs Barton might crack you over the head with a blunt instrument — although I can sympathize with her point of view.'

Amanda stared at him for a long moment, her face white in the moonlight.

She said in a small, frozen voice: 'If you are thinking of driving us back, I think we'd all like to get home. Persis, are you ready?'

'And how!' said Persis. 'Anita honey, will you sit in front by the driver? And I guess it might be a good idea, when we get back, if you and I doubled up for the night just to keep each other company. We'll get a spare bed put up in my room and order up a bath of hot coffee and a quart of chloroform. This has been quite a party, and the sooner we sleep it off the better.'

Amanda got haughtily into the back of the car and said: 'Come on Persis!'

Persis closed the door on Anita Barton and looked at Steve Howard.

'Steve honey,' she inquired softly, 'how much am I offered to drive this car?'

Steve laughed.

'Persis honey,' he said, 'you will drive this car or else——!'

'Okay,' said Persis. 'It's a stick-up!'

Amanda attempted to descend but Steve was too quick for her. He slammed the door behind him and pulled her very roughly into his arms.

Amanda made a small, sobbing and unintelligible sound that was abruptly silenced, and presently said breathlessly: 'Steve, please——!'

'My heart,' said Mr Howard, 'shut up! You can keep the conversation for later. We are not alone.'

'Don't mind us,' said Persis cordially, starting up the car and backing it expertly on the sandy verge. 'Go right ahead and kiss her.'

'What do you think I'm doing?' inquired Steve with pardonable irritation.

Persis laughed, and having tactfully twisted the driving mirror until it faced the roof, headed the car down the long white moonlit road towards Kyrenia.